信

Faith

李无名

Li Wuming

大秦景教流行中国碑摘录

贞观十有二年秋七月,诏曰:

"道无常名,圣无常体,随方设教,密济群生。大秦国大德阿罗本,遠将像,来献上京,详其教旨,玄妙无为,观其元宗,生成立要。词无繁说,理有忘筌,济物利人,宜行天下。所司即于京义宁坊造大秦寺一所,度僧廿一人。宗周德丧,青驾西昇。巨唐道光,景风东扇

大唐建中二年岁在作噩太蔟月七日大耀森文日建立

Excerpt from the Stele to the Propagation of the Luminous Religion (Christianity) in China

In Autumn, in the seventh month of the twelfth year of the Zhenguan period of the Taizong Emperor's reign (638 AD), the emperor proclaimed:

"The way does not have a constant name, and the holy does not have a constant form. Teachings are established according to the locality, and their mysteries aid mankind. Aluoben, the virtuous man of Da Qin, has brought scriptures and images from afar and presented them at the capital. He has explained the doctrines, so that nothing is left obscure. We have observed its basic teachings. They set forth the most important things for living, their words are not complicated, and their principles, once learnt, can be easily retained. Everything in them benefits man. It is appropriate that it should spread throughout the empire."

As a result, a church was constructed in the capital, in the district of Yining. This church had 21 monks. The virtue of the house of Zhou had come to an end, and the black chariot has ascended into the western heaven. The way of the great Tang dynasty shone forth, and the Luminous teachings spread into the East.

This stele was erected on the 7th day of the 1st month in the second year of the Jianzhong period of the great Tang Dynasty (781 AD).

Contents

Page		
6	观音佛	Goddess of Mercy
13	宣传部	Propaganda Department
21	鬼街	Ghost Street
29	幼儿园	Kindergarten
36	怀孕	Pregnant
48	饺子馆	Dumpling Museum
64	兰会所	Orchid Club
72	合眼	Sleep
79	眼泪	Tears
87	姐妹	Sisters
99	盼望	Hope
107	基督徒	Christian
116	天坛	Temple of Heaven
125	家庭教会	House Church
132	认知失调	Cognitive Dissonance
141	司马南	Sima Nan
150	圣诞节	Christmas
159	归心者	Convert
166	耶利哥	Jericho
174	描绘	Temple Fair
182	逮捕	Arrest
191	天安门	Tiananmen
199	社会信用体系	Social Credit System

Page

207	上善若水	The Supreme Good is Like Water
216	思想工作	Thought Work
232	黑手	The Black Hand
242	招供	Confession
251	温柔的人有福了	Blessed are the Meek
261	救救孩子	Save the Children…
271	中国梦	Chinese Dream

观音佛
Goddess of Mercy

A seemingly endless stream of cars zipped past Shao Huan as he stood on the wide sidewalk waiting for his wife. They were married exactly five years earlier, and Shao knew it was the best decision of his life. Shao spotted his beautiful bride walking toward him in the cool dusk air. The fading sunlight behind her cast a dim halo around Zhang Ying's slender silhouette. Zhang wrapped her arms around Shao Huan's neck and greeted him with a kiss, "Happy anniversary! You waited for me here? I thought you would be waiting inside."

"It's no problem, I thought the two of us should go in together," Shao kissed Zhang's soft white cheek and took her by the hand. Her smile told him that she was glad he had waited. As they approached the white tent draped over the entrance to the restaurant, a hand reached out and pulled the folds of fabric to the side.

"Welcome! Please enter," the hostess at the entrance greeted them with a courteous voice and a deep bow. She was dressed in a silk qipao with elaborate brocade and asked them to place their hands over a silver basin as she poured rose scented water over them. Shao Huan and Zhang Ying had never washed their hands in rose water before and laughed quietly to each other, enjoying the novelty. The hostess led them into the large restaurant, dimly lit with colorful fabric hanging in folds and large green plants between the tables. The room smelled like sandalwood incense and a statue of Guanyin, the Goddess of Mercy, stood illuminated and radiant near the center of the restaurant. The hostess seated the happy couple at a small table with a lotus blossom candle floating in a bowl of perfectly clear water.

"Wow, this is really fancy!" Zhang Ying was excited and impressed, "I hope it's not too expensive."

"It is definitely too expensive, but it is our anniversary. We should celebrate," Shao Huan reached across the table and took Zhang's rose scented hand again. "I really can't believe it has been five years. It feels like just yesterday we got married at the West Lake."

Zhang Ying's eyes sparkled with the flame from the candle and the light reflected from Guanyin, "I think it feels exactly like five years. Hangzhou seems so far away now."

"Do you still miss Hangzhou?" Shao asked.

"Of course, it will always be home. I don't mind Beijing so much even though I really do miss the south. But don't worry, wherever you go I will follow you," Zhang squeezed Shao's hand as a waiter approached and handed them a digital menu.

Shao didn't bother to turn on the menu and handed it back to the waiter, "We really don't know what to order here. Can you recommend some good dishes for two people?" He asked.

"Oh, of course, is tonight a special event?"

"Yes, it is our five year wedding anniversary," Shao looked at his wife's smiling face as he spoke.

"Congratulations!" The young thin waiter looked at the couple lost in each other's eyes, "I suggest beginning with the mock duck, and black fungus in vinegar sauce for the cold dishes, Buddha's delight and sizzling black pepper fake beef for the hot dishes, and carrot and mushroom dumplings with brown rice and mung beans for the main."

7

"Isn't it too much?" Zhang asked.

"The dishes are not so big, but they are all delicious. Also, to drink, I suggest our Tibetan eight treasures tea."

"Okay, we will have all of that," Shao nodded his agreement with the waiter's suggestion. "Don't worry, if it is too much, we can always take it home. Let's just enjoy the experience."

"I thought temple food was supposed to be simple, this is all so fancy," Zhang laughed, "But I do like this place. It is so peaceful. Not peaceful like a temple, but still very nice."

"How were the kids at the kindergarten today?" Shao asked.

"They were so busy! Even during nap time they didn't want to stay still. It was exhausting, but they were still so cute. Even when they are naughty, I can't stay angry at them. They are just children after all. I just wish they would stop running… sometimes," Zhang took her eyes off of Shao's attentive face and looked at the image of Guanyin, standing on a lotus blossom and holding a sheath of rice in one hand and a vase of water in the other, the embodiment of peace and kindness in her long white robes.

"Aren't you going to ask what I did today?" Shao Huan teased as he saw Zhang Ying's eyes wander over his shoulder.

"No, why should I? You never talk about your work," Zhang still looked over Shao's shoulder.

Shao Huan knew that it always bothered Zhang Ying that he didn't talk about his work. He felt sorry for her about that, but she had known that soon after they met and it wasn't worth explaining or apologizing any more, "I met Sima Nan for tea near the bookstore. He is dating a new girl. He says he is sure they will get married."

Zhang Ying rolled her eyes and refocused on her husband's strong angular face and high cheekbones, "He has been saying that since when you were both young and you still had hair. He will find some way to get that poor girl to run away."

Shao chuckled, his wife was right, Sima Nan couldn't seem to keep any relationship going for more than a few months, no matter how well they started, "You said it well, it also doesn't help that he keeps trying to date women who are in their 20s even now that he is more than 30 years old."

"Exactly. He needs to find someone suitable for him. Not just someone who is pretty," Zhang Ying didn't like Sima Nan, but he had been her husband's best friend since university and she had accepted long ago that she would not be able to change Sima Nan or to break his friendship with Shao Huan.

Zhang and Shao sat in silence. She looked down at the candle floating in front of her while Shao Huan watched her delicate black eyebrows arch and a furrow form in her porcelain brow, "Dear, what is the matter, you can tell me."

Zhang Ying's eyes returned to Shao's calm and happy face. She had not wanted to burden him on such a happy night but staring at the image of Guanyin, she couldn't put the thought out of her mind that she wanted the blessing of a child, "I really love you and the last five years have been the best years of my life, but I am almost 30 years old now and I want to have a baby. My parents ask every time I talk to them, everyone at work tells me that I should have a baby soon, but I don't really care what they say. I really want to have a baby. I want to be a mother. I know you have been happy with just the two of us, but don't you want a child to fill our lives with crying and laughter?"

Shao Huan kept the calm smile on his placid face, and nodded with compassion and sincerity, "Ah, that's what it is. These five years together have been the best of my life too. Since we met at the cafe in Hangzhou, you have made me so happy. My work is a little more stable now and I am not traveling so much these days. I think it is a good time for us to have a child. Since the Party has changed the one child policy, we could even have two or three children if we start soon."

"Really? You mean it?" Zhang Ying's voice filled with hope and the surprise on her face washed away the worried lines that had crept across her forehead.

Shao nodded, "Yes, of course. You said it exactly right. It is the right time for us to have a child. My parents will also be very happy. We should be filial children to make them happy too. I have been selfish waiting so long to have a child. Thank you for being patient with me."

Zhang Ying wanted to stand up and hug Shao Huan, but took both of his hands in hers and held them tight, "Okay, we will be good parents, but let's not tell anyone that we are going to have a baby until we are sure that I am pregnant. And let's just have one baby. Children are so expensive, and hard to care for. I see it at work at the kindergarten, only a few families have more than one child and they all seem so tired."

The waiter brought out the tender mock duck and the cold crisp black fungus on thin white china dishes and set them between the couple as they stared into each other's eyes, silently affirming their resolve to begin a family. After a minute, Shao looked down at the food, "We should eat," he said and picked up a piece of the carefully folded vegetable protein between his chopsticks, "It doesn't taste like duck, but it is still good, come on eat."

Zhang Ying chewed the crunchy black fungus and felt the light sting of the strong vinegar on her lips, "Do you want to have a son or a daughter?" She asked.

"What I want doesn't really matter, does it? If we have a daughter, that is good. If we have a son, that is also good," Shao Huan tried to brush off the question.

"Of course, regardless of whether we have a boy or a girl we will love them, but wouldn't you like a son to carry on your family line?"

Shao put his chopsticks down beside the small plate in front of him, "Family lines are kind of an old way of thinking, I am sure my father would like me to have a son to carry on the family name, but if I had to pick I would probably want a daughter. I think daughters are much better to their fathers than sons. I was a very naughty child. I am sure that if I have a son, he would be naughty too."

Zhang was relieved to hear that her husband would prefer a daughter, "Good. I want a daughter too. The boys are always naughty, at least when they are little. Maybe girls are naughty when they are older, but I think that would be easier to manage."

The waiter cleared away the cold dishes and brought the sizzling plate of fake beef and the bowl of stewed mushroom, bamboo shoots, bean curd sticks, cellophane noodles and day lily bulbs. Shao

Huan looked over his shoulder to where Zhang Ying's eyes had lingered before her admission that she wanted to be a mother.

"Do you want to go to Dongyue temple to ask for a blessing to get pregnant?" Shao Huan was not superstitious, but wanted to show Zhang Ying that he supported her desire to have a baby.

Zhang took a bite of savory bamboo shoot soaked in the rich mushroom broth, "No, you know I don't believe in any of that. It's okay. I was just sitting here tonight, looking at the statue of Guanyin…after five years as husband and wife, I couldn't keep quiet any more. I really want to have a baby. I know that you have other things to look forward to at work, but I am tired of just taking care of other people's children. I want to take care of my own child."

"I understand. We'll have a baby, okay? I promise," Shao felt a warmth deep in his stomach as he held Zhang Ying's hand and looked into her sparkling round eyes and saw her cherry lips drawn into a huge smile on her round face, already glowing with the thought of being a mother.

宣传部
Propaganda Department

The summer heat was already radiating off the sidewalk as Shao Huan walked up from the Xidan subway station. Shao enjoyed the stroll as the crowd surged past and around him. Shao usually found his commute between his apartment in Chaoyang and his office at the Propaganda Department was a pleasant one. The trains ran on time and it wasn't a long walk on either side.

Shao greeted the guards as he did every morning and badged in to the conspicuously nondescript building just to the west of the Chinese Communist Party's leadership compound behind the imposing red walls that surrounded the historic grounds at Zhongnanhai. Shao took the elevator to the top floor and turned to his office, just down the hall from the Head of the Propaganda Department for the Central Committee of the Chinese Communist Party.

Shao's office was cool and quiet, the secure servers that connected the Propaganda Department headquarters to the Party's nation-wide secure communication network hummed quietly as Shao began working through his morning checklist. There were only a handful of classified reports for the Head of the Propaganda Department, Ye Hongqi. Shao printed them off and placed them in the classified reading folder for Ye. Shao usually couldn't be bothered to read the reports, but had to at least make sure that any messages from the Politburo Standing Committee were placed at the top of folder so Ye Hongqi would read those first. The reports from the provincial propaganda offices or Party secretaries were always of less importance than any new directives from the Center.

Ye Hongqi's office was large and luxurious, with a long conference table and a plush couch set for less formal conversations over tea. His secretary, Liu Wuqing, sat in the small office just outside of the entrance to Ye's office. Shao delivered the classified folder to Liu. Ye Hongqi relied heavily on Liu Wuqing and had kept him close since he spotted Liu's talent as a junior cadre. Shao Huan had only started working for Ye Hongqi when he was the Deputy Party Secretary for Zhejiang Province and Shao was assigned as his communications officer.

Liu Wuqing was always at the office early and stayed late. Shao got to the office early as well, but the only times that Shao Huan had ever seen Liu's office empty were when Ye Hongqi was traveling and required Liu to accompany him. Shao Huan admired Liu's diligence, but was glad that he was was a technical officer and was not on a political track like Liu. Shao only had to work late hours when there were specific communications requirements.

"Good morning buddy," Shao Huan greeted Liu Wuqing and handed him the day's reports.

"Morning. Did you have breakfast yet?" Liu asked politely even though Shao could tell Liu's thoughts were already focused on the folder in his hands, "Anything important today?"

"There is only one Top Secret document from the Center. The rest are reports from Xinjiang, Tibet, and… I think there are a couple from Guangxi as well," Shao looked at Liu's tired face and felt some sympathy for his comrade. Ye Hongqi was not a bad boss, but he had high expectations for Liu Wuqing and Shao didn't know how he managed to do everything, "Hey, it looks like you are pretty busy, but I am going to get a coffee in a little while. I'll bring you a cup too, okay?"

Liu Wuqing's lips curled into a half smile, "Okay, only if it is no trouble. Can you get me a latte with two shots of espresso? I think I need the extra energy today."

"Of course, no problem at all. The editors-in-chief are all coming today aren't they?"

Liu nodded and slipped the Buddhist prayer bead bracelet off of his wrist and started slowly running the smooth wooden beads through his fingers, "Yes, they all think they are so important, and they are so competitive with each other. They never miss the weekly instruction session. Today should be okay though, they will just be receiving updated guidance on promoting the Party Chairman's ideology. Some were too eager to please the Center and started to go overboard creating a cult of personality, but now they seem to understand where the line is."

"I admire you, but I don't envy you," Shao Huan smiled, "Those are a lot of self important people to deal with all the time, especially when you are smarter than them."

Liu Wuqing's smile faded and he moved the beads more quickly, "Even Zhuge Liang would run out of stratagems with them." Liu sighed, "Ye Hongqi should be here soon, I must continue getting ready."

"Okay, I'll bring that coffee by a little later," Shao said and returned to his office. He continued on his check list, monitoring the network latency, reviewing the log files, and ensuring the secure telephone was working properly. The job had changed so much since he had been hired to work for the CCP Central Committee's General Office as a communications specialist. Shao Huan enjoyed that the technology kept changing and he had to keep up with the newest tools, but it had taken him a little while to master the new secure voice over internet phones.

After checking the schedule to confirm there were no secure calls scheduled, Shao slipped out of the office to the Starbucks behind the giant bookstore that anchored the northeast corner of the Xidan Station intersection. The cafe was always so packed, and the staff turned over so quickly that even though Shao was a regular customer, they never seemed to remember him. His phone buzzed with a WeChat message while he waited for his coffees. Sima Nan wanted to have dinner.

Shao didn't feel like texting and called back, "Hey buddy, what's up? No, I can't do it. I can't have dinner tonight. I promised Zhang Ying that we would try to have a baby, so I have uh, work, to do tonight."

Sima Nan's deep voice almost turned to a whine, "What? No way! You didn't even talk about it with me first. It's a bad idea, you should wait until after we've had dinner to do that."

"Look at yourself, you sound like a baby. Let's have dinner tomorrow night. Okay?"

"Okay, okay. Forget it. Let's meet at 7 at the old place on Ghost Street."

"Good. That's settled then. See you tomorrow," Shao hung up and picked up three coffees.

Shao handed one coffee to the guard standing duty at the reception desk. Shao had known him since he returned to Beijing and started working at the Propaganda Department. They weren't exactly friends, but Shao felt sorry for him being stuck at the desk all day and brought him coffee and snacks from time to time.

The door to Ye Hongqi's office was closed as Shao approached Liu Wuqing's desk. Liu wasn't there and Shao assumed he was in Ye's office with the top editors from China's main media outlets. Shao Huan set the coffee on Liu's desk and returned to his own office. There was always enough work to keep Shao active, but he almost never felt too busy. Most days he had at least a little time to review training manuals and to keep up with the new protocols.

There was a knock on Shao Huan's door and he opened it to find Liu Wuqing standing there with the coffee. Shao wasn't normally allowed to let anyone else from the Propaganda Department in to the communications office, but he and Liu were quite comfortable so he let Liu come in to the office, "Hey, I hope the coffee wasn't too cold."

Liu shook his head, "No, it was just about right when I got it. They always make it too hot. Thanks. That instruction session went much longer than usual."

Shao put his hands in his pockets, "Oh yeah? Don't those things always go long?"

"Well, it's like this, the People's Daily editor and the China Youth Daily really don't get along. When Ye Hongqi provided the instructions for how to cover the Party Chairman's speech, the People's Daily editor recommended they include some images of the Party Chairman shaking hands with local cadre but the China Youth Daily editor wanted to argue that the images should only show the Party Chairman's face delivering the speech so that there is no distraction from him being the center of the Party."

Shao Huan shrugged, "That seems a bit silly. Does it really matter? I mean, I don't think people really read those articles anyway. They skip over them and go to the sports and lifestyle articles."

Liu Wuqing nodded emphatically, "It is very important. Thought work isn't just about informing the ordinary people, it is about setting the tone for how Party cadre across the country should act, and to signal to them what the Center is doing and thinking. If we let them see the Party Chairman greeting local cadre, then it will signal a greater emphasis on support for local officials, if we show the image is only the Party Chairman speaking, it will signal continued focus on strengthening the Center."

"Wow, okay. I still don't quite see how that is all connected, but that is why I don't do your job buddy. So, who won out in the end?"

"Ye Hongqi supported the China Youth Daily editor, and everyone else quickly fell in line. Ye said it is not good to confuse the message and the core message remains the importance of the Party Chairman's ideology, not his personal charisma and showing him shaking hands with other cadre who are looking at him admiringly might make some people think it is okay to return to the cult of personality again," Liu took a long sip of coffee and continued, "I personally also don't think it is a very big difference really, but Ye thinks the People's Daily editor is getting too confident and forgetting his place as a tool to implement thought work."

Shao Huan laughed and bobbed his head slightly, "It's too complicated. I have been here for so long now and I really don't understand thought work, but it seems to be going okay. The boss seems to be doing very well. I wonder if he will take us with him to Zhongnanhai when he makes it to the Politburo Standing Committee."

Liu's eyes flared with concern and he lowered his voice, "Buddy, you shouldn't talk like that. We don't know what will happen, and just saying something like that can start rumors. If the Center thinks Ye is getting too confident, they might not elevate him, they might send him to be a Deputy Party Secretary in Anhui, or maybe just force him to resign completely. Please, don't say anything about that again. That isn't our problem to worry about. Do you understand?" Liu was from Guangdong but had mastered a perfect standard accent.

Shao had known Liu for several years, and thought that they had reached a point of familiarity where they could joke with each other. Liu's nervous and almost angry response surprised him, "Oh. Okay, I wasn't being serious, just kind of joking a little. Don't worry, I won't say anything else about it."

Liu nodded gravely, "Good. I know you were just joking, but be careful. Like any senior cadre, Ye Hongqi has many enemies who are jealous of him. We are so close to him, that we must be very careful and protect him. Okay, I should get back to work. Thanks again for the coffee."

Shao Huan typed a few classified messages from Ye Hongqi to the provincial Party secretaries and the official guidance from the instruction meeting which would be relayed to editors across China and to Chinese Embassies overseas. Shao Huan set the alarm and locked the office. He liked being so close to Zhongnanhai that he didn't have to work with a second communicator and that the General Office could send a back-up for him whenever needed.

Shao stopped by Liu's office before leaving for the night, "Alright buddy, I'm going home. Hopefully you can leave while the sun is still out."

Liu grimaced, "I hope so too. See you tomorrow." Shao noticed that Ye's office door was closed again.

The evening buzz around Xidan was electric. Streams of workers returned down the stairs into the subway station while others came up to go to the restaurants and shops. The large windows of the bookstore were well lit and showed dozens of people with their faces buried in books. Shao marveled that even when most people could read books on their phones, so many people still flocked to the giant bookstore.

Zhang Ying was already at home when Shao Huan returned to the apartment. "My dear, you are home! I've been waiting for you," she teased him, "I thought you might be avoiding me."

Shao Huan set down his bag and took off his shoes at the entrance, "Avoiding you? I've been looking forward to this moment all day."

Zhang wrapped her arms around Shao's neck and ran her thin white hand along his square jaw, then kissed him, "Are you sure you want a baby?"

Shao laughed and kissed her back, "It is hard work, but I am ready."

"Wait a minute, what is hard work?" Zhang slapped his arm playfully.

"I mean looking after a baby is hard work, what did you think I meant?" Shao smiled again and kissed his wife.

鬼街
Ghost Street

The red paper lanterns along Ghost Street swung gently over Shao Huan's head as he walked to Sima Nan's favorite hotpot restaurant. Zhang Ying didn't really like spicy food and definitely wouldn't touch it now that she wanted to get pregnant. Shao was looking forward to the burn on his tongue, the sweat beading on his forehead and hearing Sima Nan's stories.

Sima Nan already had a table and had started the fire under the pot of thick red soup, "Buddy, over here!" Sima Nan waved Shao Huan over to the small wooden table. "So, shit, you are really going to have a kid?" Sima asked as Shao sat on the wooden bench across from him.

"Yeah. I am," Shao Huan answered simply and took a drink of ice cold Snow Beer from the bottle that Sima Nan had ordered for him.

"Dammit," Sima Nan drug the curse out until he had to take a breath, "I thought we were going to make the band really happen finally."

"Brother, we have known each other for more than a decade and we haven't made the band happen. It is fun to jam together, but I can't tell Zhang Ying that we can't have a baby because I still want to become a rock star. I'm satisfied. This will be good."

A waitress brought plates of thinly sliced mutton, beef balls, squares of congealed blood, fresh cilantro, golden needle mushrooms, cabbage, and potato slices and stacked them on the table around the steaming soup.

"You always order too much!" Shao Huan laughed and put his hands on his keens, his shoulders squared to the pot.

"Well, I always eat everything. Even if you don't help very much."

"Fine, fine. Let's see who can't eat so much," Shao took a sip of beer, "It is exhausting trying to have a baby, I have a big appetite now."

Sima Nan smirked, "You just get tired too easily. You should have had more girlfriends so you could build up your stamina."

Large bubbles started slowly rising under the thick layer of red chili oil and black peppercorns floating on top of the soup. Shao Huan started to put in the potatoes and mushrooms, "You mean lots of girlfriends like you had? That isn't really how I remember it buddy!"

Sima Nan ran his hand along the close cropped hair on the side of his head, "You remember wrong. I've had lots of girlfriends. But I think that little Hua is the one. She is really cute and sweet. Maybe if you are ready to have a kid, I am ready to settle down."

Shao Huan took a spoonful of thick peanut sauce and mixed it in his bowl with fresh cut cilantro and sesame oil, "That's good brother, that is really good. How did you meet little Hua?" The fragrant smell of the spices rising from the soup made their mouths water and the boiling chilis made their eyes sting.

"We met through WeChat. Dating now isn't like it was when you met Zhang Ying. It's all digital. It's how everyone meets now," Sima Nan mixed in the mutton and beef balls as the soup returned to a rolling boil.

"I get it, that is the way things work now. How old is she?"

"She is only 21!" Sima Nan exclaimed proudly.

"So she is more than 10 years younger than you?" Shao Huan used the large ladle to fish a thin slice of mutton that had turned a delicious brown out of the scalding hot broth and cooled it in the peanut sauce mix before putting the warm tender meat in his mouth.

"Yeah, that's about right, but that just means I am lucky, right? I mean after all, Zhang Ying is younger than you. Men should always have younger wives," Sima Nan took a big bite of a beef ball.

Shao Huan gave a half hearted shrug, "Well, I guess it is usually that way. It takes so long to get financially stable that most women end up marrying someone a little older who already has their own apartment and car. You should be fine now, you have everything you would need to find a good wife."

"You got really lucky that Zhang Ying was willing to marry you before you had all of that and that she didn't make you stay in Hangzhou," Sima tried to cool his burning tongue with a big gulp of cold beer.

Sweat started to form on Shao Huan's high forehead. Shao Huan coughed as a pepper flake glanced against the back of his throat, "Wow, this is spicy. Did you get extra spicy soup?"

Sima Nan laughed and almost spit his beer over the side of the table, "Of course! We can take it!"

Shao Huan shook his head with a chuckle and took a bite of long stringy mushrooms covered in thick paste and sesame oil, "I hope little Hua is good for you brother. Hey, what is her given name?"

Sima Nan paused to think a moment, "Hmm… Hua Chunbao. Yeah, I'm pretty sure it is Chunbao. I always just call her little Hua. You know, you never did introduce me to your boss's daughter. She is real pretty right?"

"She is fair, rich and pretty, but she is way out of your league. Even if I could introduce you, would you would never have a chance," Shao Huan knew that Sima Nan could talk about his failed romances all night but wanted to talk about some changes he was trying to understand.

"Hey, I was reading about some of the changes that we are going to have to make to our network because of 5G technology. It sounds like it is going to catch up even to the secure network eventually. On the one hand, we might be able to enable secure communications on mobile devices, which I know the senior cadre would love, but on the other hand it seems like it will be very hard to secure. What are you guys doing at the Internet Information Office?" Shao Huan always appreciated Sima Nan's insights on technology. Sima had been the better student at Beijing Communications University and Shao wasn't surprised at all when he was selected to help set up the body that administered China's cyberspace.

"It's a thorny issue. The 5G networks are already running, and the data transfer speeds are so fast. It is incredible, but it makes our job so much harder. The telecommunications companies love it because they are able to sell more data, but we have had to increase our data storage and analysis capacity to keep up," Sima slicked back the long hair on top of his head. "The social credit system has helped to reduce the number of people who send or store prohibited information, but bad people who want to get around the controls can do it much more quickly and it takes us longer to catch up. What we are doing in Xinjiang is working, and we can control individual devices and keep a close eye on anyone who we are suspicious of, but that is only with a population of 11 million Uighurs. We don't have the capacity yet to deal with 1.4 billion people," Sima Nan took a breath and started to eat again, his face was red and covered in sweat.

"That is a much bigger problem than what we are dealing with. We just need to make sure the network stays closed and that none of the devices enable a link outside of the network. I guess, I really won't have to be part of the development and will just work on implementing the new equipment and policies once they are approved. It is interesting to think about," Shao Huan finished his beer and ordered another bottle for each of them.

"The real problem is the device to device communication. So many of the 5G devices enable direct communication to create mesh networks and reduce data latency and power usage for data transmission. For us, they are hard to control, but for you guys you'll have to prevent the mesh networks from being used as a vector to attack the cadre's communications. I've heard the Americans are already working on ways to hack us through mesh networks. I suppose the Fourth Department of the Joint Staff Department is doing the same thing to them, but our 5G networks are already so much more advanced than theirs. Those American bastards are so worried about our 5G networks that they keep trying to stop other countries from buying them. They can't compete with us anymore, all they can do is complain."

Shao Huan laughed and had to agree, "Yes, it is amazing how far we have come. Remember all the time we spent learning about CISCO routers? I haven't touched a CISCO router in years." He noticed the Sichuan peppercorn from the soup had numbed his lips.

Sima Nan lay down his chopstick and took a napkin to wipe off the sweat running down his face, "It's like this, the Americans think that the next war is going to be fought on the oceans or in the sky, maybe even in space, but they are wrong. The next war is already happening in cyberspace and we are winning. I really don't know about what the PLA is doing, but just seeing what we are able to do at the Internet Information Office, even with 5G networks, our systems are more secure and stronger than anything the Americans have. By the time we are actually at the point of shooting missiles or bullets, or whatever, the war will already be over."

Shao Huan clapped for Sima Nan, "Well said. I hope you are right. I spend all of my time working on protecting our communications that I don't think about how we are preparing to deal with foreign threats. But you are right, our infrastructure has improved so much and the Party has done a good job of centralizing control over the Internet."

"Hey brother, you can give the Party credit but you and I both know that I'm the one really working on keeping our cyberspace secure from the Americans and from poisonous thoughts within China." Sima Nan laughed and looked at the boiling soup that had nearly evaporated from the bowl. "You said I ordered too much," Sima teased.

"And you said I couldn't eat so much!" Shao Huan retorted.

"Okay, fine. You ate a lot. Good job," Sima stood up to leave, "Dammit that was really spicy. I need to get some yogurt."

"Good idea, let's go."

The evening air wasn't cool, but both Sima Nan and Shao Huan were sweating so much that the evaporation of the sweat from their skin in the gentle breeze was a relief. They walked down the street, past the crowds that were starting to spill out of the little restaurants along the way, and stopped at a convenience store. Shao bought two big glass bottles of cold yogurt and stood with Sima Nan outside, leaning up against the brick wall and watching the people pass by.

"Oh my god, that is exactly what I needed," Sima said with relief after a big gulp of the thick yogurt washed the heat from his tongue. "So have you thought about what you will name the kid? Shao Nan has a nice ring to it."

Shao Huan also relished the cool relief of the yogurt on his lips and in his stomach, "Brother, you know my father will pick the baby's name. You can make your case to him," he slapped Sima Nan on the back. "Maybe he'll agree if you promise to name your first born after him!"

Sima tilted his head, "Sima Youping… Yeah, that's okay I guess. I will talk to your father."

Shao Huan burst out laughing and hunched over, "I'm not sure if it is hot pot or the laughing, but my stomach hurts."

"Brother, it is definitely the hot pot. It's always the hotpot. That is one of the reasons Zhang Ying doesn't like you to go out for hot pot."

Shao Huan laughed again, "No, she doesn't like me drinking with you. She thinks you are going to get me to go to a bar to help you meet girls."

Sima Nan blew air between his lips, "I did that one time. Just one time! She will never forget that."

"Not for her whole life, brother. Never," Shao kept laughing and saw Sima Nan's face twist in annoyance in the glow from the red neon lights along the street.

"Dammit. Well, tell her you only had two beers tonight, and no girls. I can't believe you are going to be a father. You know you won't be able to go out like this anymore when you have a baby and an angry wife at home."

"Yeah, it will definitely be different, but you'll get to be uncle Sima. That will be fun, right?"

Sima Nan rested his head against the brick wall, "Yeah. Okay brother, you'll be a good dad but I'll be a better uncle. I'm not changing any damn diapers though."

幼儿园
Kindergarten

The summer slowly faded to autumn, and Zhang Ying had settled in to the new school year at the kindergarten. She loved her job. She woke up each day excited to see the children, and even though she was exhausted at the end of every day, she felt happy and fulfilled. The old courtyard house in the Dongcheng District with its slopping tiled roofs, long covered corridors and heavy wooden doors felt so connected to the past and such a perfect place for children to prepare for the future.

The job didn't pay much, but Zhang Ying knew she was lucky to work there and was grateful that her professor from Zhejiang Normal University had given her a good recommendation. She also knew that it didn't hurt that Shao Huan worked for a senior Party cadre, and that most of the parents were either already connected to the Party or aspired to build those connections through their children's education.

Joy filled Zhang Ying's face as she welcomed the children to her classroom every morning. The school's owner, Fang Zhitai walked around the courtyard throughout the day to check on the classes and usually lingered in Zhang Ying's classroom longer than the others. Fang was impressed with how Zhang Ying maintained order in the class without ever raising her voice and that Zhang's students still excelled on all of the evaluations.

The only part of her days that Zhang didn't like was dealing with overbearing parents. She tried to remind herself that they were just doing what they thought was best for their child, but it wore her down all the same. One day after the first frost, Fang Zhitai looked on with a smile as one of the mothers angrily berated Zhang Ying for not making sure that her son was dressed warmly enough while playing in the courtyard.

"Ma'am, I understand what you mean, it really is getting colder. I asked little Bao to put on his coat but he refused. I offered to help him put it on, but he still didn't want to. I can't make him wear a coat if he doesn't want to. Is there a sweater or something else warm that he likes to wear?" Zhang Ying met the scolding with grace and patience.

After the parent left, Fang Zhitai approached Zhang, "You handled her very well. She is always angry about something, her husband left her a few months before school started. Don't be too upset with her."

Zhang Ying appreciated Fang's support, "Yes, little Bao has mentioned that his father doesn't live with them any more. It is very hard for him too. I know she isn't really angry with me. I will be okay," Zhang Ying continued to tidy up the classroom while keeping an eye on the children that remained.

She tried to be kind and sweet to all of the children, and patient and understanding with all of the parents, but she couldn't help getting more attached to the sweeter children and feeling more connected to the kinder parents. She also knew the kind parents usually had the sweetest children. Zhang's favorite child in the class was Bai Xiaorong. He was smaller and quieter than the other boys in the class, but was so observant and clever. She liked to hear his laugh and always knew that after the other children shouted out incorrect answers, she could call on little Bai for the right answer.

Zhang finished preparing the classroom for the next day and saw Bai Xiaorong playing by himself in the courtyard. She approached him and smiled, "Can I play with you?" Xiaorong nodded and Zhang squatted down next to him and picked up a toy car, "What are we playing?"

A bashful smile crossed Xiaorong's little round face, "I'm playing race cars. Do you know how to play race cars?"

"Of course! But I have to tell you, my race car is very, very fast."

Xiaorong's joyful laugh rang out, "No way, my car can go faster!" He shouted and started running around the courtyard driving his car on the pillars and along the floor. Zhang Ying chased him with her car, keeping half a step behind him and blowing air between her tightly pressed lips to make engine sounds.

Zhang got so caught up in the game with Xiaorong that she didn't notice when his mother arrived, "Oh my goodness! I am so late, I am very embarrassed to arrive so late."

Xiaorong immediately stopped racing around the courtyard and ran to his mother. He squeezed her legs tightly, "Mama, you came!"

She leaned over and picked him up in her arms, and pressed her face against his, "Of course I came!"

Zhang Ying caught her breath and smiled watching Bai Xiaorong nuzzle against his mother, "Mrs. Jin! You interrupted our game, but it's okay. Xiaorong's car was much too fast for me."

"Thank you so much for staying with him. I am really so sorry. Xiaorong's father is out of town on business and so I am a little too busy right now. I should have been here sooner."

"It's really no problem. I was glad to have a little extra time with Xiaorong. There are so many other children all day, that I don't get to play with him much. You are very fortunate to have such a clever child," Zhang Ying stepped closer to Jin Xishan and put her hand on Xiaorong's back. Jin Xishan had short bobbed hair, fair skin and warm eyes. Zhang Ying thought Mrs. Jin had the kindest face she had ever seen.

"Well, shall we go? Principal Fang will lock the door," Zhang Ying motioned to the heavy wooden front door with large iron handles and black iron belting.

Mrs. Jin nodded, "Come on Xiaorong, you can walk too. Don't forget your bag!" She set her son down and he scrambled to pick up his dusty backpack.

"Where did your husband go for work?" Zhang Ying asked while she and Mrs. Jin stepped over the high threshold of the old wooden door. Xiaorong laughed as Mrs. Jin swung him up and over the threshold.

"He went to Seoul. He has business there sometimes," Mrs. Jin smiled at Zhang Ying as Xiaorong reached for her hand. "He really likes you!"

"He is a very sweet boy," Zhang Ying squeezed Xiaorong's hand, "I have never been to Seoul, I hear it is such a modern city."

Zhang and Jin walked along with Xiaorong swinging between them, "I have only been there once many years ago with my husband, but it is a very nice place if you like Korean food."

"I don't know, I haven't really had much Korean food, just Korean pickled cabbage. That is good, but a little spicy."

"Well, if you want, someday Xiaorong and I can take you for Korean food in Wangjing. There is a lot of good Korean food there."

Zhang Ying had never thought much about eating Korean food, but she decided that she liked Jin Xishan almost as much as she liked her son, "Okay. I would like that. Are you ethnically Korean?" She asked.

Jin Xishan nodded, "Yes, I grew up in Jilin, not far from the border with Korea. My grandparents moved to China during the war against the Americans and never went back. I am glad they stayed in China. They always said they wanted to go back, but it was so hard then. At least they could see Changbai Mountain from China before they died." Jin Xishan smiled, "We are really very lucky to have been born in China and not in Korea."

Zhang Ying agreed, "Yes, you said it well. I would really like to have Korean food with you sometime."

"Okay, we can arrange it when my husband returns. I am sure I will see you at school. We will take the bus from here. Thank you again for looking after Xiaorong today… and every day really," Jin Xishan reached out her arms and embraced Zhang Ying. Zhang was surprised, she barely knew Mrs. Jin but felt kindness radiating through her and then felt Xiaorong squeeze her legs, "Good bye teacher!"

Zhang Ying said good bye to them both and continued on her way home. The clear sunlight reflected low on the tall glass buildings as she walked east toward Chaoyang. She decided not to take the subway but to enjoy the evening and the wind rustling in the yellow and brown leaves above her.

Shao Huan was already cooking dinner when she got home, "Hey, there you are! Are you really tired?" He asked.

She hung up her coat and nodded, "I am tired, but it was a good day. I wish I was pregnant already. You know when we were young, everyone made it seem like as soon as you have sex you would get pregnant. But now, I want to get pregnant so badly and it is not so easy after all."

Shao turned the flame down on the stove and set down the pan he was using to fry strips of pork and eggplant. Steam rose from the rice cooker quietly counting down on the counter. Shao Huan took his bride by the hand and pulled her toward him, she buried her face in his chest, "Maybe there is something wrong with me. I should go to a doctor."

Shao sighed and held her tight, "Dear, we have only been trying to have a baby for a few months. Let's give it some more time. It isn't so easy after all."

Zhang Ying pulled back, "No, I mean it. I think I should go to a doctor to check. Why spend so much time trying to have a baby if I really can't have a baby anyway."

"If you go to a doctor, then I will go to a doctor. It could be that I have a problem," Shao ran the back of his hand along Zhang Ying's soft, fair face, "Don't worry my dear, we will have a baby. We just need to be patient. What happened today? Was it a hard day?"

Zhang firmly shook her head and sighed, "No, it was a wonderful day, really a wonderful day. I just saw how one of my students loved his mother so much, and the look on her face as she held him close. It made me want to have a baby so badly."

"Was it a little boy or a little girl?" Shao Huan asked.

"It was a boy."

"So do you want a boy now?" Shao kissed Zhang Ying on the cheek, and she playfully slapped him.

"Maybe. Maybe I want a boy. Most of the boys can be too much trouble, but some of them really are very sweet with their mothers. I think I would like that."

Shao Huan nodded, "Okay, well let's eat, and then try to make a baby boy."

Zhang Ying loved how Shao Huan set her at ease and made everything feel like it would be okay. She didn't tell him that the eggplant was overcooked, only that she was so glad he had cooked for her. She watched him lift up his bowl and shovel the last few bites of rice into his mouth and was glad he would be the father of her child.

怀孕
Pregnant

Shao Huan didn't mind the cold and dark days of January, his office didn't have windows anyway and was always at the same cool temperature. For Zhang Ying, however, the cold days were exhausting. The children couldn't play outside and their energy nearly burst through the walls of the small classroom. Even though Fang Zhitai had refurbished the old courtyard home, the cold crept through every seam in the building.

Zhang looked forward to seeing Jin Xishan every day and even though they hadn't been able to go out for dinner together, she felt like they were becoming friends. Jin wasn't that much older than Zhang Ying and she hoped to be as good of a mother as Jin was for Xiaorong. Zhang had not made many friends in Beijing since she moved from Hangzhou. She liked some of Shao Huan's childhood friends and liked his parents, but was glad to have a friend of her own. Zhang also looked forward to her evenings at home with Shao Huan, curled together on their sofa in the warm and comfortable apartment, watching silly shows on television or reading books. She especially loved when Shao Huan would play the guitar for her.

Zhang Ying felt like every day in January was colder and more tiring than the day before. She didn't mind Beijing most of the time, but she missed the mild winters in Hangzhou. One evening at home with Shao Huan, she admitted, "I am so tired, I don't want to go to teach tomorrow. I just want to sleep."

Shao Huan put his strong hand on her back, "I know, it is so cold. Maybe you should take a taxi to work during the winter?"

Zhang Ying rested her head on his shoulder, "I don't think I need to do that, I am just complaining. I wish spring was already here."

Shao kissed her forehead, "Me too. Do you want to try to make a baby tonight?"

Zhang just shook her head weakly, "No, I just want to go to sleep," she said and let Shao Huan help her to bed.

The next morning was dark outside and Zhang dreaded leaving her warm bed and cozy apartment. She heard Shao Huan cooking breakfast in the kitchen and pulled herself out of bed. She felt her stomach turn as she stood up and she rushed to the bathroom, her hair fell over the toilet bowl as she leaned forward. She wanted to vomit and wretched a few times but nothing came up.

Shao Huan heard Zhang Ying's coughing and moaning and rushed to the bathroom, "Dear, are you sick? Can I take you to a doctor?"

Zhang Ying placed one hand on his outstretched wrist and with her other hand on the toilet bowl. She pushed herself up from the toilet. Shao Huan put down the toilet seat and Zhang sat down. She wiped her mouth and ran both hands through her fine black hair, "I don't think I need to go to a doctor, I think I am pregnant."

"What? Really? Are you sure?" Shao Huan was elated.

Zhang was too uncomfortable to show her excitement but hope welled up in her as she asked Shao Huan to get a pregnancy test kit. She had bought several when they started trying to have a baby and had even used a couple of them so she would know how they worked. "When should you have your next period?" Shao asked as Zhang opened up the test kit.

"A few days ago. I hoped that maybe I was pregnant, but my period doesn't always come on time anyway," Zhang Ying touched the tip of the test kit in her morning urine and Zhang and Shao waited together anxiously. The two minutes that they waited in the small bathroom seemed impossibly long, but the moment that a second pink line started to appear on the test kit Shao wrapped his arms around Zhang and cheered, "You are pregnant! We are going to have a baby!"

Zhang was too overwhelmed to speak. She put her hand over her mouth and began to cry. Shao Huan was not expecting her tears, but he quickly recognized them as tears of joy, "It's okay my dear, it's okay. We will have a baby. This is wonderful." Zhang Ying stood and hugged him tightly.

"Maybe you shouldn't go to work today?" Shao suggested.

Zhang couldn't answer for a moment, but after taking a few deep breaths said, "No, I want to go to work. I feel better already. I feel sick, but I also feel wonderful. I want to see the children today," she paused, "but I will take a taxi if that is okay?"

Shao leaned back to look at his exhausted, uncomfortable, beautiful wife, "Of course! I am steaming some buns and was heating up the soy milk. Do you want to eat before you go? Maybe eat just a little?"

"No, I don't think I can eat now, but I will take some of the steamed buns for later. Those should be easy to eat once I feel hungry."

"Okay, no problem. Hey, should we call your parents? They will be so happy."

Zhang tilted her head thinking about whether to call her parents, they had agreed they wouldn't tell anyone until she was at least 13 weeks pregnant in case something went wrong, but was now torn between the desire to share her joy and the fear of disappointing her parents if the pregnancy didn't last, "No. I think we should still wait. We shouldn't tell anyone yet. But I should make an appointment with a doctor. I will do that this afternoon."

Zhang Ying squeezed her husband tightly and started to laugh, "We are going to have a baby. I thought it would never happen. But I'm pregnant. I am sure I am pregnant." She looked up at Shao Huan, "Hey, aren't you going to be late for work?"

Shao Huan looked down at his watch, "Aya! You are right, I have to go. I love you, take the buns to work!" Shao Huan turned off the stove and dumped the buns on top of a towel resting over a plate, "Okay! Let's celebrate tonight!" He shouted and left a kiss on Zhang Ying's check before he raced out the door.

Zhang Ying moved slowly getting ready for work and her stomach felt uneasy, but she couldn't stop smiling. She was grateful that Shao Huan had suggested she take a taxi to work and even though traffic heading in to the city was heavy as always, she felt much more comfortable in the back of the warm taxi than walking through the cold.

The children were as rambunctious as ever and Zhang found herself sitting and resting more than normal throughout the day. She looked forward to the relative quiet of the afternoon nap period, and sat in the comfortable bean bag where she read stories to the children as they listlessly turned on their mats. She had not expected that she would feel so tired and fought to keep her eyes awake in the warm, dark room with just the soft grey light from the courtyard outside.

Zhang was relieved to reach the end of the day and helped the children put on their heavy coats as parents started arriving to collect their precious little ones. Jin Xishan arrived a little late as usual and greeted Zhang Ying with a hug. Jin's hugs had seemed strange at first, but as they grew closer Zhang had come to look forward to them.

Jin's face was flushed pink from the cold outside and she lifted Xiaorong up in her arms and held his warm face to hers, "Come on baby, you are so warm, can you help warm up mama?"

Xiaorong laughed and struggled against her, "I can't! I can't! You are too cold, put me down!" Jin set him down and tousled his hair. She looked at Zhang Ying, "Are you okay? You look very tired."

Zhang Ying smiled and nodded gently, "I am okay, I am just very tired. I think it is the cold. It makes me tired."

Jin Xishan studied Zhang carefully, and then said "You are pregnant. Aren't you?"

"What? How? I… I just found out this morning," Zhang was too amazed by Jin's guess to argue and too tired to try lying to her.

"I thought so. You have been a little different for these last couple of weeks. I had wondered if you were pregnant, but seeing you today it is clear you are pregnant. You look so tired but your face is still glowing. Congratulations!"

"Thanks. I haven't told anyone and want to wait a few months before we tell anyone…" Zhang Ying's voice trailed off.

"I understand, really. I waited a few months before I told my family that I was pregnant with Xiaorong. Don't worry, I won't tell anyone.

But we really have to go out for Korean food to celebrate. Okay? Can we go out tomorrow? I can take you to Wangjing and your husband can meet us there."

Zhang Ying was so tired, but celebrating with Jin Xishan and Xiaorong sounded like a wonderful idea, "Okay. I will tell Shao Huan."

Xiaorong gave Zhang a hug and put his face against hers before he left, "Your face is really warm," he said and then waved goodbye as he left with Jin.

Zhang was still very tired and felt a little sick the next day, but she was increasingly excited about the new life growing inside her. She looked forward to dinner with Jin and to introducing her to Shao Huan. After school, Jin arrived a little earlier than usual and read with Xiaorong in the classroom while Zhang waited for all of the other parents to collect their children.

"Okay! Let's go!" Zhang Ying said after the last child had left.

Jin called a taxi and a cold gust raced along the old alley way, blowing dried leaves into the air, "It is so cold, we have to get you out of this weather!"

The ride to Wangjing was short and fast along the wide boulevards, and Xiaorong lay on the back seat between his mother and his teacher, basking in the attention from both of them. The hostess greeted Jin Xishan in Korean as they entered the restaurant and after a short conversation with the hostess, that almost sounded like an argument, they were led to a small private room at the back of the restaurant. They took their shoes off and stepped onto the raised wooden platform and sat on cushions around the low table. The hostess closed the sliding rice paper door and left them. Xiaorong sprawled out on the warm floor.

Zhang Ying was impressed with Jin Xishan's Korean language, "What did you say to the hostess?" Zhang asked.

"I asked for a private room. She said they were all booked, but I told her that you are pregnant and need to warm up on the ondol. It is like a kang heated bed in northern China, but heats the whole floor. She said there is a booking for this room at 8 p.m. and I told her we will be gone by then, so she agreed to let us sit here."

A waitress appeared with a pot of hot barely tea and earthenware cups. She poured the tea for Zhang and Jin and gave Xiaorong a bright green plastic cup with sweet bubbly Sprite. Jin explained that they were waiting for Shao Huan to arrive before they ordered.

"Are you going to try to find out if it is a boy or a girl?" Jin asked and took a sip of the smooth and light golden barley tea.

The warm tea and heat radiating from the floor felt good. Zhang Ying felt her muscles loosen and noticed Xiaorong crawling under the table, "No, it is too much trouble and we really don't care if it is a boy or a girl. I am just so happy to be pregnant. I thought it would never happen, or that something was wrong with me. But now, I am happier than I have been since Shao Huan and I first got married."

Jin nodded, "Any child is a blessing, and you will be a wonderful mother. Everyone says you are the best teacher at the kindergarten and I see how you are with Xiaorong. Regardless of whether you have a boy or a girl, you will be a wonderful mother."

Zhang heard Shao Huan's voice outside of the paper door just before the waitress slid it open and Shao Huan stepped in side. He hugged Zhang Ying and greeted Jin Xishan, "It is really good to finally meet you. Zhang Ying talks about you and Xiaorong all the time. Hey, by the way, where is Xiaorong?" Shao Huan looked around the room.

Xiaorong started giggling under the table, and Shao Huan kneeled down to look under the table, "Hey! There you are little friend! I am teacher Zhang's husband." Xiaorong rolled over under the table and emerged next to his mother. He laughed and buried his face in her back.

"I think he is a little jealous to meet teacher Zhang's husband. Sometimes I think he likes her too much," Jin joked.

The waitress entered with a menu and started setting out little dishes of cold pickled cabbage, mushroom, mashed potato, cold boiled beansprouts, and stir fried fern shoots. She poured a cup of barley tea for Shao Huan. "Is there anything you don't eat?" Jin Xishan asked.

"I don't like too much spice, but Shao Huan loves spicy food," Zhang Ying reached for Shao Huan's hand and looked at him while Jin ordered in Korean.

After the waitress left, Jin explained, "I didn't order anything spicy but Shao Huan, you can add some of this fermented chili sauce to anything you want to make spicy."

"Good! I hope you ordered some meat, I like Korean barbecue," Shao Huan waved at Xiaorong as he poked his head out from behind Jin's back.

"I ordered grilled pork belly and grilled short ribs for you. If it is too much you can take it home. Congratulations on the baby! That is really wonderful. I have been telling Zhang Ying what a great mother she will be."

Zhang Ying blushed as Shao Huan agreed, "Me too. I have told her that for months. I am glad we think alike. Let's drink a toast to Zhang Ying and our baby," Shao Huan lifted up the sturdy clay cup and clinked it against Zhang's and Jin's cups. Xiaorong emerged from behind his mother, "I'm coming!" He shouted and lifted his red plastic cup to join the toast.

Xiaorong grew more comfortable with Shao Huan and they played together while Jin Xishan and Zhang Ying talked and laughed. The waitress entered with a black clay pot still boiling with a hearty tofu stew, a plate of cellophane noodles stir fried with strips of beef, and a large plate filled with leafy green vegetables, carrot sticks and slender green chilis and sliced garlic, and another plate with thick dumplings. She placed silver bowls of rice in front of each of them and closed the door.

"It looks so delicious!" Zhang Ying admired the food on the low wooden table but Shao Huan followed the smell of meat grilling on a charcoal stove near by, and opened the rice paper door to see the waitress grilling long strips of thick pork marbled with fat, "It smells delicious too," Shao rubbed his hands together, "Let's eat!"

Jin Xishan filled a bowl with the boiling tofu stew and placed it before Zhang Ying, "Wait until it cools down, but this is good for you and the baby. It isn't so spicy."

Zhang Ying hadn't really eaten much for two days except for the steamed buns, but the warm stew looked delicious and she took a spoonful of the soft white tofu and blew on it until it was cool enough to eat. Shao Huan took the flat metal chopsticks and placed some noodles and beef on Xiaorong's plate, "I am guessing you like this." Xiaorong nodded and also reached for a long strip of crisp carrot.

Shao Huan and Zhang Ying noticed that Jin Xishan lowered her head in silence for a moment before she lifted her own chopsticks and began to eat. The waitress opened the door and placed a plate of grilled pork and juicy ribs in front of Shao Huan, "Wow! This is really great. All for me!" He joked and then moved the meat to the center of the table.

Jin Xishan took a large lettuce leaf and smeared chili sauce in the middle of it. She then took a piece of meat and rubbed it in the small dish of sesame oil and salt beside her plate, placed the meat in the leaf, folded it up and popped the morsel in her mouth. Shao Huan copied her and savored the feeling of biting through the cool crisp leaf and the taste of the well marinated meat inside.

Jin paused from eating to ask, "Shao Huan, Zhang Ying has told me how you two met, but I want to hear your side of the story."

Shao Huan laughed, "Hopefully it is the same. My friends from Beijing all teased me that I would meet Bai Suzhen at the West Lake when I moved to Hangzhou. But, luckily, I met Zhang Ying at a cafe instead."

Zhang Ying lightly hit his shoulder, "You always used to tease me about us being the characters from the Legend of the White Snake. But it's true you really don't like the sweet dumplings and would have spit those immortality pills back into the lake."

"It's true. I really don't like sweet dumplings, and fortunately you aren't an immortal snake. It's a romantic legend though. Anyway, it wasn't long after I moved to Hangzhou that I went to the West Lake on a weekend afternoon and took my guitar to play by the water. I didn't know many people in Hangzhou. I sat by the lake by myself and just played and played, I didn't pay attention to anyone else, I just watched the light on the lake. Eventually I got tired and went to a cafe nearby. As I was waiting for my coffee this pretty girl told me that she really liked listening to me play. We started talking and then sat by the lake and talked for what seemed like only a moment but it had been hours. It wasn't just love at first sight, it was like finding my soul mate," Shao Huan's brown eyes sparkled as he recounted meeting Zhang Ying. She always loved to hear him tell the story.

"How romantic!" Jin Xishan exclaimed, "It really was fate for you two to meet." Xiaorong had finished his noodles and a few pieces of meat and lay his head on Jin's lap.

Zhang Ying had nearly eaten all of the tofu soup and felt warm and content sitting on the soft cushion and listening as Jin told them about childhood growing up in a small village in Jilin, about the cold winters, the beautiful summers, and the clear river where she played with her friends. Jin told them how she had gone to university in Shenyang, and how she met her husband there. Xiaorong started to snore softly while Jin Xishan gently raked her fingers through his thick hair.

"We should let you go home, Xiaorong is already sleeping and I know Zhang Ying is also tired. Thank you for such a wonderful meal. Next time is our treat. Let me help you get Xiaorong to a taxi," Shao Huan stood up and carefully lifted the sleeping boy on to his shoulder. He held Xiaorong while Jin Xishan put on his coat and shoes, "I wish I could sleep like that," he marveled.

Jin laughed, "Sleep as well as you can now, soon you won't be sleeping at all!" She hugged Zhang Ying farewell and wrapped an arm around Shao Huan's back as well when he passed Xiaorong to her, "I am so happy for both of you, please let me know if you ever need anything, even a few hours sleep."

In the taxi on their way back to their apartment, Shao Huan held Zhang Ying's hand in his lap, "I like her. And I understand why you want a little boy."

饺子馆
Dumpling Museum

The morning sickness gradually passed and Zhang Ying felt her energy returning as the days grew longer and the first few buds appeared on the trees around Chaoyang park. Her doctor assured her that the baby was growing well and that all the tests showed Zhang and the baby were both in perfect health. Zhang Ying and Shao Huan decided that the pregnancy was going well and that it was time to tell their friends and family.

Shao Huan's parents were thrilled with the news. Zhang Ying's parents pledged to travel from Hangzhou to be in Beijing for the birth and to help Zhang Ying during her month of postpartum confinement. Shao Huan's mother started making plans to look after the baby when Zhang went back to work. Zhang and Shao agreed that she would tell Fang Zhitai and to request leave for the delivery, and that Shao would inform Ye Hongqi.

That morning, Shao Huan stopped by Liu Wuqing's office to deliver the daily reports. "Hey buddy, here you go. Looks like some important communications from the Center. It sounds like the thought work is getting very focused on religion."

Liu nodded and accepted the folder, "Yes, the Party Chairman is deeply concerned about the uncontrolled spread of religion since the reform and opening era began. He has directed us to use every tool to reeducate the people about the five official religions and to stop the spread of evil teachings. He wants religion to be a tool of the Party, and not an alternative power center competing with the Party."

"Wow, it's really like that? I thought Falun Gong was the only evil teaching the Party really cared about."

Liu sighed, "The Party Chairman is very serious about the ideological struggle. He wants to ensure that all Party members adhere to the Party's doctrine completely, and that the people's superstitions are controlled within the approved official religions. We already have established quite firm control over the Daoist and Buddhist temples, though there are always some monks who are hard to control. We have made great success in limiting Islam, but are only now really beginning to try to control Christianity. It is perhaps the biggest threat, and the Party Chairman has reminded Ye Hongqi several times of the Taiping Rebellion."

Shao was shocked and forgot that he wanted to request a meeting with Ye Hongqi, "The Taiping Rebellion? Is he really worried about peasants rising up against the Party because they think they want to establish a heavenly kingdom? That doesn't seem possible."

"The Party Chairman is a student of our history. He is very aware of the Yellow Turban uprising against the Han dynasty, the invasion of the Yuan, and the collapse of the Qing. He thinks the ideological threats are more dangerous than the military threats, and that every dynasty collapsed because it strayed from its ideological center and lost the mandate of heaven," Liu stretched out his hands and Shao noticed his prayer beads were gone. "The Party Secretaries in Xinjiang, Gansu and Ningxia have done a good job of controlling the Muslims and the provincial propaganda offices have supported them, but Christianity is a problem across China. The Party Chairman has placed a great responsibility on Ye Hongqi to bring the Christians under control. The Bureau of Propaganda and Culture has already completed revisions to the Bible to ensure it does not contain thoughts that might undermine the Party. I think the Party Chairman puts more responsibility on our Department than on the whole military."

Shao shook his head, "I know I tell you this often, but I really don't envy you. That sounds like it must be impossible."

Liu Wuqing grimaced, "Whether it is possible or impossible, it is vital to the Party and we must make every effort." Liu checked his watch, "I am sorry, I must do some work."

Shao suddenly remembered his purpose, "Of course, I shouldn't distract you. I wanted to ask if I could have two minutes with the boss? I need to tell him something."

"Of course, I can arrange that, but first you should tell me what you need to tell him. If you are going to resign or there is some problem he will be angry at me for not informing him first," Liu said nervously.

Shao Huan laughed, "Oh buddy, no, no. I am not resigning. I… it's just, well, my wife is pregnant. I wanted to let him know directly."

Liu Wuqing appeared relieved, "Oh! Oh good! Congratulations. That is great news. Yes, I will not tell him, but I will let him know it is good news. He will probably guess. I will come get you this afternoon in between his meetings. Okay?"

"Thanks. Okay, yes that would be great. And I'm sorry, I didn't mean to scare you. It is good news."

Shao Huan returned to his office and began processing messages that Liu had drafted for dissemination to the provincial propaganda offices. He slipped out of the office for a bowl of hot and sour noodles for lunch. The early spring day was refreshing, and it felt good to get out and walk in the sunlight. He liked to watch the crowds of people coming and going around Xidan, and the fast and delicious food from little shops tucked away in the neighborhood. Shao was excited to tell his boss the good news.

Liu knocked on his door a little before 4 p.m. "Hey, the boss should be finishing a meeting soon. Can you come wait in my office? Then when he is done, we can go in so you can tell him."

Shao stood and followed Liu Wuqing to his office, "Hey, who is he meeting by the way?"

"He is meeting the Head of the United Front Work Department. We need to ensure our thought work is coordinated with them so that the overseas Chinese media they control follows the same line, and that their agents overseas can emphasize the correct ideology," the door to Ye's office opened and a slender man with glasses and a hairline that started near the middle of his head walked out and nodded a brief farewell to Liu and Shao.

"Come on, he should be ready now," Liu knocked on the open door, "Director Ye, Shao Huan is here and would like a few minutes of your time."

"Okay! Please come in!" Ye called from inside the office and Shao followed Liu Wuqing into the large office, with televisions nearly covering one wall, all on different channels.

Ye Hongqi greeted Shao Huan with a handshake and asked him to have a seat, "It's okay, this shouldn't take long. I just wanted to let you know that my wife is pregnant. Our baby is due in October. I know it is a busy time with the anniversary of the founding of the People's Republic of China, but I would like to take a couple of weeks off then. I can arrange with the General Office to have another communicator sent over from Zhongnanhai for a short while."

Ye stood and smiled while he waited for Shao Huan to finish, "Congratulations, congratulations! That is wonderful news. I hope you have a son! My daughter was wonderful when she was little, but now she is making me grow old so quickly!" Ye joked. "Of course you can have the time off. It is important. I wish I had taken more time off when my daughter was born. I was so young then, I didn't understand how I would never get those days back. You have my full support and blessing."

"Thank you, I really appreciate your support."

Liu Wuqing signaled to Shao Huan that it was time to go, but Ye Hongqi stopped him, "It is good to see both of you, I have been so busy these days that I have not had the chance to talk with either of you very much. Liu Wuqing, what is on my schedule this evening?"

Liu always knew Ye's daily schedule by heart, down to the minute, "You are scheduled to have dinner with the head of the propaganda department for Guizhou Province and the director for China Radio International. The dinner will be held in the restaurant for the Guizhou Province representation office."

Ye sighed, "I am really tired. Every meal is not about eating, but about work. Call them and tell them that I am not feeling well and I must cancel dinner tonight. Can we include them in another dinner next week?"

Liu quickly calculated the political arrangements of Ye's dinner meetings in the week ahead, "Yes, we could include them in the dinner with the Hunan and Guangxi representatives. The only question would be where to hold the dinner."

"Okay, let's hold the dinner at the Guizhou Province representative office since I am cancelling on them. Let's go out for dinner tonight, just the three of us. We can celebrate Shao Huan's good news. Okay?"

Liu Wuqing and Shao Huan looked at each other, they used to go out to dinner with Ye occasionally in Zhejiang but since he had been so busy since he returned to Beijing that they never really saw him outside of the office. Liu took the lead to answer, "Yes, of course. Where would you like to go?"

Ye thought for a moment, "Nothing fancy. I am tired of fancy food. Maybe that dumpling place that you like? Do they have a private room?" He asked Liu.

"Yes, they do."

"Great! Okay, let's leave here at 6 p.m. then. You can both ride with me."

Liu and Shao left the office and gave each other puzzled looks but couldn't say anything more than, "Great, see you at 6!"

Shao Huan went outside so he could use his cell phone to call Zhang Ying. She was just tidying up the classroom when he called, "My dear, I told my boss about our baby, he is really excited. He wants to have dinner tonight to celebrate. I will be home a little bit late, please don't wait for me. I should be home around 8 or 9, okay?"

"Of course dear, that is great. I am glad he wants to celebrate with you. I haven't told Fang Zhitai yet. I will tell her soon. I will see you at home later. I love you!"

"I love you too! See you later!"

Zhang Ying hung up the phone and put on her jacket. She walked to Fang's offie and knocked on the door, "Come in!" Fang's voice rang out.

"Principal Fang, I have something I need to tell you," Zhang started anxiously.

Fang looked up from her laptop and smiled, "Have you finally come to tell me that you are pregnant?"

"I... I... How did you know?" Zhang Ying was surprised and at first nervous but Fang's comfortable smile set her at ease.

"Teacher Zhang, it is obvious to everyone. I wanted to speak with you about it earlier, but decided that you would tell me when you were ready. And, now you have come! Congratulations! When is the baby due?"

"In October. I can work until the baby comes and then I will stay home for one month. My mother-in-law will help look after the baby, though, so I can come back to work after that."

"Don't be anxious about returning to work. Rest assured, whenever you are ready to come back, your job will be waiting for you. I want our little school to be like a family and I am so glad you will bring another baby to join our family," Fang had stood from her desk and placed her hand on Zhang Ying's shoulder, "If you need anything, please just let me know."

"Thank you so much. I really do love working here. Thank you for letting me come back to work after the baby."

"Of course, whatever you need. You are one of the best teachers I have ever worked with. Maybe one day you will have your own school. And being a mother will make you an even better teacher. I know it won't feel like that at times, but it will. It really will."

Zhang Ying walked home, relieved, happy and excited. It felt good to share her news with everyone, and to know that they supported her. She was curious about Shao's dinner with Ye Hongqi. She had only met Ye a few times, and she was glad that he had helped Shao Huan's career but in their brief interactions, he just seemed like every other senior cadre she had seen on television.

Shao Huan waited with Liu Wuqing in his office. "Hey, buddy, you know, we have known each other for years but I just realized I have no idea what kind of music you listen to. You do listen to music, right?"

Liu laughed, "Of course I listen to music, I'm not a machine... even though I sometimes feel that way. When I was younger I listened to pop music from Hong Kong like Wang Fei and Leon Lai. But now, speaking frankly, I am so tired that I listen to music to relax. Usually traditional Chinese zither or sometimes Buddhist chants. It helps me to take all of the things happening here and put them to the side so I can focus."

Shao Huan looked at Liu's naked wrist and Liu understood the unasked question, "I can't wear the bracelet here anymore. It isn't convenient, but I can still meditate on my own if it helps me to be a better cadre."

"Yes, of course. I don't really meditate, but I think you know I play the guitar. That is how I relax. I like to listen to Yang Xuefei play. She is amazing. I used to listen to Cui Jian and the old rockers, but now I really prefer Yang's complexity and art."

The door opened and Ye emerged, "Okay! I'm done, let's go. Did you make a reservation?" Ye asked Liu.

"Yes, I did. It will be quiet and low profile, but I did promise the owner that she could take a picture with you, but that she couldn't put it up in her restaurant, otherwise we would not be able to return."

The three men took the elevator to the basement parking garage where Ye's black Audi was waiting. His security detail was in another black Audi behind. Shao Huan sat in the front passenger seat while Ye sat in the rear passenger seat and Liu sat next to him. Liu told the driver where to go. Liu explained to Ye Hongqi that the security detail had agreed to park the car around the block and that they would have a meal in the main dining room and try to look like normal customers.

Ye nodded, "Okay, good plan. It is always so hard getting out. It is even harder for the Party Chairman though. Do you remember when he went to one steamed bun shop? That shop had lines around the block for months afterward. When you go there, you can see they still have pictures of that visit. I think that was probably my first big mistake as Head of the Propaganda Department. I underestimated how much the people longed for the Party Chairman to be a celebrity and not just a leader."

Shao Huan sat quietly in the front seat and admired how the driver worked his way through the heavy traffic toward the little dumpling restaurant. The restaurant looked nearly empty when they arrived, but the owner was waiting at the entrance. She bowed deeply and shook Ye Hongqi's hand, "It is a great honor to have you visit our restaurant. I hope you enjoy your meal."

Ye easily snapped out of his brief moment of relaxation and resumed his officious air as he greeted the owner, "This is a fine shop. My secretary Liu has told me your dumplings are the best in Beijing. I only regret I have not come sooner. Thank you for your hospitality. May I take a picture with you?"

The restaurant owner beamed with pride as she stood next to Ye, and it was all the better that he had asked her for a photograph. Liu used his phone and the restaurant owner's phone to take the pictures. She ushered Ye, Liu and Shao to a small private room at the back of the restaurant where ice cold beer and small cold dishes were already waiting.

"This is just right, thank you," Ye said to the owner, then turned to Liu, "Would you order for us and make sure to order something for the guards and drivers as well." He then signaled for Shao to have a seat, and his carefully crafted facade fell away again.

"So, you are going to be a father. Are you nervous?" Ye asked.

Shao shifted in his seat, "Speaking honestly, I am very nervous. I haven't told Zhang Ying that, but it is a big responsibility."

Ye nodded solemnly, "It really is a big responsibility. It is the biggest responsibility of your life. It's not just about being a filial son, more importantly it is about your child's future. You will want to give them every opportunity you can."

Shao started to pour three glasses of beer as Liu entered the private room, "Okay, the dishes will be here soon. She wants to impress you so much, I had to argue with her a little bit to get normal dishes and that she should not try to make anything different. I think she understood."

"Good, thank you. First a toast to Shao Huan's wife, may her pregnancy be easy and the baby healthy!" Ye raised his glass and Liu and Shao were careful to tap their glasses beneath the lip of Ye's glass. Ye finished his first small glass of beer in one shot, so Liu and Shao followed suit. Shao poured another round.

"Let's eat!" Ye said and picked up a fat piece of clear mung bean jelly dripping with chili oil and vinegar, and flecked with spring onions. Shao put some spiced peanuts on his plate and a clump of sliced kelp and tofu skin. Ye asked, "Wuqing, when are you going to have a child? You have been married for nearly ten years now. Don't you think it is time?"

Liu Wuqing squirmed in his seat and Shao Huan could see him struggling to respond and tried to come to Liu's aid, "Hey boss, I think Wuqing is working so much these days he probably doesn't even see his wife."

Ye looked up surprised, "Is that true? I know things have been busy since we came back to Beijing. How often do you see your wife?"

Liu sighed, "I usually see her for a few hours on weekends. It isn't a problem. She understands that this is important work for the Party and the country. She is willing to wait to have children until things are a little more stable."

Ye took a bite of crisp cucumber, "I know that you have been working hard. I appreciate it and the Party Chairman has commented to me what a good secretary I have. I am working with the personnel department to find an appropriate position to reward you for your work. You can start a family then."

"Thank you, I know you will find an appropriate position for me. I will go wherever the Party decides."

The restaurant owner knocked on the door and entered with several plates of steaming dumplings, "Be careful, they are still hot!" She said as she set them down in the middle of the table. The three men all poured black vinegar into the dipping dishes by their plates and Shao Huan added a spoonful of chili oil.

Ye took a steaming dumpling and set it on his plate. He pierced the thick skin to let the heat escape, "It is good that you have faith in the Party. We all must trust in the Party, even though you never know where the Party will put you or where fate will take you. When I got assigned as the Deputy Party Secretary in Zhejiang, I was upset that I was not made the Party Secretary in Guangdong. I had worked hard to get that position, but because of the time in Zhejiang I got to work closely with the Party Chairman. Now, he has brought me to Beijing and given me this important job. I know it is hard on all of us," Ye's usual efficacious tone was gone and his voice was sincere, " I really couldn't do it without both of you. The Party Chairman needs people who he trusts in key positions, and I need people who I trust close to me."

Shao Huan finished a bite of pork and cabbage dumpling, "Boss, of course. We will do anything we can to help you."

Liu Wuqing echoed Shao, "Anything at all. We are here to support you."

Ye took a bite of pork and chive dumpling coated in the tangy vinegar and then had a drink of beer, "The Party Chairman really values our work, but it is hard work. Very hard. We must educate the people and guide their thinking, but it has never been harder. There are so many groups, platforms and media. So many of our people go overseas, and now they return. Before, they would stay overseas and their foreign ideas would not be so influential. But now, they come back. We must use their social credit score to keep a close eye on them, and we must not allow any ideology to rival the Party's supremacy. If we fail, it could mean the end of China. Our enemies want to split us apart. The Americans want to take Taiwan from us, the Indians want to take Tibet, even the Russians want to take Heilongjiang. It is our ideology that holds us together."

Shao Huan nodded intently but had to wonder what Ye meant, Shao had never really cared about the ideology. He had studied Party slogans throughout school and saw them around Beijing, but most seemed empty to him. He was grateful Ye Hongqi didn't ask him what the Party's ideology actually was. Under Chairman Mao Zedong it had been the revolution of the peasants against the feudal elite, under Deng Xiaoping's leadership it was reform and opening up, under Jiang Zemin and Hu Jintao it seemed that the ideology didn't matter at all and the Party was just overseeing a race to accumulate wealth. But he couldn't possibly explain what the ideology meant any more.

Fortunately, Liu Wuqing knew exactly how to respond, "Quite right boss, quite right. We must strengthen our thought work across China. The people will follow where we lead. We must lead them away from danger, away from foreign influence. Our work is even more important in Hong Kong and Macao. The foreign influence there is so strong, we must be more firm and vigilant."

Ye Hongqi's eyes sparkled and he laced his fingers and rested his hands on his belly, "Maybe we should send you to the Hong Kong Liaison Office. You do speak Cantonese after all, right?"

Liu's face started to turn red, "That wasn't what I meant. I was just…"

Ye waved his hand at Liu Wuqing, "I know, I know, we are all friends here. Take it easy. I'm not saying you were asking to go to Hong Kong. I am asking if you would like to go to Hong Kong."

Liu took a drink of beer and Shao refilled his cup, "Yes, I would like to go to Hong Kong," Liu stated plainly.

Ye smiled, "Good. In the Party we usually talk around things. It feels good to speak directly, doesn't it?" He turned to Shao, "And what about you Shao Huan? Where would you like to go next?"

Shao laughed, "It is nice to speak frankly, and to be honest I am very happy here. I will work for you as long as I can, and then if I could go work for the General Office in Zhongnanhai, I would be content."

The restaurant owner knocked on the door, "Do you want more dumplings?"

They all laughed, "No, they were so delicious. We ate too many, thank you so much," Ye answered for them.

"Okay, I will bring the last dish," she yelled to the kitchen and then started clearing away their plates.

After she left the room, Shao said, "I really don't think I can eat anything more. I am so full."

Liu Wuqing turned the question back on Ye, "Boss, how about you. You have had such a good career, what do you want to do next?"

Ye sighed and leaned forward, "There is only one more step up that I can make. I don't know if that will happen, but since we are speaking frankly, I would like to finish my career from the Politburo Standing Committee."

The restaurant owner didn't bother to knock on the door and walked in to the small room with a plate of sizzling toffee apple, she put the scalding hot plate down in the middle of the table and then placed a bowl of cold water in front of each guest. An assistant brought her a plate of sliced oranges that she set alongside the caramel colored apples.

Liu Wuqing took a piece of the breaded fruit and twisted the sugar coating leaving long sticky strings behind it. He dunked the morsel in the cold water and the candy coating hardened instantly, the strings of sugar snapped off and he gingerly bit into the apple and almost whispered, "It's so delicious."

Ye and Shao both laughed at the satisfied look on Liu's face and started to eat the toffee apple with him. It didn't take long until the candy coating had hardened and locked the last few remaining pieces to the plate.

Ye's face was slightly red and he seemed only a little bit drunk "I am glad that we could have dinner together tonight. I really do appreciate everything you both do. I am so happy that you will be a father Shao Huan, and Liu Wuqing, I know what a sacrifice you are making right now. I want you to have time in your next job to start a family. You have a bright future in the Party but the Party won't love you like a child will. Remember that, okay?" He reached out and put his hand on Liu's shoulder.

Liu nodded, "I will never forget it. You have another busy day tomorrow boss, we should get you home. Liu stepped out of the room to get the guards and drivers ready.

Shao Huan helped Ye Hongqi to his feet, and as they left the restaurant, Ye's heartfelt thanks to the owner for one of the best meals he had in months nearly brought her to tears. Shao Huan and Liu got Ye into he car and waited until he had driven away before they both breathed a sigh of relief.

"Hey buddy, I hear Hong Kong is pretty nice," Shao said and patted Liu on the back.

"Yeah, why not? He asked me. Thanks for helping me out in there. Sometimes I think he forgets how much I work at the office. My wife would love to have a baby, but I barely get to see her."

"Well, I hope you can have a baby in Hong Kong."

兰会所
Orchid Club

Zhang Ying and Shao Huan enjoyed that spring more than any they could remember and Zhang felt healthier and stronger by the day. The baby growing inside her increased her own vitality. The cherry blossoms in Chaoyang park were softer and the pansies were more vivid. Zhang's stomach seemed to be bottomless, and she kept craving tofu stew. The children at the kindergarten all knew she was pregnant and she liked how they pressed their ears against her stomach trying to listen to the baby inside.

Shao Huan requested an afternoon off of work to accompany Zhang Ying to her 18 week check up at the Dongcheng Maternity Hospital. Zhang Ying got nervous before every appointment at the hospital, but Doctor Deng Xiayi's calm and comfortable manner set them both at ease. After the phlebotomist had taken Zhang's blood to screen for birth defects, Doctor Deng had Zhang recline on the hospital bed and lift up her shirt. Doctor Deng squeezed a cold gel over Zhang Ying's stomach and began moving the ultrasound probe over her abdomen.

Zhang and Shao treasured the grainy images from her first ultrasound and they couldn't wait to see how the baby had grown. They watched eagerly as the screen next to Zhang turned from static to shifting lines and then as an outline of a spine and feet gradually came in to view. Shao Huan held Zhang's hand tightly, their eyes fixed to the screen while Doctor Deng positioned the probe and captured the outline of a tiny nose, cheekbones, face. She turned the probe to the baby's chest, and the rapid heartbeat racing over the speaker was like music.

"Your baby appears very healthy," Doctor Deng said reassuringly, "it has a strong heartbeat, and there don't appear to be any abnormalities. It is developing as it should. Do you have any questions?"

A tear ran down Zhang Ying's check as her eyes locked on to the the image that Doctor Deng had frozen on the screen. Shao Huan shook her hand gently, "Dear, do you have any questions?"

"What? Oh. I'm sorry. I was just thinking about the baby."

Doctor Deng smiled, "It's no problem. The nurse will print the images for you. Everything looks perfect. I don't expect any problems from the blood tests, but I will let you know if there are. Is there anything else you want to know?"

Zhang wiped the tear from her cheek and sat up while Doctor Deng used a towel to clean the gel off of Zhang Ying's slightly bulging abdomen, "What should I be doing or eating? I am trying to think only positive thoughts, and to avoid spicy food, and cold foods."

Doctor Deng put her hand on Zhang Ying's, "You should eat well and rest well. You are young and healthy. Your body is an amazing thing. It will take care of the rest. You should start to feel the baby move soon and it will get harder to sleep. You will need to go to the bathroom often. That is all normal. Don't worry. Okay?"

"Thank you, really thank you so much," Zhang squeezed Doctor Deng's warm hand. The doctor excused herself and left them to schedule the next appointment with the nurse.

The light outside was clear and bright, Zhang Ying smiled and breathed a deep sigh of relief, "It is beautiful! Our baby is beautiful!"

Shao Huan held her hand, "You have to listen to the doctor and eat a lot and sleep a lot okay?"

Zhang Ying laughed gleefully, "Of course! You have to bring me lots of good food and let me sleep any time!"

"Okay, I can do that," they started walking out to North Dongsi street and saw a few monks in Tibetan Buddhist robes headed toward the Yonghe Temple, "Shall we take a taxi or subway?"

"I feel great, but my feet are already tired. Let's take a taxi."

Shao Huan hailed a taxi from his phone, "By the way, Sima Nan has been asking me to go out with him since I told him about the baby. It has been a long time since I've seen him. Is it okay with you if I go out with him tomorrow night? He wants to go to listen to music."

The taxi pulled up and Shao Huan opened the door for Zhang Ying. She slid into the car, "Okay. It is good for you to see your friend. But tell him you have to be back by 9 p.m. He always gets into trouble after 10 p.m. and if you tell him 9 p.m., he will think he has won if he keeps you out until 10 p.m."

"Okay, yes he will be very happy," Shao Huan laughed, "Thanks dear, I will let him know."

Shao Huan had caught up with Sima Nan for coffee a couple of times since he and Zhang Ying started trying to have a baby, but hadn't been able to see him since Shao shared the news that Zhang

Ying was pregnant. Sima Nan was waiting for Shao Huan in front of the LG building near the Eternal Peace subway station.

"Brother! Aya, it has been way too long!" Sima greeted Shao Huan slapping their hands together and embracing in a half hug.

"Yes, too long. Things have been busy helping Zhang Ying. She eats so much! It is really amazing."

Sima Nan put his arm around Shao Huan's shoulders and started walking him in to the building to go up to the Orchid Club, "It's okay buddy. I have been really busy too. Technology keeps changing so quickly and it is so hard to keep up."

They took the elevator up to the club and the doors opened to reveal a dimly lit and well decorated space with graceful paintings in elaborate frames on the walls and covering the ceiling. A hostess seated them at a table underneath an ornate chandelier near the back.

"You know, I always thought we would play here one day," Sima Nan sighed wistfully.

Shao Huan laughed, "Brother, the only way they would let us play here is if we paid them. This place may be getting old, but they'd have to be pretty desperate to let us play."

Sima Nan ordered two Heineken beers, looked around the club and leaned back in his chair, "It's too early. This place is still too quiet… so, shit. You are really going to be a dad. Are you guys getting a bigger apartment?"

A pretty waitress with sharply cropped hair delivered their drinks and brushed off Sima Nan's attempt to flirt with her. He watched her walk away and shrugged.

"Brother, I thought things with little Hua were still good," Shao Huan clapped his friend on the back.

"Yeah, sure. They are fine, really. I guess you can't stop a dog from eating shit though," Sima laughed at his own philandering ways, "Anyway, are you getting a bigger place?"

"No, no way. It's too expensive. Besides, our apartment already has two bedrooms. We will keep the baby in our room at first, but can use the other room later. It is crazy brother, Zhang Ying can eat so much now. I think she can eat more than you."

Sima Nan took a big swill of beer and tried to get the waitress' attention again, "No way. You are just talking nonsense. Are you going to ask for time off of work?" He caught the waitress' eye and ordered two glasses of Laphroaig scotch whiskey, neat.

"Buddy, there is no need, let's just drink beer."

"No way! We are celebrating tonight. My best friend is going to be a dad, we are at least going to drink one glass of whiskey." They clinked the necks of the beer bottles together.

"I already asked my boss for a little time off. He agreed. It is good, I was worried he wouldn't let me. I know they are so busy with all of the thought work. I understood what he did in Zhejiang and I read what he is doing at the Propaganda Department, but I don't think I will ever understand it."

"Thought work is really important. You should study it more," Sima Nan took another long drink.

"Okay, you know me and know how I think. Explain thought work to me. I can't really ask anyone at work."

Sima Nan leaned forward, "Okay, okay.." He ran his hand along his chin, "It's like this, it's not that complicated. Think about people like they are computers, okay?" Shao Huan didn't see where Sima was going, but indulged him and leaned forward as well. "Okay, so with computers you have input and output, right? To get the output you want, you must have the right input. Thought work is like the programming, the input. If you want the output to be loyalty to the Party, or going to fight a war, you need the thought work to prepare people first. Look, in my job we are trying to find and stop people who are providing bad inputs. People outside of China, sometimes people inside of China, who want a different output that does not support the Party. Your office does the thought work to make sure the inputs are right and that people support the Party. Look, its like your office writes the source code, and my office is the anti-virus software. Got it?"

The waitress set two glasses of scotch on the table. The peaty smell wafted up as Shao and Sima swirled the amber liquid in the short thick glasses and toasted to Shao and Zhang's baby.

"Wow, that is good…" Shao swirled his scotch gently again and set it back down. "I understand what you are saying, I hadn't thought of it like that. That makes logical sense, but people aren't really computers. They have experiences and ideas that the Party can't control. Right?"

Sima Nan sipped his whiskey, "Of course, that is obvious. I was just trying to explain it so you could understand it. What the Party thinks is a threat always changes too. Like, Winnie the Pooh. Because some bad people decided to use Winnie the Pooh to make fun of the Party Chairman, we had to remove all references to Winnie the Pooh on China's Internet. It was not easy, but at least it was something that most Chinese people didn't care about. Imagine if the Party needed to remove references to Jackie Chan or the Monkey King, it would be really hard."

Sima Nan continued, "That is why the thought work never stops, every newspaper, every broadcast, every speech, every text book, every religious book, are all part of it. It happens all the time, all around us. Most people don't even realize it. They don't realize the thoughts they have are guided by the Party. But sometimes, they get sick. It is like catching a virus. We used to try to stop the information from the source, and we still do that, but there are so many sources now it is almost impossible. Last month we found people using the video game World of Warcraft to share anti-Party information. Now we are shifting to focusing on the individual and the people around them. We even hired an epidemiologist."

Shao Huan couldn't believe it, "No way. That's not possible. Now look at who is talking nonsense."

Sima Nan slapped the table, "Really! It's like just like a disease. Anti-Party thoughts spread like the flu or the novel coronavirus, maybe even more contagious than the novel coronavirus. It is why everyone's social credit score is linked to the people around them. If someone you know has a problem, there is a much higher chance that you will have a problem too. There is too much information to control, but we can study social networks and then focus our attention on that network when there is a problem. It is like putting a population into isolation. If someone in a group starts to read about Falun Gong, we don't just look at that person but also everyone around them. They may not all get arrested, but they will become targets for more intense monitoring and efforts to reeducate them."

Shao Huan sat silently, trying to wrap his head around everything that Sima Nan had said. Sima saw his skepticism, "Look, like right now, we are talking and I am sharing ideas with you. That personal contact is stronger and more influential than the best propaganda. If I were filling your head with anti-Party thoughts, there is no way the Party could find that. But, the Party can look at me and if they see that I am reading about the Dalia Lama, or splitting Tibet from China or that I start going to a Tibetan temple regularly, they can know that I might be a danger to them. Then they would step back and see who my closest contacts are, and they would see that you are my best friend. They would know there is a high chance that I started to get you thinking about Tibet."

Shao Huan shook his head, "Wow. That is really amazing. I had never thought of it like a disease. I see what you mean. So, if your job is to find and stop viruses, my office keeps the body healthy and able to resist disease?"

"Yeah brother! Exactly! You got it!" Sima Nan raised his glass to toast Shao Huan's realization. "It's really important work. You should be proud of your boss and what you guys do. People must have faith in the Party, and your offices gives them that."

"For me, it makes more sense to think about it like a body than a computer, but I understand what you mean."

The band started tuning up on the stage and two skinny black guys with shaved heads walked out. "Yes, about time. I wish we were playing, but they are probably better," Sima Nan conceded.

合眼
Sleep

Zhang Ying's energy and enthusiasm faded as her stomach bulged and the hot summer months passed, slow and sleepless. She had felt such a thrill the first time she felt the baby move but could not muster a flicker of that excitement when it kicked and turned all night, and she lay in bed next to Shao Huan, exhausted and unable to sleep.

Shao Huan still loved to put his hand on her stomach and to feel the baby's foot brush against his hand and to feel the baby turn towards the sound of his voice. He knew how tired Zhang Ying was and did everything he could to help her, but there was nothing he could do to get her what she needed most.

They stopped going to any social engagements and even when Shao's parents came by the apartment they kept the visits short to deliver food and well wishes. In her exhaustion, Zhang felt more easily upset and emotional than she had ever been before. Some nights she would abandon all hope of sleeping and sit on the sofa watching soap operas on her phone. She was embarrassed how she cried at even the silliest and most predictable points.

Zhang Ying didn't want to go out, but she was glad to video call with her parents and friends in Hangzhou and was always happy any time Jin Xishan and Xiaorong called to check on her. She had tried working through the summer, but by late July had stopped going to work and she just wanted to be done being pregnant.

She only caught sleep in brief moments when the baby rested and when she didn't need to go to the bathroom. The 10 or 20 minutes of sleep she was able to get were sometimes worse than staying awake, but she slept in the moments of stillness whenever she could. One evening in early August she sat on the sofa and felt the baby settling down. Zhang Ying closed her heavy eyelids and immediately fell into a deep, still and unknowing sleep.

Zhang Ying woke up to see early morning sunlight filling the living room and a quilted blanket tucked around her. Her stomach hurt and she pushed herself up from the chair but pain radiated from her stomach and felt like a spike piercing her lower back. She went to the bathroom and pulled down her sweatpants, sticky dark red blood was all over her legs and pants, she screamed, "Shao Huan! Shao Huan!"

Shao Huan rushed to the bathroom, sleep still heavy in his eyes, "What? What is the matter?" Before Zhang Ying could answer he saw the terrified look on her face and the blood on her legs, "Put your pants back on, let's go to the hospital." Shao Huan grabbed his phone and ordered a taxi that was waiting for them when they got downstairs. He put a towel on the back seat of the cab as Zhang Ying got in. The cab driver asked in a thick Beijing accent, "What's the matter?"

"I think the baby is about to be born," Shao Huan closed the door and the cab sped through the quiet streets to the Dongcheng Maternity Hospital. Zhang Ying held Shao's hand tightly, fear and worry gripped her, "I can't feel it moving, I can't feel it moving," she began to sob.

"I'm sure it is okay, we just have to get you to the hospital. It's okay," Shao Huan did his best to stifle his own worry. Zhang Ying's face was more pale than usual, and she grabbed at her stomach like she was trying to reach in and pull out the pain.

They got to the hospital and Shao Huan carried Zhang inside, "Help! Help! She needs to see a doctor!" Shao Huan set Zhang Ying's feet on the ground and hunched forward to keep her arm around his neck. "Quickly! Quickly!" Shao Huan shouted as a nurse came to help him and asked "What is her name?"

"Zhang Ying, she is about 30 weeks pregnant," Shao Huan said and helped lower Zhang into a wheelchair. They pushed Zhang down the wide hallway to a delivery room.

Shao Huan got her in to the delivery room and the nurses lifted Zhang Ying on to the table, one of the nurses tried to talk to Zhang but she just screamed in pain. A nurse put his hand on Shao Huan's shoulder and tried to guide him out of the room, "No. No. I am staying here."

The nurse's voice was calm and assuring, "I need to ask you some questions, please it will help her and will be easier out here."

Shao Huan looked on anxiously as the medical team pulled down Zhang's blood soaked pants and started getting her on an IV. He nodded and let the nurse guide him back into the hallway.

"Can you tell me about what happened?" He asked calmly.

Shao Huan took a deep breath, "I... I really don't know. She fell asleep on the sofa last night. She woke up this morning and when she went to the bathroom saw that she was bleeding. She screamed and I woke up and... and we came here," Shao Huan paused, "She said she couldn't feel the baby moving..." his voice trailed off.

"I know this is scary, but that information is very helpful. You did the right thing to come here. Has she had any other problems with the pregnancy?" The nurse asked as a doctor walked in to the room and nodded assuringly at Shao.

"No. No problems at all. Doctor Deng Xiayi has been her doctor. Everything was fine."

"Okay, thank you. I understand that you want to be in the room, really I understand. But it will make it harder for us to help her and the baby. You have done everything you can. Now it is our job is to help her. Please wait in the waiting room, we will get you as soon as we can," the nurse returned to the room and closed the door. As the door closed, Shao Huan only caught a glimpse of people and equipment around Zhang Ying's still body on the bed.

Shao Huan tried to sit in the waiting room but couldn't stay still. He realized that he needed to let Liu Wuqing know he wouldn't make it to work. He called Liu's office phone, "Hey. It's me. I am at the hospital. Something is wrong."

Concern filled Liu's voice, "Okay, I will call the General Office and ask for your back-up. Let me know if you need anything."

"Thanks. I will," Shao Huan was relieved that was taken care of and hung up, but knew he needed to call Zhang Ying's school. He found Fang Zhitai's phone number and let her know Zhang was at the hospital and wouldn't make it to work. Shao had only met Fang a few times, but he liked her and was grateful for her understanding and support.

It was a beautiful morning and the trees around the hospital were filled with light and the sounds of the city stirring to life echoed along the street outside. Shao Huan returned to the waiting room and made eye contact with the nurse at the receiving desk who gave him

75

a sympathetic look and shook her head that they weren't ready to call him.

Shao Huan sat, stood, paced and anxiously checked his phone. The cool morning light became a beam of heat radiating through the window on Shao's back. At last the nurse who had spoken with him came through the waiting room door and waved him over, "Please come with me."

Shao had so many questions, but from the nurse's solemn tone, Shao was sure he didn't want the answers. The nurse led him through the corridors, and stopped in front of a solid door, "Doctor Huang Bin will see you in his office. He will explain everything," the nurse opened the door and the doctor stood up from a desk. He nodded to the nurse who closed the door and Shao listened to the nurse's footsteps receding on the hard hospital floor.

"Hello, I am doctor Huang Bin, you are Zhang Ying's husband, is that right?"

"Yes. That is right. My name is Shao Huan," the calm in the office was almost as terrifying for Shao as Zhang's blood curdling scream that began his day.

Doctor Huang pointed to a seat for Shao and sat in his own chair, "Mr. Shao, first let me tell you your wife is alive and okay but we could not save the baby," the doctor's steady voice delivered the news that Shao had been dreading. Doctor Huang continued, "The placenta, which delivers nutrients from the mother's body to the baby, became detached and the baby could not get oxygen. We performed an emergency c-section, but the baby was already dead. There was nothing we could do. Your wife had also lost a lot of blood and was in shock. It was good that you got here when you did, we were able to stop the bleeding and she received a blood transfusion. We had to give her general anesthetic and she is unconscious now, but her vital signs are all stable. The general anesthetic should wear off in a few hours, but she might sleep longer than that. She will be okay."

Shao Huan slumped forward in the chair and cradled his face in his hands and mumbled, "How could that happen? Why did that happen?"

"We don't know what causes the placenta to detach prematurely. Unfortunately, there is no way to predict it or to stop it. Your wife is very lucky to be alive. While it is not impossible for her to get pregnant again, women who suffer this kind of stillbirth have a harder time getting pregnant and a much higher risk of their placenta becoming detached again with the next pregnancy."

"What gender was the baby?" Shao Huan pulled his hands away from his face, red with grief and effort as he tried to restrain his tears.

Doctor Huang answered calmly, "It was a girl."

Shao Huan couldn't hold back his tears any more and began to sob, he squeezed his eyes shut tight but the tears poured out all the same. His body shook and he muttered through short breaths "It was a girl…"

Doctor Huang waited until his gasps for breath and deep sobs slowed, "You can wait in your wife's room if you want. We will have to keep her overnight. There is a chair there that you can sleep in."

Shao Huan wiped his eyes and nodded, "I will do that. I'm so embarrassed to cry like this… thank you for saving my wife's life. I can never repay you," Shao Huan stood.

"It's no problem to cry. You should cry. The next few weeks and months will be very hard. We have psychiatrists who can help both of you. Nurse Peng will show you to the room," Doctor Huang opened the door and Shao saw that nurse Peng had returned. He stepped through the door and shook doctor Huang's hand, "Thank you. I really can't think what I would do if they both died today." Shao turned his face away before he started to cry again and followed Peng down the corridor.

Peng opened the door to the delivery room where Shao had last seen Zhang Ying. She lay on the table, motionless. Her clothes were gone and she was draped in a thin hospital gown. An IV ran to her arm, and her chest and flat belly rose and fell gently with each breath. Shao stood by her bed and stroked the back of his hand along her silent, peaceful face.

"My dear, she is gone. She is gone… I am so glad you are still alive," Shao Huan whispered as tears started to fill his eyes again, "We were going to have a little girl, but… not any more. You can rest now," Shao leaned forward and kissed Zhang's smooth forehead, his tears fell down on to her motionless face.

眼泪
Tears

Shao Huan sat in the comfortable chair and imagined all of the new mothers who had nursed their newborns there. He desperately wanted Zhang Ying to wake up, but was terrified of what he would tell her. He practiced the words in his mind, he whispered them to himself, but nothing sounded right. The doctor had stated everything so simply and directly. He tried to do that, but knew he couldn't.

Just before mid-day, Zhang started to stir. Shao Huan walked to her bed and gently held her hand. She turned her head and slowly opened her eyes. She saw Shao's face and the worry in his eyes. Zhang tried to speak but her voice caught. She felt dizzy and like the world had collapsed into a dim fog and a faint pain. As she looked at Shao, she remembered that he had brought her to the hospital. She lifted her heavy arm and tried to touch her stomach. Shao Huan caught her hand in his and he started to cry again, the tears chased away all the words that he had prepared for the moment.

Even through the fog clouding her mind, Zhang immediately understood his sadness. She wanted to scream and beat the bed but all she could do was whisper, "No… no… no…" She felt Shao Huan's lips on her forehead and she let go of his hands, her voice growing stronger, "No! Where is my baby?" She asked, her eyes filled with fire and anger, sure she already knew the answer.

Shao Huan tried to answer, but the words caught in his throat. Zhang Ying pleaded, "My dear, tell me. Please tell me the baby is okay"

"The baby was stillborn," Shao Huan managed to say. He felt his face turn hot and felt the weight of those words as they fell on both of them, "I will call the nurse. They wanted to know when you woke up."

Shao Huan pressed the call button and a moment later a different nurse appeared at the door. She looked in and saw that Zhang Ying was awake, "The doctor is nearly finished with his shift, I will get him now."

Zhang Ying stopped struggling and looked in Shao Huan's heartbroken eyes. Doctor Huang arrived with a nurse. The nurse started checking Zhang Ying's vital signs and Doctor Huang explained for Zhang everything that he had told Shao Huan a few hours earlier. While Shao Huan had time in the waiting room to worry and work through his shock, for Zhang Ying it only felt like a few minutes since she sat down in the wheelchair. All she heard from Doctor Huang's explanation was that her baby was dead. She didn't feel fortunate at all when he told her that she was lucky to be alive.

Doctor Huang understood that Zhang Ying was in shock and looked to Shao Huan, "We will keep her here tonight, but her vital signs are still strong. You should be able to go home tomorrow."

Shao Huan nodded, "Thank you, we are so grateful." Doctor Huang and the nurse left them alone again. Zhang Ying put her hands on her stomach and felt the baby's absence and the bandages over her skin. She could feel the cool skin of her stomach, but realized that her stomach didn't register her hands passing over it and she that she couldn't feel her legs.

"I'm so tired," she murmured. "I am really so tired."

Shao Huan stroked her hair, "Go to sleep my dear, just rest. I will be here when you wake up." Shao Huan held his hand to her head until she fell asleep again. Shao called Liu Wuqing and explained what had happened and Liu organized for Shao to take the rest of the week off. Shao anxiously watched Zhang Ying for the rest of the day. He knew he should call his parents, and call Zhang's parents but he couldn't bring himself to tell them the news. He decided to wait until Zhang was home from the hospital and they could tell them together.

Nurses came to check on Zhang every few hours, and Shao gradually felt the muscles in his back and neck relax. He hadn't noticed how tight they were until he lay back in the comfortable chair and closed his eyes. Shao Huan tried not to think about the daughter they had lost, but the harder he tried, the more he imagined what she would have been like. He drifted to sleep slowly, all the hope and happiness he had felt the night before replaced with grief and futile thoughts about what might have been.

When Shao Huan opened his eyes early the next morning, he saw Zhang Ying reclining on the recovery bed, staring vacantly into space. He couldn't tell what she was looking at, but she seemed to know he was awake, "I thought it was a bad dream. I wanted it to be just a nightmare… but every time I touch my stomach I know it is real."

Shao stood and walked to her, and took her hand. Zhang Ying looked up at him, "Was it a boy or a girl?"

"It was a girl," Shao let out a heavy sigh. Shao sat down on Zhang's bed and stayed with her in silence.

A nurse poked her head in the door and saw they were both awake. He turned on the bright lights, "Good morning. I was getting worried that I would have to wake you up. Wait a moment, I have breakfast for you."

Shao was hungry and he knew that Zhang needed to eat too. The nurse set a tray in front of Zhang with a bowl of rice porridge and shredded chicken, stir fried pork liver, and green tea and offered Shao the same menu.

Zhang looked at the food but didn't eat, "I can feel my legs again," she said.

Shao started to eat the rice porridge, "That's good. The doctor said you will recover well."

Zhang didn't answer. Shao ate in silence and when he had finished his meal and saw that Zhang still hadn't touched her food, he encouraged her, "Dear, please eat a little. Maybe just the pork liver?" Still, Zhang didn't answer. Shao Huan sighed and put his hand on her leg, "I am so glad you are alive."

A stream of tears started running down Zhang's checks, but she still didn't speak. They sat in silence, Shao Huan hoped the nurse would return to collect the trays and that Zhang could get discharged to go home.

"I'm not," Zhang eventually said. Shao Huan looked at her, perplexed. She didn't look at him directly but she saw that he didn't understand her, "I'm not glad to be alive."

Shao Huan reached for her hand and squeezed it, but Zhang Ying didn't return his affection. Her hand lay limply in Shao's hand, "Dear, don't say that. I am so sad too, but the only thing I am happy about is that you are alive."

Zhang Ying shook her head and looked into Shao's eyes, "I should have died with the baby. I wish I had died with the baby."

Shao sat silently next to his wife. Her devastation and despair cut him as deeply as the death of their baby. He knew how to hold her when she cried, how to comfort her when she wanted comfort. Her cold despair, however, left him uncertain about what to say or do. He worried that the wrong words would only hurt her more, and quite certain that all the words he wanted to say were wrong. He was relieved when the nurse returned to collect the trays, "Hey, you sure you don't want to eat?" The nurse tried to coax Zhang Ying to eat. She simply shook her head.

"Okay, that's okay. The doctor will come by soon, you can eat at home later," the nurse cleared the trays and Shao Huan followed him in to the hall.

"She is really sad. I don't know what to do, the doctor yesterday mentioned there is a psychiatrist at the hospital. Can we see them?"

The nurse nodded, "No problem, I will let the doctor know. I am sure he will recommend talking to the psychiatrist when he comes through.

Shao needed to stretch his legs and take a break from the ghosts and sadness in the delivery room. He walked outside and found a warm summer rain falling slow and steady and he breathed in the earthy smell of wet concrete. Shao stood under the awning and watched as expectant mothers and families with newborn babies arrived for their appointments. Shao didn't begrudge them their happiness, but he envied them more now than ever before.

When Shao Huan returned to the delivery room, Doctor Deng Xiayi was speaking with Zhang Ying, "Ah, you've come back. Good, I was just speaking with Zhang Ying about everything that happened. I am so sorry for your loss."

Zhang Ying looked away from Deng as she spoke, "I just recommended to Zhang Ying that although she should not do postpartum confinement, her body still needs to recover slowly. She needs to eat well and to rest. She should not exercise for the next few days, and will need to take medicine for the pain. But after a week, she should start to walk and to exercise her body. Qigong is a good exercise to help recover. She is young and may recover more quickly."

Shao Huan nodded his understanding as Doctor Deng Xiayi continued, "We cannot change the past, but we can help Zhang Ying recover. I also want Zhang Ying to return to meet with our psychiatrist. After such a loss, it is important to treat the mind and body. Okay?"

Zhang didn't offer any indication of response, so Shao Huan answered, "Okay. Thank you."

"Good. It will take us some time to do a few last checks and to prepare Zhang Ying to go home. Perhaps you can go home and get some fresh clothes for her? She should be ready in about an hour, I will stay with her a little longer," Doctor Deng offered Shao Huan a sympathetic smile and he realized that she was right. They had left in such a rush, Zhang didn't have any clothes, she didn't even have shoes.

Shao stared out of the back window of the cab as it drove through the rainy streets taking him back to their apartment building. He fell into a trance listening to the tires turning on the wet asphalt and the windshield wipers swishing the rain away. It took him a moment after the cab arrived at the apartment to thank the driver and get out.

Shao Huan turned on the lights in the apartment and saw the drops of blood on the floor at the entrance. He took off his shoes and got a large plastic bowl and a rag. He kneeled down and started scrubbing the blood off of the tile floor and followed the trail back to the bathroom. The blood came off of the tile easily, but he couldn't get the spots out of grey rug in the center of the living room, and the dark stain on the sofa only faded slightly. He sat on the sofa and hunched forward, his elbows on his knees, rested his head in his hands and cried slowly. He wanted to have it all cleaned before he brought Zhang Ying home. He wanted to try to remove the stains that would remind them both of that terrible morning. All Shao Huan could do, however, was to throw a blanket over the stain.

By the time Shao returned to the hospital, the nurses had taken the IV out of Zhang's arm and given her a white paper bag filled with medicine and vitamins. Zhang dressed slowly. Shao Huan tried to help her and she rested her weight on his shoulder while he helped her pull up her sweatpants. Shao tied her shoes and helped her out to another taxi. Zhang barely spoke and that cold distance that Shao first felt when he woke up had only hardened.

The rain kept falling on the drive home. Zhang avoided Shao's eyes and although she let him rest his hand on her leg, she didn't offer any response. When they got back to the apartment, Shao bent down and took off Zhang's shoes and then tried to guide her to the bedroom to rest, but she looked at the sofa. She pulled her arm away from Shao and staggered slowly to the sofa. Zhang Ying leaned forward gingerly and pulled the blanket away.

Zhang Ying stood silently looking at the dark stain on the sofa and began to sob. She sat down on the sofa next to the bloody mark and threw her head back, her whole body shook with grief. Shao Huan sat next to her and put his arm behind her back. Zhang Ying's hair caught in his whiskers and tickled his face as she leaned in to him, pressed her face into his shoulder and wailed. Shao Huan smelled her tears and the sadness on her breath. He listened to her cries and the rain falling outside.

姐妹
Sisters

Zhang Ying cried until she had run out of tears. Her grief filled the silence all the same. Shao Huan still didn't know what to say to her, but was glad that she was at least letting him hold her. He knew that she still hadn't eaten, but he didn't want to cook. He didn't want to stand up and leave her side. Shao took out his phone to order food for them both.

"Don't call anyone," Zhang Ying finally said.

"I'm not. I'm just ordering food. We both need to eat."

Zhang watched as he ordered Hangzhou braised pork belly, sweet and sour carp, and lotus root powder nut soup. The food at the hospital hadn't appealed to her at all, and she was too upset to eat anyway, but Shao Huan knew her favorite dishes and she started to feel her appetite return.

Shao Huan set down his phone and kissed her forehead, "We have to tell our parents."

Zhang Ying knew that he was right, but she couldn't bear the thought of calling her parents to tell them their baby had died before she ever got to breathe. That she had died before they had even given her a name, "I know, but not tonight, okay?"

"Of course. Whenever you are ready… It has been more than a day since you checked your phone. I bet your mother has already tried calling you."

Zhang Ying put her hand in Shao Huan's and squeezed gently, "I don't want to see. If I see it, I have to ignore her or lie to her. I will check it tomorrow."

When the food arrived, Shao Huan pulled the low coffee table close to the sofa and set the food and a glass of warm water out for Zhang. The layers of pork fat, tender meat and skin melted in Zhang's mouth. Once she started eating she finished the whole dish. Shao Huan was relieved to see her eating again, and planned on eating a packet of boiled noodles as she started eating the soft white fish and the tangy red sauce.

Zhang Ying looked up at Shao Huan and sighed, "I am so embarrassed, I am eating everything."

"It's no problem, the doctor said you need to eat well. Have some of the soup too," Shao moved the bowl of thick, sweet, and nutritious soup toward her. Zhang picked up the bowl and took a spoonful with a cashew and fragrant Osmanthus flower.

"Don't forget your medicine," Shao Huan had prepared her first doses and set them next to the glass of warm water in front of Zhang Ying.

She picked them up, "I was so mean to you today. You have done everything for me. I am tired, and very sad, even very angry. But I'm not angry with you, okay? Whatever I said today, whatever I say tomorrow… I love you and I'm not angry with you."

Shao felt his lower lip shake as he tried to smile, he couldn't speak and just nodded. Zhang Ying took her medicine and Shao Huan helped her to bed. Shao Huan sat by Zhang Ying until she fell asleep.

He took a look at her phone and saw that her mother had called several times, he didn't know what to do but decided he had managed enough problems for one day and that was a problem for tomorrow.

The sunlight slipping around the curtain woke Shao Huan up early. He got up and tidied the apartment. He wanted to tell his parents, but knew they would want to talk to Zhang Ying. He tried again to get the blood stains out, and while they faded further, they didn't disappear as he hoped. Shao Huan tried to keep himself busy around the apartment, but soon found there was nothing more to do. He watched a police drama on his phone and started to reread Mao Dun's "Midnight."

The longer that Zhang Ying stayed in the bedroom, the more worried Shao became. He checked on her several times throughout the morning and couldn't tell if she was sleeping or just laying in bed. At midday he sat on the bed next to her and she opened her eyes, "I don't want to get up."

"It's already after 12, come have lunch or at least sit on the sofa with me," Shao Huan rested his hand on her shoulder.

Zhang Ying shook her head, "No. I don't want to."

"Okay, but you need to take your medicine again. Please?" Shao Huan stood and pulled aside the curtain to show the beautiful blue sky that followed the rain.

Zhang Ying rolled over to face away from the window and closed her eyes tightly, "It was my fault she died. I was too tired. I wasn't strong enough. I should have died, not her."

Shao Huan lay down on the bed next to her and looked up at the ceiling, "Dear, it's not your fault. No one knows why it happens."

"I don't care that they don't know why it happened, I should have noticed she had stopped moving. I shouldn't have slept. If I had woken up earlier, she would have lived," Zhang's voice was cold and tired.

"It isn't your fault. It isn't anyone's fault," Shao Huan whispered and then lay next to her in silence.

Zhang Ying finally broke the quiet, "You should go to the other room, or go out for lunch. I will stay here."

Shao couldn't remember any time when Zhang had asked him to make space between them, and didn't want to leave her but didn't know what else to say. He stood up next to the bed and reached for Zhang's phone, "Okay, but you should talk to your mother. She has called a few times and I think she is getting worried." Shao set her phone next to her on the bed, "And please, take your medicine, okay?" Zhang didn't answer him and Shao left the room.

Even with her eyes closed, Zhang couldn't hide from the bright August sun outside. The light shown red through her thin eyelids and the heat beat down on the quilt. Zhang Ying hated to push Shao away but she knew he would be better off away from her. She didn't want to take the pain medication, she wanted to feel the pain radiate from her empty stomach and cut through to her grieving heart.

She felt her phone buzz on the bed where Shao had left it next to her chest. She opened her eyes and saw the list of missed calls from her mother and a few WeChat messages from Jin Xishan. Zhang Ying didn't want to talk to anyone, but picked up her phone and looked through the messages more out of reflex than conscious choice. Jin Xishan had sent her a dozen messages, at first they were just pictures of Xiaorong but grew concerned when Zhang didn't respond.

As Zhang held the phone, it buzzed again with another message from Jin, "Little sister, I'm really worried about you. Call me."

Zhang lay the phone down and rolled on to her back. She wanted to answer Jin, but she didn't know what to say and wasn't ready for what Jin would say. She didn't want to hear any words of comfort. Even Shao Huan's words that it wasn't her fault echoed in her thoughts and felt like a hollow lie. All she felt was emptiness and pain, and that was all she wanted to feel.

Zhang Ying didn't know how much time had passed when Shao Huan returned to the room, but the harsh midday light had faded and turned to a softer gold. Shao saw that Zhang hadn't taken her medicine while he had gone out to walk around the park. He sat near the foot of the bed and put his hand on her leg. He had thought a lot about what to say to his despondent wife, "Dear, please drink something. Drink a little water. I know you are so sad, but I need you to live. Okay? I can't live without you. I beg you, drink this."

Shao Huan's words stung. Zhang Ying had failed her baby and she realized she was failing her husband. She slowly lifted herself up in and sat on the edge of the bed next to Shao. The water felt good on her dry lips and in her empty stomach.

"Good, good. I will get some more water so you can take your medicine, okay?" Shao Huan stood and walked to the bathroom.

When he returned Zhang looked at him, "You should call my mother. I can't do it. Tell her I am okay. Call your parents too," she reluctantly placed the pills in her mouth, took a drink of water and swallowed. The pills felt like gravel going down her throat.

Shao Huan knew that her parents would recognize the lie immediately if Zhang Ying didn't call, "Dear, they will want to talk to you."

Zhang shook her head firmly, "I don't want to talk to them. I don't want to talk to anyone."

Shao Huan decided that at least Zhang had taken her medicine and that it was better to tell their parents the terrible news than to hide it from them any longer. He stepped into the living room to make the calls and hoped she would come eat the meal he brought back for her.

Shao made a video call to his parents first because he thought it would be easier to begin telling them. His mother, however, started crying immediately and the tears that Shao had held off all day overcame his attempt at stoicism. He told them what the doctors had said, that Zhang was young and would recover well, but couldn't tell them about the darkness that filled Zhang's eyes or the coldness in her voice.

He waited to regain his composure before he called Zhang's mother. He knew that seeing her face would only make him cry more, so he just called her. He told her the baby was dead, that it was a girl, that Zhang Ying was recovering, that she was resting. He explained that it wasn't a good time for her to come from Hangzhou and promised that they would let her know when she should come. He promised that he was feeding Zhang Ying well. He choked back his own tears again as she started to cry, and finally let his tears return after he hung up.

Shao Huan saw the calls and messages from Jin and decided to call her too, "Jin Xishan, this is Shao Huan. I should have called you sooner. The day before yesterday, Zhang Ying went to the hospital but the baby was stillborn."

Jin's voice on the other end of the line was comforting, "Shao Huan, I am so sad for you both. I know there are no words to help right now. I am coming over."

"No, it's okay. Don't bother. We are okay. I will let you know when it is a convenient time to visit."

"Shao Huan, don't be so polite. Zhang Ying is not okay. It is more than two days later and she hasn't answered any of my messages. I can understand that she feels like she needs to be alone, but she shouldn't be alone. I will be there as soon as I can," Jin's voice was firm and Shao Huan was so tired of trying to deal with Zhang Ying's despair and his own grief that he didn't try to argue any further.

Shao was glad to hear Jin Xishan's knock at the door and happier still to see Jin's concerned face when he opened it. Without saying a word, Jin stepped inside and wrapped her arms around Shao Huan. Shao Huan knew Jin was there to see his wife, but her embrace was the first comfort he had since the mad rush to the hospital.

"I am so sad, I can't believe the baby is gone. I can't imagine how sad you are," Jin said as she pulled back from Shao. Shao nodded slowly, "I didn't tell her you are coming. She is sad, really very sad.

I don't know what to say or do. She is different. She says she wishes she had died. She won't talk to me… maybe she will talk to you."

Jin took off her shoes and set them by the entrance, "Even if she doesn't talk, it will be better that she isn't alone."

Shao Huan showed Jin to the bedroom where Zhang Ying lay on the bed, facing the window, "Dear, Xishan came to see you." Jin nodded to Shao and shut the door before she sat down next to Zhang.

"Little sister, I… I don't know what to say, but I don't want you to be alone. You don't have to talk to me, but I am going to stay here with you a while. Okay?"

Zhang Ying wanted to tell Jin Xishan to leave, to let her be alone. She didn't want to talk to anyone, but she didn't want to argue with Jin, and so she lay there in silence. Zhang stared out of the window watching the golden light soften and fade to night. Jin kept waiting for Zhang to speak, but after the last of the sunlight had gone and the city lights shown brightly against the black sky, Jin stood up to look out of the window, "The lights are pretty, aren't they?" Zhang didn't respond.

Jin lay down on the bed next to Zhang Ying again, "I know you don't want to talk. It's okay. I will come back tomorrow. You don't have to talk then either." Jin placed her hand on Zhang's arm, then stood to leave.

Shao Huan was sitting in the living room reading and looked up from his book, "Are you okay? You were in there a long time."

Jin's voice sounded tired, "I am okay. You are right, she is so sad. She didn't want to talk. I will come back tomorrow. You should go to work tomorrow, or at least go out. Okay? I will come early and will spend the day with her. Try to get her to eat something tonight."

"Okay. Thank you so much. Even if she didn't say anything, I am sure she was glad to have you there."

"How are you?"

"I am sad about the baby, but I am more worried about Zhang Ying. I have never seen her like this and I don't know what to do."

Jin sighed, "For you, the baby was still an idea, and the baby's death hurts, but for her, it was a part of her body, a part of her soul. It will take her longer to recover. She will recover and we will both help her. Okay?"

Jin Xishan left and Shao Huan tried to coax Zhang Ying to join him for dinner, but eventually gave up and ate alone. He was grateful for Jin's help and her words. He wasn't sure that he was ready to go back to work, but he wanted to get out of the apartment and away from the terrifying ghost that he felt Zhang Ying was becoming.

Shao Huan lay down and fell into a deep sleep next to his wife. When he woke in the morning, Zhang Ying appeared to be in the exact same position as when he went to bed and she didn't respond at all to his voice, his touch or his warmth. She had floated through the apartment at some point during the night and eaten the food he had brought back for her. She left the empty dishes on the table and the kitchen faucet dripping water. She had not, however, taken any of her medicine.

Shao Huan messaged Liu Wuqing that he would return to work and waited for Jin Xishan to arrive. Shao felt guilty for wanting to escape the dark apartment, but that guilt didn't stop him from nearly running out the door when he heard Jin's knock.

"Did she eat?" Jin asked as she entered with a bouquet of white lilies.

"Yes, she ate a lot last night, but after I was asleep. I cleaned everything up this morning. I will come back early today. Thank you so much for staying with her."

"It's no problem. You need to be away from her a short while, and she needs to be away from you too. She isn't ready to share her sadness with anyone. I can stay as long as needed," Jin hugged Shao Huan and hurried him out of the door. She went to the kitchen and found a vase for the flowers. She cut the stems and arranged the large fragrant blossoms.

Zhang Ying heard Shao Huan and Jin Xishan talking about her. She had heard everything they said, and she knew that Jin was right, she was not ready to share her sadness with anyone and she resented that Shao Huan was somehow still able to eat, to sleep, to go to work as if it was a normal day. Her life had changed completely and it made her angry that he wanted to go back to a normal life so quickly.

Jin entered the bedroom and set the flowers on the nightstand by Zhang Ying's head. She pulled open the curtain and let the bright light from another summer day chase the darkness away, "Good morning! I sent Shao Huan to work, so it is just us two girls today." She sat down on the bed next to Zhang, "It is a beautiful day. I'm glad you ate last night. I was worried that you wouldn't eat anything, but you ate a lot. That is really good. Something inside you still wants to live. I know life is hard, and times like this the sadness seems like it will never end, but it is worth living."

Zhang Ying's voice, weak from laying mute for so long, creaked "No, it isn't."

Jin's heart leapt to hear Zhang's voice again, "I understand it feels that way, but believe me, life is worth living. You have a handsome husband who loves you more than anything in the world, parents who love you and are worried about you, a school full of children who miss you, and friends who care about you."

Zhang pushed herself up and sat against the headboard, her hair was matted and greasy from not showering for days, "I should have died, not the baby. It is my fault. I want her to be alive. I want to trade my life so she can live," Zhang's voice was still cold and distant but Jin was happy that at least she was talking.

"I understand little sister, I really understand. I would give my life for Xiaorong's without any hesitation. But we don't get to make those decisions. Life is filled with sadness, but full of happiness too."

Zhang shook her head slowly, "No, life is full of sadness. I don't want it. I don't want this sadness. I want to die with my baby."

Jin Xishan reached out and took Zhang Ying's hand, "I want you to live. Shao Huan wants you to live. Live for us."

Zhang Ying squeezed Jin's hand lightly, "You both will be better without me," tears started to run down her cheeks, "the world will be better without me."

Zhang's words broke Jin Xishan's heart and she began to cry with her, "No. No. The world will not be better without you. You have a purpose in this world. Your life is valuable, more valuable than you know," Jin threw her arms around Zhang's shoulders and pulled her close.

Zhang lay her head on Jin's shoulder and started to sob, "I was so excited to be a mother. I... I... I don't know what to do. Everything feels empty. I feel so empty."

Jin Xishan cried with her, "I know, I know. Life isn't empty. There is hope."

盼望
Hope

Zhang Ying gingerly pulled her bandage away and looked at the thin red line of cut flesh where the doctors had opened up her stomach to take her baby's body out. She ran her hand over her smooth flat stomach and her index finger along the wound. Jin Xishan had persuaded her to take a shower while Jin fixed breakfast, but Zhang hadn't thought about taking her clothes off, taking off her bandage or what lay under it. She couldn't cry any more, but her sadness returned. Even the hot water on her face and the smell of her clean hair didn't distract her from the grief that consumed her.

Zhang stared at herself in the mirror and was glad for the scar to remind her of her pain and loss. She put a clean bandage that the hospital had given her and took the pain killer and antibiotics that she had avoided. Jin Xishan was cooking in the kitchen when Zhang returned to the living room.

"There you are! You look so much better!" Jin's fair face beamed with satisfaction seeing Zhang Ying clean and out of bed. "Come over to the table, I've made Korean seaweed soup for you! It is so good for you, come on."

Zhang stood and shuffled to the table. Jin placed a large bowl of thick soup with chopped seaweed and large pieces of boiled beef, "Eat up!"

Jin sat down across from her, "I'm glad you are up. I know you don't feel better, but you look better."

Zhang simply nodded and took a spoonful of the salty soup. The slippery seaweed and tender beef felt good in her mouth, "This is good. I am a little hungry."

"Good! I made plenty, so eat as much as you can. It is a good soup to help restore the body. Xiaorong doesn't like it though, he thinks the seaweed is not so delicious."

"Where is Xiaorong?"

"I left him with my neighbor. She is older and doesn't have grandchildren. She loves to look after Xiaorong, and she spoils him so he likes it too," Jin laughed. "I thought it would be better if we were alone to talk. Xiaorong wouldn't really understand."

Zhang Ying nodded, "It's no problem. She reached out and put her hand on Jin's soft white hand, "I am glad you are here. I thought I wanted to be alone. I was wrong."

Jin turned her hand over to hold Zhang's "I understand. I can never understand how hard it is to lose your baby, but I do understand what it is like to want to push everyone away. To hold on to pain like some treasure that you can't let go…" Jin's voice softened, "And to want to punish yourself. To feel like you have done something so wrong that no one can forgive you. I understand that."

Zhang kept eating while Jin looked on, smiling, "Good! You finished it! Can I get you some more?"

"No, I'm full. I just want to sit down for a bit."

"No problem, this soup will keep for a few days. You can eat it tomorrow too," Jin cleaned up the dishes and put the remaining soup in the refrigerator. She sat down on the sofa next to Zhang and saw the stain, "Can I clean this up?"

"No. Shao Huan already tried to clean it. I don't want it gone though. I want to remember."

"Okay. No problem. I will leave it."

Zhang Ying lay back on the sofa and looked at Jin Xishan, "You said there is hope. I don't feel like there is anything to look forward to. The only thing I want is to have my baby back, and I can't have that."

Jin Xishan smiled softly and sighed, "There is hope, but let's go for a walk in the park and talk outside? It is a nice day," Jin saw the reluctance on Zhang's face, "It's okay, we won't go far and will come back whenever you want. Okay?"

Zhang paused and slowly nodded her assent. She allowed Jin Xishan to help her put on her shoes, but thought it was strange when Jin asked her to leave her phone behind. They took a taxi to the south gate of Chaoyang Park. Zhang's legs were tired from spending so long in bed, but it felt good to stretch them out.

The park was busy with people exercising and groups of children playing. Zhang Ying usually loved the park, but seeing the children and hearing their shouts of laughter made her heart ache. Jin Xishan guided her to the right, over the canal and down along the sports fields.

"When I was a teenager, I was very angry and so sad," Jin began while walking slowly and offering support to Zhang whenever she appeared to falter, "I hated our little village and didn't see any point in living. I thought about killing myself. I thought it would be romantic, somehow, to end my life while I was young and beautiful. I thought that I would never get out of there and I didn't want to stay there, have children there, grow old there. A South Korean family moved to the town near by and I thought that South Korea must be like heaven. Our area was so backward then. They started holding meetings at their house and invited people from the village. I wanted to know everything about South Korea, and so I went. They talked about how hard life can be, and how we all need to find some purpose in life. I knew they were right, and that I was so sad and angry because I didn't feel like my life had any purpose."

Jin saw that Zhang was struggling and guided her to a bench shaded under the thick green sheets of cherry leaves. "I stayed after the meeting and talked with the mother in the family. She was so kind, so full of love. She gave me a Chinese translation of a book to read and asked me to come back to have dinner with them. The book told the story of Jesus. I had never really studied religion. I mean, we had our traditions and offered respect for our ancestors, but I didn't know anything about Jesus and when I read the story of God's love and how he traded his son's life to save all of us… I cried. I couldn't imagine that anyone would give their child's life to save someone they didn't know, but even more than that I couldn't have imagined how much God loves all of us that he allowed his son to be punished so much for the horrible things that people do."

Jin stopped and looked at Zhang, "I know this must sound strange to you, and it may not make sense now. I don't usually tell anyone about my faith. The Party has made it very hard for Christians and I have to be very careful, but seeing you in so much pain hurts me too. I don't know if my faith can help you, but I want you to know that whatever sadness you feel, whatever grief, and no matter how much you want to punish yourself, God loves you and his son already died to take that punishment. Life is hard and full of sadness, but God has also given us so much joy and purpose… After I read that book, I went to dinner with the missionary family and held hands with them while they prayed a blessing over the food. They were so grateful to God for everything, even the hardships that they endured there. They had so much love for each other and for all of the people there. I decided that I didn't want to be angry any more, I wanted to be like them. I wanted to feel that love and to have that kind of purpose."

Zhang listened intently to Jin's voice, even as she stared ahead of her through the trees and the tall grass. Jin's clear and compassionate voice continued above the distant shouts from the sports fields, and the chirrups of the cicadas, "I know it sounds so strange at first, but I really believe that God created everything around us, and that he loves each and every person. I believe that he gave his own son's life to save all of us from punishment, even people who have done terrible things. I also believe my purpose in life is to share that love. Of course I still feel sad sometimes, but I never feel alone and when I do have dark times I remember that there is nothing I can do that God can't forgive and that he loves me, and loves even the people that I don't really like."

Zhang Ying hadn't cried since the morning, but felt tears filling her eyes again, "If there was a God, why would he let my baby die?" She let the tears fall down her face.

Jin Xishan put her hand on Zhang's back, "Bad things, really horrible things, happen all of the time. This world is not perfect because humanity rebelled against God, and God won't stop bad things from happening because he wants us to have a choice. He chooses to love us, and wants us to choose to love him. He loves us even though we have rebelled against him, even though we have ruined his perfect creation. He can't stop the pain in this world, but he promises us a heavenly kingdom where everything is perfect."

Zhang cried harder and a few passersby noticed Zhang's despair and accepted a knowing nod from Jin Xishan as they continued on their way. Zhang gasped "Do you think my baby is in heaven?"

Jin rubbed her hand over Zhang's back and took a deep breath, "I don't know. I really don't know. I do know that God loves you, that no matter what you feel God is always ready to talk with you. I talk with God every day, usually several times a day. And he talks back. Sometimes he answers in the still moments in my heart, sometimes I feel like he answers me through the people around me. You can ask God if you want to. "

Zhang shook her head, "No, I don't know how to talk to God. I don't even believe in God."

"It's okay. You don't have to believe in God to talk to him. He believes in you. You don't even have to close your eyes or kneel on the ground. Let's talk to him together, okay?" Jin stopped moving her hand on Zhang's back and left it between Zhang's shoulder blades.

Zhang nodded meekly, "Okay."

In a calm and even voice, just as if she was speaking with a friend, Jin began, "Heavenly Father, You know how much my sister Zhang

Ying hurts right now. She was so excited to be a mother. Please Heavenly Father, let her feel Your love. You tell us that You love even the sparrow, and I know You loved her baby too. We don't know if she will get to see her baby in heaven, but You know. Her pain is great and heart is open. Please touch Your child, my sister Zhang Ying."

Jin stopped speaking and the sound of the cicadas and rustling leaves filled the silence. "I don't hear him," Zhang Ying whispered.

"Sometimes he answers right away, sometimes he waits. Sometimes he answers like a voice in your heart, sometimes he answers with a bird song or a falling leaf. He will speak to you at the right moment," Jin patted her back.

"How are you so sure?"

"Little sister, I am sure because I have faith."

Jin and Zhang sat in the shade a little longer. Zhang was too tired to walk all the way back to the south gate, so they walked to the quiet east gate and waved down a taxi to take them back to the apartment. Jin helped Zhang sit down on the sofa and got her a glass of cool water. She got her bag and pulled out a well worn book, "This is the book that the missionary family gave me. I want you to have it. You don't have to read it, but I hope you do."

Zhang looked at the book's faded cover and pages that had clearly been read many times, "I can't take that. You can get me a new one."

"Alright, I will get you a new one, but start with this one. Okay?"

Zhang nodded and gave Jin a long embrace as she accepted the gift and opened herself again to Jin's friendship and love.

基督徒
Christian

Zhang Ying started to read the book immediately after Jin Xishan left. She carefully turned the well loved pages, and read about the most important angel who decided to challenge God, how he led a rebellion and was cast out of heaven. How God created the earth and gave humans free will, how that angel entered the perfect world and seduced the first humans away from following God. How God blessed Abraham and his children and how God worked through the Israelites. Zhang was immersed in the story when Shao Huan returned.

"Hey! You are up!" Shao Huan was relieved to see her out of bed. "Did Xishan already go?"

"Yes, she left. She was so kind to stay with me."

Shao Huan kissed Zhang Ying's head and sat down next to her, "What is this?"

"Oh, just a book that she gave me to read," Zhang wasn't ready to tell Shao Huan about everything Jin Xishan had told her and not even sure that she should, she didn't want to cause Jin any trouble. "I took my medicine," Zhang tried to muster a faint smile, but only managed to bring her face to a neutral expression.

"Good. That is really good. You need to take your medicine to recover. Can you do that every day?"

Zhang Ying nodded, "Yes. I will. I promise. I am still so sad, but I really love you and I want to live for you," Zhang nestled in to Shao's shoulder and put her arm around his slender stomach.

Shao Huan had been so worried that he would return to the apartment to find Zhang still nearly catatonic in the bed, that he was unprepared for her affection. He wrapped his arms around Zhang Ying, "It's okay to be sad. I am sad too. I need you to live… Did you eat?"

Shao Huan took left over vegetables and some beef that was left over from Jin Xishan's seaweed soup and made fried rice. Zhang sat at the table with Shao, "I think I am ready to talk about it."

"Are you sure?"

"No, I am not sure… but I was so tired the last few weeks. The baby was so busy, I was miserable and already sad then. I tried to pretend that everything was okay, but it wasn't. I just hoped for the baby to come soon. I wanted the pregnancy to be over so I could sleep…" Zhang's voice faltered, "I feel so guilty for that. I should not have been so impatient. After she died, I only wanted to sleep. I didn't dream, I didn't think of anything. When I was awake, I only felt pain and emptiness. When I slept, I didn't feel anything."

Shao Huan listened carefully but didn't speak. Zhang Ying continued, "I wanted to be a mother so much. I felt like my purpose in life was to be a mother. Ever since I was little, everyone has told me I will be a great mother. Even at the kindergarten, I felt like it was all practice for when I have my own child. But now, I don't think that I can be a mother at all. I don't want to go through that again. I don't think I can give you a baby."

"My dear, I just want you. Whether or not we have a baby is not as important as you staying healthy," Shao Huan thought to offer that they could adopt a baby, but held back. "Whatever you want, I will support you."

A dim light returned to Zhang Ying's eyes, and for a moment Shao Huan felt that she would be okay, "My dear husband, you have been so kind and have done everything for me. Let me clean the kitchen."

Shao Huan started to protest but saw the resolve on Zhang's face, and acquiesced. Shao had carried his anxiety about Zhang Ying deep in his muscles and as she cleaned the kitchen he lay down on the sofa and let his muscles relax and his exhaustion carry him to a deep sleep.

Zhang Ying sat on the sofa by her sleeping husband and continued to read. She read about how God chose a kind young woman to bear his son, how Jesus was born and how he showed kindness and love to everyone around him. Zhang Ying didn't understand how a God could have a mortal son, or how Jesus could be mortal and divine, but she loved the stories of Jesus calling the little children to him, healing the crippled and his kindness toward the poor and the outcast. Zhang finished reading the thin book and carefully put it away before she lay down in bed. She still felt the incredible loss, but now had something else to think about and she had so many questions for Jin Xishan.

Zhang woke the next morning while Shao Huan was showering. She sat on the couch and started to read Jin's book again. Shao Huan came out of the bathroom and smiled when he saw Zhang Ying was already up, "Good morning my dear, I am going to the office. Are you still reading that book?"

Zhang nodded, "Have a good day at work, Jin Xishan will be here soon."

"Good. You can tell me about that book later. I have to go now," Shao Huan lightly kissed Zhang's lips and rushed out of the door.

Zhang was drawn to a speech that Jesus made on a mountain and read it several times, 'Blessed are the poor in spirit, for theirs is the kingdom of heaven. Blessed are those who mourn, for they will be comforted. Blessed are the meek, for they will inherit the earth…' The words were so simple and beautiful, and so different from anything she had ever heard before. Zhang didn't know if she felt God speaking to her, but she found so much comfort in those words.

Jin Xishan knocked at the door and greeted Zhang Ying with a hug, "Did you sleep okay?"

"I slept okay, but I read your book and I have so many questions."

"That is good. I may have some answers, but I am sure you will have more questions. That is how it should be. I want to get a jianbing for breakfast, and it is a beautiful morning. It is better to talk about this outside anyway."

The thought of the fresh hot crepe wrapped around crunchy fried cracker and seasoned with coriander and scallions made Zhang Ying's mouth water, "Okay. We can talk there. It won't take me long to get ready."

After a quick shower and change, Zhang Ying and Jin Xishan made their way to an intersection near Chaoyang park and found a street vendor making crepes on the hot plate at the center of his push cart.

They watched the grey wheat batter cook into a thin crepe and the eggs sizzle and spread over the crepe.

"Good morning! How many?" The swarthy vendor asked in a heavy Beijing accent.

"Two. One without chili sauce," Zhang stepped forward and paid. The vendor smeared chili sauce over the crepe, sprinkled soft coriander leaves and sesame seeds across it before he placed a thin piece of fried dough in the middle of the crepe, folded it over, crunched the fried bread, folded it in half again, picked it up with a clear plastic bag and handed it to Zhang.

Jin Xishan took the bag from Zhang, "I love these. I don't eat them very often, but this morning I had such a craving for jianbing. Let's eat in the park."

Zhang took her breakfast crepe and they found an empty bench by the lake on the west side of the park. Jin sat down, "So what are your questions?" She bit through the soft wheat and egg crepe to the fried bread in the middle that crumbled in her mouth with a satisfying crunch.

"Jesus was a Jew? Is that right?" Zhang Ying asked. The steam from the crepe had clouded the plastic bag.

Jin swallowed quickly, "Yes, Jesus and all of his disciples were Jews. Most of the first Christians were Jews."

"Why did the other people turn against him?"

"There were many people who wanted Jesus to save them from the Romans. They wanted to use him like a political tool, but he wasn't concerned with the politics of this world, he only looked to the kingdom of heaven. He didn't want people to seek power, or to use their religion to make them rich. He wanted people to love each other, to treat each other kindly, and to forgive each other."

Zhang ate her crepe slowly while Jin talked, "They were scared of him too. Jesus had attracted so many followers, the other religious leaders worried that he would take away their own power. Love is more powerful than politics."

"Does the Party let people be Christians?" Zhang asked.

Jin took a long deep breath and exhaled slowly, "No. Not really. The Party realized they couldn't get rid of Christianity. The Romans tried that and failed. They learned from the Romans and have made an official Christian church that is controlled by the Party. The Party tries to make Christianity seem like a foreign disease, but there have been Christians in China since the Tang dynasty. The Taizong Emperor welcomed Christians to China. The Party's version of Christianity doesn't really teach about God's love, it uses a shadow of the story of Jesus to support the Party. They even edited the Bible so that it supports the Party. For the Party, it is just another kind of thought work. Real Christians are dangerous to them, because we love God, not the Party, and because we aren't afraid of them. We have to be careful, but if I had to trade my life in this world to save another soul… I would do it. Real Bibles are illegal. Real churches are illegal too."

Zhang set the rest of her crepe down on the bench, "Are you scared?"

Jin smiled, "No, I'm not scared. The Party is scared. I know that whatever happens in this life, God has promised me a better life. The Party knows that if people can worship freely, they will lose control. I am careful, we are all careful. The Party arrests any leaders they think are becoming a threat to them. If I get arrested, I can't work for God like I am now, but I know he will also use me for his glory inside prison. "

Zhang sat quietly next to Jin and watched the morning light sparkle on the lake, "You know that Shao Huan is a Party member, right?"

"I know. But he is a good person. There are many Christians who are in the Party too. It is how we have learned to adapt and continue to spread God's word even though the Party is always trying to stop us. Have you told Shao Huan that I am a Christian?"

"No. He is curious about your book, but I haven't told him what it is yet. Should I tell him?"

Jin smiled, "Of course you should tell him. You two are so close, I don't want you to have a secret from him. I know he won't report me."

"Is that book a Bible?"

"No, it is just some stories from the Bible. The real Bible is long and it can be hard to read, but it is beautiful too. There are so many stories, and songs, and poems. That book is a little easier to start with, and it isn't actually illegal. I can give you a real Bible if you want, but you will have to be careful with it."

Zhang weighed the risk but was drawn to the stories and Jin's bravery inspired her, "Okay. I would like that. I will be careful."

"From the very beginning, Christians were persecuted, but no matter what, God's love always wins in the end. The Party thinks they are more powerful than God. They are wrong. So very wrong," Jin Xishan's normally sunny voice took on a gravity that surprised Zhang.

"How do you love your enemies? Jesus said that we have to love our enemies, but I don't know how to do that."

"It is hard. Very hard. Speaking frankly, we can't do it alone. It is only after we accept God's love and forgiveness that we can really learn how to love our enemies," Jin took a long pause and then asked, "Would you like to come to church with me? Part of being Christian is being part of a community. We aren't supposed to bring new people to our church, but I am sure they will be so glad to meet you."

"Are you sure? I… I haven't been to a church before. I don't know what to do."

"It's okay. You don't have to do anything. Just go with me and open your heart. That is all. You don't have to come this weekend, you can come next weekend, or any other weekend."

Zhang Ying thought about it carefully, "Can you get me a Bible? I want to read it and to talk with Shao Huan first. Then maybe I can go with you next time?"

Jin's radiant smile made Zhang feel so accepted and loved, "Of course. It is good you want to read the Bible first. I will bring it for you tomorrow."

天坛
Temple of Heaven

Zhang Ying waited eagerly at home for Shao Huan. She read the new copy of the book that Jin had given her, and found such comfort in Jesus' words. She still hadn't heard God speak to her and didn't know if he ever would, but she liked the ideas in the book. Jin Xishan's words of caution also raced through her mind. She didn't know how Shao Huan would react.

Shao Huan returned later than normal and was tired from a long day but relieved again to see Zhang Ying sitting in the living room, "How was your day with Xishan?"

"It was good. We went back to Chaoyang Park. It was good to get outside, even though it was hot. We talked a lot. I really like talking with her. She understands me so well. How was your day?"

"Very busy. The boss had lots of calls and messages. Did you eat today?" Shao Huan sat on the sofa next to Zhang.

"You don't have to worry about me so much now. I know I made you worry so much for those days, but I am eating now. I also took my medicine. Okay?"

"Okay. I won't worry so much," Shao Huan noticed a new book on sofa beside Zhang, "Another book? What is this one about?"

Zhang Ying handed the thin book to her husband, "It is a new book, but the same story. Jin Xishan told me a lot, and she trusted me a lot too. I don't know if I believe everything in this book, but I like it a lot. I think you should read it and we can talk about it. How do you think?"

Shao Huan started to thumb through the pages slowly, "Wow. I wondered about Xishan after we went to dinner. I… I don't know. I shouldn't read this."

"I know you aren't supposed to read this kind of book, but this story has helped me so much the last two days. These words have given me comfort, and if you wonder why I am a little better, it is because of Xishan and this book. Will you read it for me? It isn't very long. We can go for a walk and talk about it when you are done."

Shao Huan was so glad that Zhang Ying was feeling better. Over the years he had also come to see the Party's rules and limits as excessive, "Okay. I will read it for you. We can't tell anyone though, okay? Not your parents, or mine. Especially not Sima Nan."

Zhang Ying hugged Shao tightly, "Good. I hope you like it too. I want to hear how you think about it. I made thin sliced potatoes and shredded pork with garlic sauce."

"Wow, you are feeling better. I really will have to read this book," Shao stood as Zhang pulled his hand toward the table.

The thin strips of potato were perfectly flash fried and coated in sweet clear vinegar and the pork was tender and the sauce had soaked deep into the strips of meat. Shao Huan was tired and his belly was full, but he wanted to see why Zhang Ying was so interested in the book from Jin Xishan. They had never been religious. Shao Huan appreciated the traditional celebrations and had his paternal grandmother had kept an image of the Kitchen God in her house, but he didn't think of them as anything more than quaint superstitions.

He sat on the sofa and began to read. He was soon engrossed in the story and kept reading after Zhang Ying went to bed. It was not like any book he had ever read. Shao finished the book and lay down beside Zhang, her peaceful, steady breathing helped guide him to sleep.

Zhang Ying was up and getting ready for the day when Shao Huan woke. Shao walked in to the bathroom as Zhang was taking her medicine, "Good morning," he greeted her with a kiss on the cheek.

"Did you finish the book?"

"I did. Maybe we should go for a walk this morning?"

Zhang Ying's smile was the brightest Shao had seen since their baby died, "Great! Where should we go?"

"It is Saturday and it is still early," Shao considered the options, "Let's go to the Temple of Heaven. We can eat breakfast near there too."

Shao and Zhang reached the park while the sun was still low on the eastern horizon. They walked through large arched doorway of the east gate opening into the expansive garden, and Zhang couldn't hold back her questions any more, "How did you think about the book?"

"It was really interesting. I didn't understand the beginning too well, it seemed a little like the Monkey King rebelling against the Jade

Emperor, causing trouble in heaven, declaring himself the Great Sage and being imprisoned under a mountain. But that is just a story, and it seems like Christians really believe that Lucifer rebelled against God and was cast out of heaven. The Garden of Eden seems a little like the immortal peach garden. It was interesting to compare those things. I liked the story better when it got to the part about Jesus. It was a little bit like the stories of Confucius and his disciples, but while Confucius wanted to find a worthy ruler to restore the rites of Zhou and for a worthy ruler to receive the Mandate of Heaven, it seems that Jesus wanted to establish a new Kingdom of Heaven and became a political threat to the ruling class, so they killed him, but that Christians believe he really was God's son and his death actually was part of God's plan to offer spiritual freedom, not physical or political freedom," Shao Huan offered his analysis while they walked along the quiet paths and watched the morning mist rise through the well spaced pine trees.

Shao's comments disappointed Zhang Ying, "Okay, I can understand your comparative analysis, but how did the book make you feel?"

Shao Huan took Zhang's hand in his, and he had to contemplate her question before answering, "It made me feel like there is still so much I don't know. It was a good story, but it didn't make me feel anything special." Shao saw dejection start to pull down the corners of Zhang's mouth, "My dear, I am glad that you like the story, but it is dangerous for me. Even if I liked the story or wanted to believe it is more than a story, I couldn't become a Christian. The Party would kick me out and I would lose my job. I don't want that to happen."

"But, isn't it better to find comfort and truth than to keep a job with the Party?" Zhang Ying pleaded.

Shao heard the ache in Zhang's voice and knew it was not worth arguing, "I know that it is important to you, and I will support you. If you want to study more with Jin Xishan or even to become Christian someday, it is no problem. Really. I can't become Christian, it would make problems for everyone at work."

Zhang withdrew her hand, "Why? Why can't you follow your own heart and not your mind or the Party?"

"I can follow my own heart, and that is why I married you," they saw the golden orb on top of the Hall of Prayer for Good Harvests catch the morning light above the misty earth below and the tower's dark blue tiles as they neared the center of the park, "I just don't feel my heart is leading me to become Christian. It is a good story and I liked some of the things that Jesus said in the book, he seems like a very kind man, but can God really become a man? The emperors used to say they were the Son of Heaven, but they were just men. Maybe Jesus was different, and maybe it is possible, but it isn't something I feel."

The magnificent circular tower at the center of a wide courtyard paved with cut stone rose before them, the ornate painting and rich tiles sparkled in the clear morning light that pushed aside the last soft wisps of morning mist. Zhang Ying stood silently next to Shao Huan for a moment, watching the scene where emperors had offered sacrifices for centuries, "Our ancestors believed in things. They believed in this place and in gods. Don't you wish you had something more to believe in than work and the Party?"

"It isn't that I only believe in the Party. I believe in you. I believe that we should work hard and enjoy life. I will support you and will help you stay safe if you want to become a Christian, but I can't study with Jin Xishan together with you," Shao Huan knew how those words would hurt Zhang, but that he would put them both in too much danger if he joined Zhang Ying to find comfort in faith. "I am a little hungry. There used to be a good breakfast place outside the of the north gate. Shall we walk there?"

Zhang simply nodded and walked alongside Shao. She reached for his hand and pulled him close to her as they walked through the park. They passed an old man with a calligraphy brush as large as his leg drawing characters with water on the stone path. Shao paused to watch him finish tracing out Cao Zhi's "Verse in Seven Steps" "Lighting the bean stalk to boil the beans, and the beans then wailed: Aren't we borne of the same root; should you burn me now with such disregard?"

Zhang Ying pulled on Shao Huan's sleeve to wake him from the trance watching the graceful characters form and slowly evaporate in the morning light. They didn't say much on the rest of the walk through the park or over their bowls of fermented mung bean milk and oily fried dough. Zhang Ying was grateful for Shao's support but she had wanted so badly for Shao to also find comfort and hope in the book from Jin Xishan.

The scar across her stomach, the blood stain on the sofa and the absence in her heart kept pulling Zhang back to the grief of her loss. The sadness that she briefly thought she had escaped continued to creep back, an unavoidable agony that oozed out of her bones into her whole body. Whenever Zhang felt the darkness wrapping around her lungs and pulling her down into the despair that she had wallowed in, she read the book that Jin Xishan gave her and felt the anxiety, loneliness and guilt dissipate with the words "Blessed are those who mourn for they shall be comforted."

Zhang could see the grief still haunted Shao as well, in the quiet moments when she caught him staring off into space, his face betraying the sadness that he tried to hide from her and from himself. She wanted him to read the book again. She wanted him to talk with Jin Xishan. Zhang knew, however, that Shao would have to make those decisions in his own time.

Jin Xishan persuaded Zhang Ying to meet her in the 798 art district not far from Wangjing or Chaoyang Park. Zhang had been there once with Shao Huan when they first moved to Beijing together, but had not been back to the sprawling complex of warehouse galleries and cafes. They met at a small cafe and Jin ordered flat white coffees for both of them. They found a bench on a quiet side lane and Jin asked, "How did Shao Huan think about the book?"

Zhang shook her head and cast her eyes down at the paper coffee cup clasped between her hands, "He liked it but said he can't think about becoming Christian. It is not convenient for him."

Jin Xishan laughed, louder than she anticipated, "I'm embarrassed. I shouldn't laugh. It is just, being a Christian really is inconvenient. Being a real Christian is always inconvenient. Don't worry, God will use a different way to talk to him. It is no problem, really. I brought you a Bible," Jin pulled a heavy book wrapped in brown paper out of her bag and handed it to Zhang Ying.

"Wow, it is heavy! This will take me a long time to read."

"Of course. It will take longer than you think, and you will read it again and again."

"Okay. I will do that. Should I start reading it from the beginning?" Zhang opened the book to the start.

"It is up to you. You can start from the beginning, or you can start from the New Testament. You don't have to read it all the way through either. It isn't like a novel where you need to read it one page after the next. It is like a collection of stories that all come together, so if you get bored or tired with one part you can start another part. Sometimes I just like to read the songs and poems in the Old Testament."

The weight of the book in Zhang's hands intimidated her, and the reverence in Jin's voice when she spoke about it added to the mystique, "Okay. I will read it, even if it takes me a long time."

"Good, remember, this book is illegal. If you are caught with it, you can get in trouble. If they find out I gave it to you, I will get in trouble. You should be careful when you read it. Put a soap opera on your phone while you read it. If the government is monitoring your phone, they will think you are just at home watching a television program. Okay?"

Zhang nodded solemnly, "I promise. I won't tell anyone except Shao Huan that you gave this book to me."

"I know. Shao Huan will be okay. I also spoke with my church about you and they said that you can come next weekend if you want to. Do you want to go?"

Zhang's heart soared, she desperately wanted to go to church with Jin, "Yes, of course!"

Jin finished her coffee and stood, "Good, it is just a small house church but a church is about the people not the building. The Party doesn't understand that. I think you will like it. Come on, let's have a look at the art! I love to see the things people make here," Jin's kindness and enthusiasm continued to draw Zhang closer.

家庭教会
House Church

The morning wandering between galleries of huge paintings, elaborate sculptures and mind bending but carefully non political expressions of the human experience left Zhang Ying overwhelmed and exhausted. The cool, quiet of her small familiar apartment was a relief from the novelty and stimulation of the art complex. Just as Jin advised, Zhang connected head phones to her phone and put on a soap opera. She set the phone down on the sofa beside her and opened the Bible to the Gospel of Matthew.

When Shao Huan returned home that evening, Zhang had only finished the first gospel. She put the Bible down and greeted her husband with a hug, "Dear, you are home! You look tired."

Shao Huan smiled weakly, "I am tired. It was a long day. The boss has more calls these days. I think there are many problems."

Zhang knew better than to ask about the problems and Shao saw the thick book covered in brown paper on the coffee table. He tilted his head toward the book, "How was Jin Xishan?"

"We had a wonderful morning. I have been learning a lot today. Seeing interesting art and other things," Zhang smiled and held up the book.

Shao Huan saw how much happier Zhang was, and although he was not entirely comfortable with her interest in Christianity, he knew it was better to support her. His relief that she was finding some comfort to manage the grief eclipsed whatever concern he had about her budding faith. He thought he had put the grief of their stillborn daughter behind him, but as Zhang Ying returned to the living world, and the terror that he might still lose her faded, the sadness snuck up on him during the day's quiet moments.

After Zhang went to bed, Shao Huan sat alone and opened the book. His eyes fell on a passage of Jesus welcoming little children to him and saying the kingdom of heaven belonged to them. Shao remembered Liu Wuqing's criticism of the Taiping Heavenly Kingdom, and wondered what Jesus really meant by the Kingdom of Heaven if it was to belong to little children and not to kings or generals.

Zhang Ying continued reading the gospels as the week progressed and Shao Huan would read short passages on his own after Zhang had gone to bed. As Zhang Ying's porcelain smooth face started to glow again, Shao felt his own heart sinking deeper with the long hours supporting Ye Hongqi and the sadness that grew a little heavier each day.

By the weekend, Zhang Ying felt ready to go to her first church meeting. She didn't know what to expect but she hoped that the other people would be as kind and friendly as Jin. Jin had given Zhang Ying directions to an intersection and told her to meet there at 9 a.m. on Sunday morning. Shao Huan agreed to go with Zhang to the intersection and once they spotted Jin Xishan from a distance, Shao took Zhang's phone and went to a nearby Starbucks to wait for her.

Zhang's heart raced as she walked up to Jin, her hands were warm and her face beamed. Jin greeted her with a hug, "Great! You are here, let's go. One of our members owns a small restaurant and today we are meeting in her restaurant before it opens. We change the meeting times and locations to make it a little bit harder for the Party to find us. They have taken down the crosses from even the official churches and have arrested a lot of house church leaders. That is why our house church doesn't really have a leader. Each of us takes a turn. You'll get to meet my husband finally, Xiaorong is there with him already."

Jin Xishan led Zhang Ying down a side street and to a small Chengdu snack restaurant. Jin pulled open the glass door that was still covered by a dark curtain and Zhang stepped inside. A small group of people stood talking together inside and Xiaorong's joyous voice rang out, "Teacher, teacher! You came!" He ran up to Zhang Ying and hugged her leg. Zhang Ying kneeled down to put her face next to his and gave him a hug, "I missed you at school."

"I missed you too, is the new teacher okay?"

Xiaorong nodded, "I wish you could have had a baby, I wanted to play with him."

Zhang Ying choked back her tears and couldn't respond to Xiaorong's innocence and sympathy. Jin patted her on the back, "Little sister, this is my husband Bai Yongcheng." Bai was thin but strong, had thick black hair and smiled like Xiaorong.

"I am very glad to meet you. I have heard so much about you from Xishan and Xiaorong, I feel like I have known you for a long time. I was too busy traveling, but now we can meet," Bai's voice was deep and comforting, "We are about to begin with prayer, come stand over here."

Jin held Zhang Ying's hand, "Sisters and brothers, today we are blessed to welcome Zhang Ying to our church. She is just beginning to learn about our Heavenly Father's love and forgiveness. She is dear to me, and I know that together we will share with her the good news."

A short middle aged woman with dark skin and her shoulder length hair tightly curled spoke, "Welcome Zhang Ying, we will pray together now," the group formed into a circle and held hands. Xiaorong stood between his father and Zhang. Zhang Ying felt warm and comfortable standing with Xiaorong to her left and Jin Xishan to her right. Everyone bowed their heads and closed their eyes, and Zhang quickly followed their example.

The woman began to speak with a slight Sichuan accent, "Our Father in Heaven, we gather together today to worship You. To stand together as brothers and sisters in Christ and to welcome Zhang Ying. We are grateful to You Heavenly Father for bringing sister Zhang to us. You tell us that we will face persecution, that we will be laughed at and cast out for worshiping You. We love You Lord in Heaven because You love us and we will worship You together and on our own. There is nothing that the rulers of men can do to stop us. We thank You Heavenly Father for all of Your blessings, and we also thank You for our trials and tribulations in this life so that we may come closer to You. Amen."

Zhang Ying's prayers with Jin Xishan had felt so casual and comfortable, but the formality of this prayer carried a reverence and gravity that deeply impressed her, and she joined the rest of the group when they instinctively responded "Amen" at the end of the prayer. They began to softly sing "Thank You Father" and Xiaorong giggled at Zhang as she tried to learn the lyrics while the group sang.

The group let go of each other's hands and some pulled chairs out from the tables that had been pushed against the walls. The woman started to speak, and Zhang listened in rapt attention to her story. She introduced herself as Duan Yide and she testified about her own experience with Christ. She explained that her parents were Christians and hid their faith during the Cultural Revolution, but she was so embarrassed that they were different. She tried to hide their family's faith to fit in with her friends and avoid the ridicule that she knew would come. She never told her parent's secret to anyone, but as her father got older he became more open about his faith and eventually the authorities in Chengdu arrested him. They kept him in detention for years. Duan described the shame and fear she felt while her father was in prison, but she went back to Chengdu when he was released. She was so glad to see him again and overwhelmed that prison had only strengthened his faith in Christ. That night they prayed together at home and her father prayed for God to bless the prison guards who had held him and treated him so badly for those years. Her father's faith in God, forgiveness of his captors, and even love for the people who had despised him moved Duan so deeply that she knew her father was right. She begged forgiveness from her father for having turned away from Christ and for being embarrassed of their faith. Duan committed to following Jesus.

Duan broke down in tears at the end of her story and Zhang Ying cried with her. She was so absorbed in Duan's story that she hadn't noticed Xiaorong fidgeting next to her. Duan regained her composure and asked the small congregation to open their Bibles to 2 Corinthians 12:10. Zhang fumbled with her Bible, unsure of how to find books and verses, but Jin Xishan opened her Bible and held it between them so Zhang could read along as Duan's voice regained strength and conviction while she read, "That is why, for Christ's sake, I delight in weaknesses, in insults, in hardships, in persecutions, in difficulties. For when I am weak, then I am strong."

The congregation said "Amen" together again. Duan turned her attention to Zhang Ying, "Sister Zhang, we are so glad you came today, I would like to offer a prayer for you… if that is okay?"

Zhang looked at Jin Xishan for assurance, and after Jin smiled and nodded, Zhang replied, "Okay. Thank you." Zhang bowed her head and expected Duan to start praying, but Duan stood and walked over to Zhang and the rest of the congregation and stood with her, "We will put our hands on you while we pray, okay?"

Zhang didn't know what to expect but nodded her consent, and Duan put her hand on Zhang's head, Jin and Xiaorong held Zhang's hands on either side and the other church members placed their hands on Zhang's back and shoulders. Duan started to pray again, "Our Father in Heaven, we are grateful to You for bringing Zhang Ying today. We know the sadness and loss that sister Zhang Ying has endured. We know this world is imperfect and that the rain falls on the wicked as well as the righteous. We do not know Your purpose Father in Heaven, but we know Your love. We know that You love Zhang Ying and that You loved her child. We weep together for her stillborn child, we pray that You will guide Zhang Ying to grow in Your spirit and in Your love. We lift Zhang Ying up to You, Heavenly Father, as a member of our church and a sister in faith. Bless Zhang Ying. Thank You our Lord and Father. Amen."

While Duan prayed, Zhang felt the hair on her arms and neck raise with an unseen energy, like an electricity gathering in her soul and radiating through her body. She felt her heart quicken and the warmth of the believers gathered around her. Zhang began to weep silently and squeezed Jin's hand tightly. After the prayer ended, Xiaorong opened his eyes, "Teacher, don't cry teacher, Heavenly Father loves you."

Zhang Ying burst into sobs and Xiaorong hugged her. Duan Yide leaned down and hugged Zhang as well. Zhang's whole body shook with relief and joy as a woman she had just met hugged her as if they were old friends, as if she was Duan's own daughter. Zhang stood up and hugged Duan, "Thank you," she whispered, "I heard God using your voice to speak to me. I didn't know what it would be like to hear God speak. I believe. I believe."

认知失调
Cognitive Dissonance

After the prayer ended, it took Zhang Ying nearly an hour to leave the small restaurant. The church members all hugged her and welcomed her with such compassion and excitement. She had never felt more accepted and at home any place else in her life. Zhang wept tears of joy and held Xiaorong in her arms for much of the morning while she spoke with her fellow believers. Duan eventually told Zhang that she had to start opening the restaurant for lunch and that it was better if no one from the church was still there.

Zhang Ying hugged Jin Xishan, "Big sister, thank you so much. I think God sent you in to my life."

Jin laughed, "No, no, little sister, God sent you in to my life!" Jin squeezed her tightly, "I will see you again soon. You should go. Do you know where we will meet next week?"

Zhang confirmed that she knew the time and location for the next church service and then stepped back outside. The sunlight felt good on her face and she breathed deeply, her shoulders relaxed and she started walking toward the cafe where Shao Huan was waiting. She spotted Shao sitting in a corner looking at his phone. She sat down on the bench next to him and gave him a kiss on the cheek, "You waited so long for me. I really didn't know it would be so long."

Shao saw the glow in Zhang's eyes and the irrepressible smile on her face, "It's no problem. It seems like you enjoyed it."

"Enjoyed isn't the right word. It moved me. My dear, I heard God speak to me. I really did. I am a Christian now. I believe."

The speed of Zhang's conversion caught Shao by surprise, "Really? Already?"

"Yes. I don't think you have to wait to believe. I felt God's love and I heard him speak to me. I wish you could have been there."

Shao Huan fidgeted with the empty coffee mug in front of him, "Wow. I don't know what I should say. I said I would support you and I will. Are you sure you are a Christian?"

Zhang put her warm hand on Shao's leg, "I know it, I know it just like I knew I loved you. I still have a lot to learn, but I want to keep learning."

Shao Huan sighed, "Well, I love you and I will support you. If you are going to become a Christian, you will need to be careful. I can help you with that, okay?"

In her excitement Zhang had forgotten the danger of her conversion, but Shao Huan's offer brought back the gravity of the persecution that she was inviting and the tribulations she would need to learn to be grateful for, "Oh yes, what you said is right. I do need to be careful. What should I do?"

"You need to prevent any of the social credit algorithms from identifying you as a Christian. Once that happens, the Party will focus more attention on you. Already we don't know if they have identified Jin Xishan as a Christian. You should stop contacting Jin Xishan on your phone. You can see each other at the school, and at church, but you shouldn't send any more messages over WeChat. Don't delete her from the app right away, but stop talking with her on it and then after a month or two you should delete her contact. You also shouldn't take your phone to church ever. In fact, none of the church members should have their phones together or have any electronic contact with each other. If they do, it will be easier for the Party to link you all together. Okay?"

Zhang focused intensely on Shao's guidance, "Okay. I can do that. What else?"

Shao thought for a moment, "Don't use your phone or any computer to look for information about God or the Bible. You should keep putting soap operas on your phone when you read the Bible. That way any software monitoring will guess you are just a normal person watching television. When you go to church, I will take your phone somewhere else. We can meet again later. That will make it look like we are just going out together every weekend to have coffee or breakfast," Shao Huan paused again, "That is all I can think of for now. If there is anything else, I will tell you."

Zhang squeezed Shao's hand, "I wish you could go to church with me, but I know that you support me. I will tell Jin Xishan all of these things. She will also need to do them."

"Every one at your house church should do it that way. It will be safer for you if they are also careful."

Zhang Ying spent the following week studying her new Bible and learning to pray. The language in the Bible felt so different and special, but as Zhang read more she started to understand the books better. Her first prayers felt awkward, but she grew more comfortable speaking with God and found that sharing her heart with the unseen creator helped her better understand her own thoughts and feelings. Zhang still mourned for her lost child, but felt a deep conviction that God would reunite them someday.

Zhang decided she was ready to return to the kindergarten and Fang Zhitai was eager to get Zhang Ying back. Zhang's second church service was just as deeply moving as her first and she felt her conviction in Christ grow deeper with each song, each testimony and each prayer. She missed her calls and texts with Jin Xishan but as sisters in Christ, she felt closer to Jin than ever. The other members of the congregation were patient and kind, and explained everything clearly for Zhang.

Shao Huan was satisfied to see Zhang growing happier and more confident every day, and secretly envied her as he continued to struggle with his own grief. After Zhang returned to teaching at the kindergarten, it almost seemed like their lives were exactly the same as they had been before Zhang became pregnant. Zhang's silent moment of prayer before every meal, however, reminded Shao that the woman he loved had grown and changed. He admired her optimism and kindness.

The summer heat broke and the cool autumn wind started to kiss the broad leaves with hints of yellow and red. Shao Huan was increasingly tired from his work at the Propaganda Department. There were more nights that he had to stay late or was recalled to manage secure calls between Ye Hongqi and other senior cadre. When he returned home he would find Zhang Ying already asleep and the dinner she made for him in the refrigerator.

Shao enjoyed the weekend outings with Zhang Ying. He found peace in the few quiet hours while Zhang went to church and joy in seeing her return to him, refreshed and excited. One Sunday morning in late September, Shao Huan was waiting for Zhang Ying at in a cafe in Wangjing when Liu Wuqing called.

Shao's heart sank as he answered the phone, "Hello?"

"Hey buddy, the boss needs to make a call in about an hour."

"Okay, I understand. See you soon," Shao Huan sometimes started to resent being on call to ensure the secure communications worked properly. The systems weren't hard to operate, and almost always worked but there was no room for error and Shao had seen how quickly the senior cadre became agitated when their calls were delayed or the connection was not clear. He wished he could explain to Zhang Ying what had happened, but knew that he wouldn't have any way to communicate with her. He walked down the block and summoned a taxi.

Liu Wuqing's face was furrowed with worry when Shao arrived at the office, "What's up? Are you okay?" Shao asked

"The Party Chairman is on a state visit to Malaysia and there was a protest along his motorcade route. He is very angry and wants to know why the Party's thought work, the United Front Work Department and the Ministry of State Security had failed to prevent such a humiliation there. It will be a conference call with Party Chairman and the other senior cadre. The boss is very dissatisfied."

Shao was surprised, "Okay, don't worry I will prepare everything."

Shao found the information for the secure conference call waiting for him in his office and then knocked on Ye's office door. Ye called him in, and while Shao connected to the conference call he overheard Ye speaking with the Director of the Propaganda Department Bureau of News, "We control the thought environment in China, but we cannot control the thought environment in another country, but we must work harder to counter and eliminate anti-China views. These protestors are supporting Uighur separatists and terrorists, the Bureau of News must use all resources and contacts to ensure the coverage of the protests in the foreign media criticizes the protestors for attacking China and for supporting terrorists."

The Director of the Bureau of News nodded grimly and took notes on Ye's guidance. Ye glanced up at Shao and confirmed the line was connected, "Okay. I will speak with the Party Chairman. I will call you again if we need to change anything." Ye stood and walked to the phone, Shao handed the receiver to him and returned to Liu's office.

"You said it right, he is very dissatisfied. Thought work outside of China must be very hard," Shao sympathized with Liu's predicament.

"It is very hard, and it is getting harder. The United Front Work Department had coordinated with the Chinese Embassy in Kuala Lumpur and the local Chinese student associations and community associations to have pro-China groups line the motorcade route to show the Party Chairman that Malaysia loves and supports China. The Ministry of State Security was carefully monitoring the opposition groups, and had sources inside the main human rights groups that gave them information that helped prevent some protests, but they underestimated the Uighur groups. There are too many

Muslims in Malaysia, it is too easy for the Uighurs to get support there. It seems that the Muslim protestors got information about the motorcade route from one of the pro-China student groups, so they knew where the Party Chairman would be. It is very embarrassing. The international media is already showing the banners criticizing the reeducation camps in Xinjiang. Most Muslim countries have strong leaders who will not allow such protests, but Malaysia's government is not so strong. It cannot control its people," Liu's voice was heavy with exhaustion. Shao felt guilty for his own frustration at being called to the office for a short time. He knew Liu had likely been at the office since the early morning and would stay all day.

"Wow. It is too complicated. What will we do?"

Liu sighed, "The same thing we always do. We will be told to strengthen thought work, the United Front Work Department will be told to increase work to influence the political parties and community leaders overseas and the Ministry of State Security will be told to recruit more sources among the anti-China forces. Whatever agreements the Party Chairman signs or positive coverage of China we are able to get in to foreign media through this visit will not matter, the Party Chairman will only remember this embarrassment. The Chinese Embassy in Malaysia will make a protest to the Malaysian government and will threaten to reduce loans and investment. We will send guidance through the Bureau of News to have all Chinese journalists overseas increase negative stories about the Uighur separatists."

Shao and Liu listened for Ye Hongqi's voice on the other side of the door, but there was only silence, Liu muttered, "He will be very angry. The Party Chairman must be talking a lot. It is never good for us when the Party Chairman provides so much guidance."

"Buddy, can I do anything to help?"

"Only if you can think of a way to make Muslims around the world love China and hate Uighur separatists," Liu's lips curled into a wry and frustrated smile.

Shao chuckled quietly, "I will think about it, but I can't promise anything."

They heard Ye's voice inside the room again and Liu Wuqing stood and carefully opened the door a crack and then slipped through. Shao Huan sat on Liu's desk while he waited for Liu to return. Shao was always impressed with how clean and well organized Liu's desk was. So many other secretaries had stacks of paper and files on their desks, but Liu seemed able to keep everything in his mind and his leather bound diary.

Liu emerged from Ye's office a few minutes later, "He is very angry. I have to organize an immediate meeting with the news directors. You can go home. Thanks for coming in for this."

Shao shrugged, "Of course, that is my duty. Call me again if you need me to come back."

Shao went back to the cafe and found Zhang Ying waiting for him, "Hey, there you are!" She welcomed him back warmly, "I was starting to worry about you. Zhang looked at him, "You look so tired my dear…"

"Yes, I feel really tired. Shall we go home?"

Zhang Ying stood and left with Shao. She seemed to be filled with energy again, "I feel better every time I go to church. It is nice to study on my own, but being together with the other church members makes me feel alive." Zhang snuggled against her husband's shoulder as a crisp autumn gust cut across the street, "You really should come with me sometime."

司马南
Sima Nan

Liu Wuqing looked completely exhausted when Shao Huan arrived at work the next morning, and though he had taken off his tie, Shao noticed he was wearing the same shirt as the day before, "Buddy, you look terrible. Did you stay here all night?"

"Doing thought work on 1.4 billion people inside China is hard enough, doing thought work on 9 billion people all around the world is like using an egg to break a stone… and I am the egg," Liu laughed at his own impossible situation.

Shao Huan set his cup of coffee down on Liu's desk, "You should drink this. It's a latte with two shots of espresso. I haven't even had a sip." Shao saw Liu start to protest, "Don't worry, I will go get another. So what is the plan to handle this situation?"

"We will provide instruction to all of the overseas journalists and especially in Muslim countries. They will run stories about the history of Islam in China and about how China has always been a tolerant country. They won't mention the reeducation camps but they will show some of the model citizens from Xinjiang and Ningxia who will talk about how they have succeeded as Muslims in China. We are also restricting the access of foreign journalists in China. They will not be allowed to travel outside of Beijing or Shanghai for the next few months until interest in this story drops."

Shao Huan nodded, "That is a good plan. Why not just deny that there are reeducation camps in Xinjiang? That seems better."

Liu Wuqing let out a tired laugh, "Buddy, we tried that for a long time, but too much information leaked out. Foreign forces got satellite pictures of the camps and the Uighur separatists got out enough information that we couldn't hide the camps. It has been better to show that the camps are humane and that the people in the camps are getting an education. We showed the common people that they were not Nazi death camps, and the United Front Work Department and Ministry of Foreign Affairs put enough pressure on the leadership in most Muslim countries that they don't say anything about the camps, but now the Uighur terrorists are trying to humiliate the Party Chairman. Whenever the higher level has a policy, the lower level will develop a countermeasure. They are very smart."

"I guess they sleep sometime too."

"They don't have to work for the Party Chairman and the Head of Propaganda," Liu Wuqing yawned and took a drink of the coffee.

"I am meeting a friend for a drink after work if you want to join us, but you should probably get some sleep," Shao Huan offered.

"I will sleep as soon as I can. Thanks for the coffee."

There were dozens of classified messages for Ye and almost all of them related to the incident in Malaysia. The new capability to include photographs in the messages was useful and the most interesting report was from the Ministry of State Security with the protestors' photos and confirmation of their identities. Shao printed them off and delivered them to Liu Wuqing.

Shao Huan was also tired, but not the sleepless, stressful exhaustion that Liu suffered. Shao slept but never felt rested when he woke up and his heart was heavy with grief. He was glad that he could see Sima Nan for a drink that evening. Sima had been busy as well, but agreed to meet.

Sima Nan sent an address for a small bar tucked in an alley near the Bell and Drum Towers. Shao Huan took several wrong turns and realized he had passed by the bar at least once when he finally got there.

"Buddy! There you are. I thought you weren't coming," Sima Nan stood up from the short bar and gave Shao Huan a half embrace.

"No way. I need to get out. What are we drinking?"

"For now, beer."

Shao Huan sat on the stool next to Sima Nan, "Good," Shao nodded to the bar tender, "I'll have whatever IPA you have on tap."

"I had a really shitty day. We had to filter out every reference to Malaysia. It was like when that plane went down, but worse. I'm guessing you have also been busy?" Sima Nan took a drink from his tall pint of dark ale.

"Of course. Those protestors wanted to embarrass the Party Chairman, but they should have been thinking about all the trouble they would make for us. Bastards," Shao Huan clinked his glass against Sima Nan's and took a long drink.

"That's right, bastards. They should know better," Sima laughed, "Well, at least we will still win. They can make small problems, but they can't close the reeducation camps."

"Do you think those places really work?" Shao Huan laughed.

Siman Nan, put his hands on the bar and tilted his head at Shao Huan, "Brother, it doesn't matter if they change anyone's mind. They keep the terrorists and separatists behind locked doors. That is the whole point."

Shao Huan enjoyed arguing with Sima Nan, "There is no way that one million people there are terrorists and separatists."

"There are about 11 million Uighurs in China and maybe another 8 million Muslims. Their loyalty isn't to China or to the Party, they believe in some crazy god. Look, look at how the Americans are killing Muslims all over the world because they are terrorists. They want to kill people like us so they can go to heaven and have a nice time. It is completely possible that 5 percent of them are terrorists and separatists, and even if it is only 1 percent, it is better to lock up the other 4 percent than to have another knife attack at a train station. At least we just have them in reeducation camps, the Americans have wars in Iraq, Syria and Afghanistan. I don't know how many millions of people have suffered there. We are working on the problem before it becomes a war. If you don't fix a small hole, a big hole will bring hardships," Sima Nan slapped the bar and took a long drink to let his soliloquy sink in.

"Okay, so if you think they are dangerous because they aren't loyal to the Party, what about Christians? There must be more of them than Muslims. Do you think they are dangerous?" Shao liked to provoke Sima and knew that would take the bait, but the question meant more to Shao as he thought of Zhang Ying and her excited face when she returned to him after every church service.

"They are even more dangerous!"

"No way. They aren't terrorists, they haven't attacked anyone with knives," Shao protested.

"Exactly! That makes them even more dangerous! We don't know who they are or what they are planning. They can be anywhere, any time. With Muslims you know who they are. They were funny hats and long beards, but Christians are sneaky. They don't believe in the Party, they believe in their own crazy god. If the Party tells them to do something, and they think their god tells them to do something else, what do you think they will do? We really don't know how many Christians there even are in China. Our best guess is there are between 50 to 70 million, so let's say 60 million. That is the same as Italy's population. They are more clever too. They are waiting quietly, not making big attacks. We have to work hard to stop them."

Shao Huan was surprised at Sima's attack offended him, "But they don't have any real organization, they can't do anything against the Party."

"Buddy, come on. If there are 70 million Christians and 20 million Muslims, that is the same as the 90 million Party members. If the Party can rule the country with 90 million people, don't you think that the Christians could rule the country with 70 million? Or at least organize to challenge the Party? Hong Xiuquan led only 30 million people in the Taiping Heavenly Kingdom, and that rebellion left the Qing empire so weak that the foreign powers had an easy time controlling the empire afterward. Hong Xiuquan drank foreign poison when he heard an American Missionary preaching about Christianity. He started to think he was Jesus' little brother. Do you know how many people died in the war he started? At least, at least 10 million, probably more," Sima Nan finished his beer and ordered another round, "You have to admit, for China, Christians are more dangerous the Muslims."

"But that is all history, more than 150 years ago. Today is different. The economy is good, people are content. The Party shouldn't be so worried about a few Christians. Christians in other countries aren't trying to change the governments," Shao Huan finished his beer just as the bar tender slid another tall glass in front of him.

Sima Nan shook his head in frustration, "This is China, history is everything. We have such a long history, but it goes in a cycle. Everyone knows that. The biggest threat to China isn't an attack by Russia or America, those countries wouldn't dare. The biggest threat is from people inside China who will weaken us and then we will be weak and foreign enemies can attack us.

The small bar was getting more crowded as people arrived for drinks on the cool autumn evening. Sima Nan lowered his voice and leaned in close to Shao Huan, "And what you said is wrong. 100 percent wrong. People aren't content. If you saw the comments and complaints that we filter every day, you would know. People are angry. It isn't just the local corruption, or fights over property, or about the novel coronavirus. People are upset with so many things. If they were able to find each other, to organize, to fight back…" Sima Nan paused, his normal bravado dimmed, "it would be really dangerous." Sima sighed, "But enough about that, how are you doing? How is Zhang Ying?"

Shao Huan didn't agree with Sima Nan's fears about Christians or Muslims, but he appreciated Sima's friendship and concern, "Zhang Ying is doing okay. The first week after the baby was stillborn was very hard. I thought I might lose her forever, even though her body was alive it seemed like her spirit was dead. But she is strong and as her body recovered, her spirit also recovered," Shao Huan chose his words carefully not to lie to Sima Nan. "She went back to work and seems really happy again. I don't think we can ever have children, and that makes us both very sad."

"Brother, you are lucky she is alive. She is a good woman, and would have been a great mother, but the most important thing is that she is still alive," Sima Nan put his hand on Shao Huan's shoulder, "How are you doing?"

Shao Huan watched the water beading on his glass gather into a drop and run down to the coaster below. He took a deep breath before answering, "Speaking frankly, I'm not really sure. I am so tired lately. Work is busy, but I also had busy times at work before. At first, I thought I was okay and was so worried about Zhang Ying… but now, Zhang Ying seems like she is okay and I am so tired. I thought I agreed to have a baby for her, but after she got pregnant I realized I also wanted to have a baby. I was excited to be a father. Now, I won't be a father. My parents still think we will have a baby some day. I haven't been able to tell them that even if Zhang Ying gets pregnant again it is very likely that the fetus will be stillborn again."

Sima Nan, usually quick with a witty response, sat silently next to Shao Huan and finished his beer. He finally said, "I was looking forward to being an uncle. I bought you guys a baby present as soon as you told me Zhang Ying was pregnant. I don't know what to do with it now."

Shao Huan felt a lump hardening in his throat as he listened to Sima Nan's admission of his own grief and saw the weight of the loss pressing down on his loud, charismatic and argumentative friend. Sima Nan rubbed both hands over his face and Shao Huan saw him trying to wipe tears away from his eyes, "Brother, you would have been a good uncle."

"I know, I would have been the best uncle. But maybe you will get to be an uncle some day. Hua Chunbao says she wants to have at least two kids."

"Wow, Chunbao huh?" Shao Huan teased his friend, "You guys have been together for a while now. She must be ready for you to propose."

"Of course. Girls always want to get married. But… I am getting old and I am tired of dating. I think I probably will propose to her," Sima Nan admitted.

Shao Huan knew that Sima Nan wouldn't admit to being in love, but Shao had never heard heard him talk about marriage with such sincerity, "That is good brother. Very good. Really."

Sima Nan, ran his hands along the short hair on either side of his head, "In the end, even the colored wolf gets captured." Sima Nan stood up and paid the tab "Speaking of Chunbao, I should get home."

Shao Huan laughed at his buddy, "She has you going home this early, it must be serious! That is great brother. But what if Hua Chunbao was a Christian?"

Sima Nan motioned to the door, "Stop talking nonsense, if she was a Christian I would find another girl."

圣诞节
Christmas

The days grew colder and shorter, and Shao Huan's exhaustion and frustration only increased. By early December, Shao Huan felt his body slowing along with his mind. The highlight of Shao's weeks were the hours with Zhang Ying after she returned to him from church. He found some rest in seeing her peace and comfort.

Most nights, Shao Huan lay in bed struggling to sleep. Thoughts of his daily frustrations at work, his fear of Zhang Ying's faith being discovered, and half dreams about their stillborn daughter kept him from falling asleep. He always had a more difficult time sleeping on the nights before taking Zhang Ying to church. He often slipped out of bed and sat on their new sofa to read Zhang Ying's Bible. He liked the new sofa and was glad that Zhang had decided to get rid of the old blood stained one, but also missed that mark of their lost child.

It hadn't taken Shao long to understand the Bible's structure and the way each sentence was indexed as a verse. The language still felt old and dense, but he found reading it took his mind away from his other anxious thoughts. Shao opened the Bible and began reading Matthew 11. He reached the end of the chapter, "Come to me, all you who are weary and burdened, and I will give you rest. Take my yoke upon you and learn from me, for I am gentle and humble in heart, and you will find rest for your souls. For my yoke is easy and my burden is light."

Shao read the passage again and murmured to himself "you will find rest for your souls…" Shao felt the burden that he had carried for months was only getting heavier and felt that verse spoke to his weary heart. All Shao Huan wanted to do was to put that burden down and find the peace and rest like his wife who slept so soundly every night. Shao lay back on the sofa, closed his eyes and imagined that rest.

Zhang Ying woke him up a few hours later. The church service that morning was at an apartment in Lidou and the cold wind cut sharp against their faces as they walked up the broad lane, the branches of the naked trees clattered above them. The cafe where Shao Huan planned to wait hadn't opened yet and he was tempted to follow Zhang Ying when she invited him to join her, as she always did. He declined and stood, waiting in the cold. He took shelter from the wind around the side of the building and stamped his feet to stay warm.

He was relieved when the cafe opened a few minutes later. He basked in the warmth inside. The warm air on his frozen face, the hot coffee in his stomach and the comfort of his heavy coat cushioning his back all made his muscles unwind a little bit and Shao Huan found himself struggling to stay awake. He tried to read, but his mind kept floating away from the copy of Lao She's 'The Philosophy of Old Zhang' and back to the words from the Bible. He regretted not following Zhang Ying to church, but knew it was better their phones did not go to the home of another church member.

The sun was near its peak and Shao Huan had switched from drinking coffee to green tea by the time Zhang returned, "It is so cold! My face is nearly frozen." Zhang sat down next to her husband and put his warm hand on her icy cheek.

"Drink this tea. It is still hot," Shao Huan was used to seeing Zhang excited after church but her eyes sparkled more than normal, "What happened?"

Zhang relished the warmth of the tea running down her throat. She smiled, "I hope you won't be angry with me. The church needed some place to have our Christmas service and I told them we could use our apartment," Zhang saw the worry flash through her husband's eyes, "It's okay. We don't have to. It is my turn to host a service, and Christmas seemed like a time we could pretend to have a party, but it's no problem. I can tell them we need to meet at another place."

"It's, it's just that I'm not very clear about what would happen at our home… I mean, would there be praying, do we need to get a Christmas tree or presents?" Shao Huan was curious but also knew the risk of hosting a Christian worship service in the home of a Party member doing sensitive work.

"I have never had a Christmas service before either, but they said we will pray and talk and have a meal together. We don't need to get a Christmas tree or anything, those aren't a part of the real Christmas, not really. It won't exactly be like a normal party, but it will be more social than our normal church services. We really could tell anyone who asks that we are just having a party. If anyone asks."

Shao Huan didn't want to disappoint Zhang Ying and against his better judgement, Shao agreed, "Okay. It seems like it will not be a problem. We can have the church service at our home."

Zhang Ying linked her arm, still in her thick coat, with Shao Huan's elbow, "Really? It is too wonderful. I know it will be very different from our usual Christmas dates, but I think it will be better."

Shao Huan was still nervous to host a church service at their apartment, but as Christmas drew closer, his excitement and curiosity surpassed his anxiety and he looked forward to the event. Shao Huan and Zhang Ying both worked Christmas Day but Shao's office was quiet and he was able to come back to the apartment early and cleaned everything. He rearranged the living room so more people could sit together. He pushed the sofa against the wall and brought all of the chairs from the kitchen and the desk chair to round out the rough circle.

Zhang Ying returned earlier than usual from the kindergarten and looked at the chairs that Shao had arranged, "It still isn't enough," Zhang worried.

"There is room on the floor. The carpet is comfortable, and we can put pillows on the floor too."

Zhang and Shao worked together in the kitchen making mutton soup and wrapping dumplings. Zhang Ying wanted to make her own dumpling wrappers, but Shao Huan had persuaded her to use the store bought wrappers so they could save time. They were both hungry and excited when Jin Xishan arrived with her family.

"It is good to see you Shao Huan! It has been too long. Thank you for letting us meet here today," Jin greeted Shao with a hug again, and he remembered how strange it seemed the first time that she had hugged him. "Let me introduce my husband, Bai Yongcheng."

Bai Yongcheng was holding Xiaorong, "Merry Christmas! I am very happy to meet you. This apartment is really not very bad. Don't worry, we won't be too loud," Bai said to Shao Huan.

Zhang Ying helped Jin Xishan to the kitchen with the bags of food that she had brought. More guests arrived and the entry way was soon filled with shoes, Shao and Zhang's bed was piled high with coats and the table and counters were covered with soups, dumplings, clay pot casseroles and fruit. Shao Huan was surprised that for so many people in such a small space, they really weren't very loud.

After the food was all set out, Jin Xishan called for everyone's attention, "Everyone, today we are blessed to celebrate the birth of Jesus together. First we will feed our bodies and then we will feed our souls. There is plenty of food, so please eat a lot, but first we will ask a blessing on the food," Jin paused and Shao watched as everyone lowered their heads together and Jin began to pray, "Our Heavenly Father, today we gather together to thank You for sending Your only Son into this world to save us. You knew everything that He would suffer, and You still sent Him. Heavenly Father, thank You for keeping us safe and healthy. Please bless this food that we will share together and bless Shao Huan and Zhang Ying for welcoming us into their home. Thank You Heavenly Father, Amen."

Shao whispered "Amen" along with the rest of the congregation and helped pass out plates and chopsticks. Zhang Ying introduced Shao to the church members, and Shao was impressed that each of them seemed so kind and gentle. They all welcomed him, even though they knew he was a Party member. Even though he could have reported them and had them all arrested, they treated him with the same love they showed to each other.

Their small apartment was full of warmth and laughter. Zhang Ying squeezed Shao's hand and whispered in to his ear, "It feels so peaceful, doesn't it?"

Shao Huan nodded and smiled, "Yes. What happens when everyone is done eating?"

"Then we'll start the service. It is at our home, so it is my turn to speak."

Shao had not expected that Zhang Ying would speak, but a few moments later, Jin Xishan caught Zhang Ying's attention and then announced to the group, "We'll start the service in a few minutes. Please put your plates in the kitchen."

Shao Huan helped collect the plates and stood in the kitchen while the rest of the group took their seats on the chairs and on the cushions and pillows on the floor. Shao suddenly felt nervous as he realized the worship service was about to begin, and then felt Zhang Ying's hand in his, "My dear, come sit with me."

Shao resisted at first, but Zhang Ying insisted and pulled him to the center of the group. She sat on the sofa and Shao sat at her feet. The room was so warm from having so many people gathered together and Shao rubbed his sweaty hands on his blue jeans. Zhang Ying spoke, "Let us pray," she bowed her head and the room fell completely silent. The church members reached for each other's hands and lowered their heads. Shao held Zhang's hand and lowered his head while she prayed, "Heavenly Father, thank You for bringing us all together today. I open my heart to You, ask for Your strength and for You to speak through me. Thank You for sending Your son to save us, and thank You for this church that has welcomed me and taught me so much about You. Everyone in this room is a blessing to me. Amen."

Shao had never heard Zhang speak like that, her sincerity, her humility and the affection she had for all of the church members gathered there with them overwhelmed him and he couldn't open his mouth to say "Amen" with the rest of the church. Shao Huan noticed that after the prayer, all eyes turned to Zhang Ying. She put her hand on his shoulder and he felt her shift her weight.

Zhang Ying coughed and began her testimony, "I know most of you have heard a little bit of my story before. I used to think that my story began in this room on a hot summer morning. On the sofa we had before this one. But, it really started before that. Ever since I was little, everyone told me what a wonderful mother I would be. It was such a big part of who I was. I waited for five years before I told Shao Huan it was time to have a baby," Zhang Ying laughed at herself and the circle of attentive and smiling faces laughed with her.

"I despaired when our baby was stillborn. I had been so excited to be a mother, to give my love to a new person. When the baby died and the doctor told me that I probably couldn't have a baby, my heart broke into a thousand pieces. I didn't know what to do. I wanted to disappear, I wanted to die, I wanted… I wanted to kill myself."

Hearing Zhang Ying recount those dark days tore at Shao Huan's soul. He still remembered that pain all too well, and now Zhang Ying was telling this group of people, good people, but people he didn't really know, all about their loss and her pain. Shao Huan hung his head and the tears that he fought so hard to hold back started to slip out of his eyes and slowly ran down his face.

Zhang Ying poured out her heart, and each word weighed on Shao Huan. Zhang Ying's joyful conversion, her finding a new purpose, her growth as a baby Christian all seemed to set her free, but reminded Shao that he was still stuck and going deeper into the darkness that she had escaped. Shao Huan didn't notice when Zhang Ying finished telling her story, but wiped away his tears as the the group quietly sang "The Road of Grace."

After the song, Jin Xishan spoke, "Because it is Christmas, everyone think for a moment about what you are grateful for or what you are looking forward to in heaven. We won't go around in a circle, just say whatever you are thinking when you want. Okay? I will start, this Christmas I am so grateful for sister Zhang Ying's testimony and for how God is already working through her."

The warm room fell silent. An elderly man spoke softly, "I am looking forward to seeing my wife and children again."

Someone else spoke up, "I am grateful for the real true gospel, and that the Party can never stop it."

Xiaorong's soft and happy voice came next, "I am looking forward to being able to sing loudly in heaven."

Everyone said "Amen" to Xiaorong's wish.

Shao Huan felt an overwhelming urge to speak and almost before he knew it said, "I am grateful my wife is still alive," and then began to sob.

Zhang Ying kneeled down next to him and held him tight, "I am alive," she whispered in his ear, "God used you to save me, he can save you too."

归心者
Convert

The congregation left slowly. Jin Xishan and her family were the last to depart. Jin and Bai both hugged Shao Huan, "Thank you for opening your heart today. You should come to church next week with Zhang Ying," Bai said and patted Shao on the back. Xiaorong hugged them both and then they left. The apartment was so quiet, and clean.

Shao Huan was exhausted. He had never experienced anything like the emotions he felt during the worship service. He had never cried in front of so many people. He had never laid his frailty and fears out for strangers. It was liberating and tiring. His eyes were heavy and he fell into a deep and restful sleep on the sofa.

Shao Huan woke early and pulled off the blanket that Zhang Ying laid over him. He saw the Bible sitting on the table near him and sat up to read. Shao opened the Bible to the Gospel of John and started to read, it was such a different book than the other gospels he had read. He liked the passage "The light shines in the darkness, and the darkness has not overcome it."

Shao contemplated those words as he got ready for work. Shao didn't want to go to work, he wanted to stay home and talk with Zhang Ying about everything that had happened, about their first real Christmas. Just as Shao came up the stairs at the Xidan subway station, a faint glimmer of sunlight started to press back against the dark. Shao stood on the cold sidewalk, and watched the sun rise until he felt the first ray of warmth touch his face.

Liu Wuqing was in his office as always, but seemed happier than usual, "Hey buddy, did you go out for Christmas?" Shao asked.

"Yes, the boss only worked a short day. I was able to take my wife out for dinner. She liked to see the Christmas lights in Wangfujing and we went to a French restaurant. It was too expensive, but she liked it. I slept before midnight, so I liked that. Did you take Zhang Ying out?"

"No, we stayed at home this year. We didn't want to go out."

Liu tried to sympathize with Shao, "It will get easier. It has only been a few months. You both need time."

"It has been a hard year," Shao acknowledged. "Hopefully next year will be better."

"It will be a busy year. The Party Chairman provided guidance for our thought work in the next year. He is still most worried about religious groups. We are going to increase education about evil religions and the Ministry of State Security will also increase its work against religious groups that do not accept the Party's leadership."

Shao Huan knew that he would already be removed from the Party if they discovered that he had hosted a Christian church service at his home, and that guilty knowledge made him worry what the Ministry of State Security might do, "How will they do that?"

Liu shrugged, "I don't know. I'm still trying to figure out what exactly we will do. Hey, did you know that the boss has a brother who is a Vice Minister for State Security? I have known him for so long but I didn't know until yesterday. He kept that secret really well."

"No, I didn't know that. I know his family is big and well connected, but didn't know he had a brother at State Security," the news surprised and worried Shao, but he tried not to show his concern, "Here are the reports for this morning. There aren't so many, but the Center sent a few messages regarding covering a corruption investigation in Shandong. It seems like a small issue."

Liu took the folder, "If the Center is interested in it, then it is not a small issue. Even if it seems unimportant to us, there is some bigger issue that we just don't know."

Shao Huan went through the motions at work, but his heart was still wrestling with Zhang's testimony and his own glimpse of the light that she had embraced. He knew that he wanted to have the same peace that Zhang had, and knew that all he had to do was open his heart and accept that he wanted to be a Christian. Liu's words reminded him, however, that it was not so simple and that he would have to be very careful to hide his faith. Shao's mind wanted to resist, but his heart kept pulling him back toward what he felt was true, what he saw was true in the light that shown from Zhang's eyes and the love that he felt from Jin Xishan and the other church members.

Ye Hongqi kept Shao at the office late that night responding to the reports of corruption by a minor official in Shandong province. Ye did not send messages to the local Head of Propaganda as usual, but asked Shao to send the messages directly to the Head of Propaganda for Jilin city, with strict instructions not to tell any of the other Party cadre in Shandong about the planned reports on corruption.

Shao was tired when he got home, but wanted to talk with Zhang more than anything. She was waiting for him with a clay pot casserole of chicken and rice and still beaming from the Christmas church service, "You're back! I was just about to eat."

Shao hung his heavy coat by the door, took off his shoes and greeted Zhang with a hug and a kiss.

"You were so tired last night! You fell asleep before we could talk about anything," Zhang teased him.

"I really was very tired, but I slept so well. I feel much better today."

Zhang took a large spoon and served Shao the rice, brown with marinade from the chicken, and the soft warm meat, and then bowed her head to say a blessing over the food, "Heavenly Father, thank You for this food and for keeping us both safe today. Amen," Shao watched Zhang as she prayed. When she opened her sparkling eyes, they locked on Shao Huan's and she asked, "How did you think about the church service?"

"I thought you were amazing. Really amazing. I have never heard you talk that way. The people were all so kind and it did feel like a family," Shao paused and waited for Zhang to speak, but she just watched him intently so he continued, "I liked it. I see why you like going to church and why you feel so happy believing in Jesus. I…" Shao faltered and finally admitted, "I want that feeling too. But it is too dangerous. If the Party finds out, I will lose my job and maybe we will be arrested. This morning Liu Wuqing told me that the Party will increase its work against religious groups in the next year. It will be so complicated…"

Zhang finished a bite of rice before answering, "I know you think about things and plan more than I do, but before thinking just tell me from your heart, do you believe? Or do you at least want to believe?"

Shao Huan answered quickly, "I want to believe."

Zhang's smile was so broad that Shao also smiled and laughed, "Okay. Yes, I want to believe."

Zhang stood and wrapped her arms around Shao Huan's shoulders, "That is all that matters. Life is complicated, but faith is not."

Shao Huan sighed, "Life is really complicated. Maybe I should resign from the Party. Maybe we should emigrate."

"No, you should keep working. You have already helped to keep us safe, and you work for such a senior cadre. You can do a lot to help all of us. Maybe it is part of God's plan for you. And I don't want to leave China. This is our home, this is our country. We should stay here."

Shao sighed, "Okay. We will be careful."

Zhang laughed at Shao, "We will be careful, but what is more important is that God will protect us. We put our faith in him."

"What should I do now?"

Zhang pulled Shao tight against her chest, "Now you should pray and ask God in to your heart. It is that simple."

Shao Huan paused, unsure what to say. Zhang put her hand on the top of his head, "I will start the prayer? Okay?" Shao nodded and Zhang began, "Heavenly Father, Shao Huan has been so sad and very tired. He wants to believe in You. Please show Shao Huan how to open his heart and accept You."

Shao looked up at Zhang, "Should I pray now?" Zhang smiled and kissed his forehead, and Shao started awkwardly, "Heavenly Father," the words felt strange and stumbled across his tongue but he started to speak more normally, "I really don't know how to pray, but I want to… I want to believe in You. I want Your peace, I want Your light. I am scared too. I know what the Party would do to me. I know what they would do to Zhang Ying. Please protect us." Shao stopped and couldn't think of what else to say and his voice rose as he looked up at Zhang Ying, "Amen?"

Zhang squeezed him tightly, "Amen," she answered.

"Am I a Christian now?"

"You are a Christian the moment you want to be a Christian. You used to work for the Party, but now you work for God inside of the Party. At the kindergarten, I used to work for the school but now I work for God at the school. I want to share God's love with the children, and I do that through the school. You will see how it is different. You will see everything differently."

Shao Huan thought on Zhang's words before he answered, "I feel relieved, but I don't feel different. I feel that I had tried not to believe for so long, but now I have given up and I accept that I want to believe. Maybe even that I already believe. But I don't feel like I am a different person."

"You are still the same person, but as you learn more about God, the way you see the world will change. Everything has so much more meaning. You will also see people in a different way. There are so many people who are sad and hurting. When someone is mean to you, it is easier to see that they aren't angry at you, they are angry at the world and at themselves. It is easy to forgive them and to let go of any anger against them," Zhang saw a glimmer of skepticism fleet across Shao's eyes, "I know it sounds strange, but it is true. And you will feel better. Every day when I wake up, I pray and ask God for strength and wisdom to get through the day. Before I go to sleep, I pray and thank him for everything and ask him to help me forgive anyone who I am angry at. Then I can let go of the little things that annoyed me during the day and I sleep so well."

Shao Huan nodded again, "Okay. I will try. It is strange for me, you already know so much about this. I still don't know anything."

"But you have been reading the Bible, right?"

"Yes, you spent so much time reading that book. I was curious."

"Keep reading and you will know more. But now, don't just read it because you are curious. Read it because you want to understand God better. God will use that book to speak to you. I know it sounds strange, but He will, really."

Shao Huan stood and hugged Zhang Ying, "Okay. I will try."

"Do you feel a little bit better?"

"Yes. I feel... I feel at peace."

耶利哥
Jericho

Shao Huan slept well that night and the next day at work he thought about what Zhang Ying had said. He was a believer and he worked for God. At first he didn't know what that really meant, but as the days went by, he started to care more about his time reading the Bible before work and grew less attached to the politics in the Propaganda Department.

Even when Ye Hongqi was angry and took his frustration out on Liu or Shao, Shao Huan didn't care. He didn't take it personally or feel like he had done anything wrong. He knew that Ye's angry outbursts were because of Ye's own failures and frustrations. He even started to feel sympathy for Ye, as Ye tried to maintain a proud family legacy within the Party, and seemed unable to see his own failures.

Shao and Zhang left their phones at home on Sunday mornings and slipped out into the cold to join the other believers for church. Shao made sure both phones were plugged in and streaming different movies, with a playlist that would continue until they returned. He quickly came to love the fellowship and worship together every weekend as much as Zhang Ying did.

Their shared faith, and their shared secret, brought Shao Huan and Zhang Ying even closer together. They studied together in the quiet mornings before work, they prayed together and talked about their struggles and questions. The discord that Shao had felt before faded and he realized that he was happier and lighter. Shao found that he liked to read the Gospel of John more than the other books. He read and re-read "I am the way, the truth and the life."

Shao thought more about how to protect themselves and the church members from the Party. He made sure that he and Zhang both spent more time than required on the Party ideology application on their phones and avoided any negative mentions of the Party or the Party Chairman even in their private chats. Shao had hated the Party meetings before, and did not like them any better after he converted, but he knew they were necessary and made sure not to miss a single one. He worked hard to present the appearance of an ideal cadre, even as his heart moved farther away from the Party and he saw the hypocrisy in the Party's doctrine more clearly than ever.

Ye Hongqi and Liu Wuqing seemed to feel the pressure from the Party Chairman more intensely than ever, but it didn't weigh on Shao at all. One morning when Shao brought Liu coffee, Liu asked, "Buddy, aren't you worried? If we fail in the thought work campaign, the Party Chairman might remove the boss."

Shao smiled and set the coffee on Liu's desk, "I am not worried. You are both very capable, and I will continue to fulfill my duty to you both and to the Party. It will be okay. Even if things don't develop in the direction we want now, in the end it will be okay. All of the Party's great leaders faced many struggles. Even Deng Xiaoping was rehabilitated." Shao's flattery was convincing, but he wanted to tell Liu that he wasn't worried because he was learning to trust in God's plan rather than his own ambition.

Liu shook his head ruefully, "Those were different times. There were different voices in the Party. There is only one voice now. If we don't make him happy, we will all be punished."

"How will we be punished? Will we be sent to a reeducation camp?" Shao joked.

"Don't joke about it. Maybe we could end up in detention for corruption," there was no humor in Liu's voice.

"No way, we would have to be involved in corruption. We aren't involved in anything like that. Are we?"

Liu looked down, "No, but it doesn't matter. Anyone can become a target for the anti-corruption campaign if they become a political threat or enemy of the Party Chairman."

Shao sat on the corner of Liu's desk, "Buddy, look, it's like this, if the Party Chairman didn't trust the boss, he would remove him. Right? This position is way too important. As long as he is the Head of the Propaganda Department, it will be okay. Maybe he won't make it to the Politburo Standing Committee, but that is okay. He has had a good career, and we will have careers after he retires. He is as old as our parents, we can't work for him forever. It will be okay, really."

Liu sighed, "I hope you are right. It is so difficult to know these days. But we will work diligently."

"Good. That is all that you can do. So how will the boss show the Party Chairman that he is working diligently?"

Liu leaned forward and nearly knocked over his coffee, "Right after the Spring Festival, the police will disrupt many religious groups that are not following the Party's leadership and arrest the religious leaders. We will publicize some of them very widely, especially the ones where the Ministry of State Security has uncovered other embarrassing personal details. Some of the Buddhist teachers are really despicable people. They pretend to be holy men, but actually have sex with many of their followers. There are some Christian church leaders who are only good on the surface, but in reality they have committed many crimes including theft, corruption and tax evasion. We will use a few of the worst cases to show the people they can't trust these so called leaders."

Shao's heart sank as Liu foreshadowed the impending propaganda campaign, "That sounds like a good plan. That should keep the people from trusting such teachers and keep their faith in the Party. Why wait until after the Spring Festival?"

"I wanted to act right away before the Spring Festival, the police already have all the information they need, but the boss said the police want to wait until after the Spring Festival when everyone goes back to work because the religious leaders won't be expecting it. There is usually not so much news right after the Spring Festival, so the boss also wants to wait a little while."

Shao Huan wanted to rush home and tell Zhang Ying about the planned arrests. The Spring Festival was just a week away, and they only had one more church service before people started to return to their old homes. He kept his usual calm at the office, and even when Ye asked him to stay late to send a secure message to the provincial Party secretaries, he didn't offer any hint of his urge to leave as quickly as possible.

Shao managed to walk calmly from the office and down into the crowded subway. He could not, however, keep his leg from bouncing nervously as his guilty knowledge made him worry that their own little church might be a target. Zhang Ying had a simple dinner of home style tofu and vegetables ready, which was normally one of Shao's favorite dishes. He hesitated to sit, however, and asked Zhang if they could go for a short walk. Zhang put on her heavy coat and followed Shao outside.

Once they reached the quiet street, Shao told Zhang about the impending crack down on unsanctioned religious groups. Zhang tried to calm him down, "Dear, our church is so small and we don't try to recruit new members or make other associations. I am sure we will be okay. The Party may arrest some of the leaders of the larger house churches, but we are so small, and everyone is so careful. I am sure they will not arrest us."

Shao was not persuaded, "The Party Chairman is very nervous and the Ministry of State Security, the Ministry of Public Security and the Propaganda Department are all coordinating closely. This is not like before when they just killed a chicken to scare the monkeys. This time they are really trying to cut the grass and pull out the roots. We have to tell Jin Xishan and the others. I don't think we should meet as a church until at least after the Lantern Festival."

Zhang Ying wanted to calm Shao down, but agreed that they should tell Jin Xishan and Bai Yongcheng the next Sunday before church. Zhang pulled her hand out of her warm coat pocket and reached for Shao's hand, "We should pray about it too," she said and then started to pray without bowing her head or offering any indication that they were having anything more than a normal conversation. "Heavenly Father, thank You for using Shao Huan to help protect our church. Please help us to use this information in a suitable way. Amen."

Shao echoed her "Amen" and felt more confident that whatever lay ahead, God would protect them, "It is freezing, we should go home," Shao pulled his icy hand back into his coat pocket, "dinner smelled delicious."

After dinner Shao put a drama about Deng Xiaoping on his phone while he read the Bible. He read the book of Judges and learned about the persecution that God's followers endured and the ways that God used the faithful and guided them. Shao felt God's voice telling him that everything would be okay and that the Party could never destroy God's church.

Shao reminded himself that the arrests were still several weeks away and waited patiently for church on Sunday. When Sunday came, however, Shao was eager to get to the church as early as possible. It was at a mechanic's shop in a quiet corner of Wangjing and the smell of grease and oil hung heavy in the air as they arrived. Jin Xishan was already there and Xiaorong was running around the empty garage and pretending to fix invisible cars.

Shao pulled Jin aside and told her what he had learned and what the Party was planning. Jin's normally radiant face darkened with concern, "Can you get a list of the targets?"

"I… I don't know. I can probably get the names of the leaders they plan to publicize, but I don't think I can get a full list of the targets. I think only the police or State Security has that."

"Okay. Please get that. Don't do it if you will get caught, but if you have a way to bring that information without getting in trouble, it would be very useful. We might be able to help," a resolve that Shao had not seen before filled Jin's eyes.

Shao had only shared information that Liu happened to tell him, he had not gone seeking out information and the task to actively work to prevent the arrests made his heart race, "I don't know. It seems dangerous, and it is like spying. God wouldn't want us to spy, would he?"

"You should read the story of the the 12 spies in the book of Numbers. God had the Israelites send 12 spies into the land of Canaan, the Promised Land. Two of the spies believed that God could deliver the Promised Land to them. God was so happy with the two spies, Joshua and Caleb, that they were the only members of their generation who were allowed to see he Promised Land delivered to the Israelites just as God promised. The Israelites also sent two spies into Jericho before they attacked. They were successful and found a woman in the city of Jericho who protected them. God delivered the city of Jericho to the Israelites. God needs brave men who will do what is right, even if it is dangerous."

Shao was still nervous but he nodded, "Okay, I will try. How can I get the information to you?"

Jin Xishan thought for a moment, "Chaoyang Park will be crowded for the temple fair. Let's meet on the bridge by Laojun temple at 2 p.m. on the second day of the lunar new year. Okay?"

Shao tried to picture the spot in his mind, "Okay. I know the place. I will go there with Zhang Ying." Shao Huan thought through passing something to Jin, "Will you have Xiaorong with you?"

"Yes, of course. He loves the temple fair."

"Good. If I have something, I will give you a red envelope and the information will be inside. If I don't have anything, I will just give a red envelope with a little money to Xiaorong. Okay?"

Jin and Shao agreed on the plan, and mixed back in with the rest of the church members as the service began. At the end of the worship service, Jin told the group that they wouldn't be able to meet again until the first Sunday in April. She said she couldn't explain exactly what was happening, but that she thought it was better to be careful. They agreed to meet at Madam Duan's restaurant in April and had another prayer asking for God's blessing over the holiday and to keep them and the other believers safe.

Shao explained everything to Zhang Ying on their way home. Zhang was also nervous for Shao. As soon as they got home, they both read the story of the 12 spies and about the battle of Jericho.

描绘
Temple Fair

The story of Joshua and Caleb gave Shao Huan more confidence as he badged in to the Propaganda Department headquarters the next morning and rode the elevator to the top floor. He greeted the guards as usual. He brought coffee for Liu Wuqing as usual. He went through his daily check list, and his little daily routines calmed his racing heart when he looked through recent classified messages for any details on the impending arrests.

Shao found a message from the Center that provided a list of ten religious leaders whose arrests would be publicized and the crimes they had committed. They were Muslims, Christians, Buddhists and Taoists and from all over China. Shao didn't recognize any of their names, but wrote them down on a small piece of paper and carefully slipped the paper in his sock, just below his ankle. He looked through the recent messages for anything more, but there was only more guidance on the planned coverage of the impending arrests that Ye had sent to the provincial Party offices.

The scrap of paper rubbed against Shao's ankle all day, reminding him that the information was secure, but also that he was sneaking classified information out of a secure Party communications office, and that if he was caught he would, at the very least, be fired, and more likely arrested. Shao remembered his training courses and the images of Party communicators who were executed for breaking the Party's trust. Shao didn't know what Promised Land God might show him, but he hoped the risk was worth while. Shao got the paper home and kept it in a red envelope between two red 100 yuan notes.

The night before the Spring Festival, he stopped by Liu's desk to wish him a good holiday, "Happy new year! I hope you have a prosperous year ahead old friend."

Liu's tired smile broadened, "It has to be better than this year! Will you go back to Hangzhou to visit Zhang Ying's family?"

"No, we will stay in Beijing this year. Maybe we will go to Hangzhou next year. We will make dumplings with my parents and see some old friends. We might go to a temple fair. Are you going back to Guangdong?"

Liu laughed, "It's not possible. I will have to stay here with the boss. But at least I can celebrate with my wife's family. It will be okay, as long as nothing bad happens. Are you coming back to work tomorrow?"

"No, I took off the first five days of the Lunar New Year, I will see you after that."

"Okay! Happy new year!" Liu stood and waved farewell to Shao Huan.

Shao Huan and Zhang Ying spent the Lunar New Year's eve at Shao's parent's apartment in Langfang City just outside of Beijing. They had moved in to a new development and got a good price on the apartment, but Shao Huan never really liked the sterility of the satellite city and missed the old family apartment in Dongcheng. It was good, however, to spend the evening with his parents. Shao and Zhang rolled out nearly one hundred dumpling wrappers while his mother and father prepared the filling. The kitchen was full of laughter and the trauma of August seemed so far away, but Shao did wonder how much happier they all would have been celebrating the new year with a baby. The restrictions on fireworks weren't so strict so far outside of Beijing and they watched from the apartment as people shot bursts of color into the sky from all directions and the sound of firecrackers echoed up from the streets below.

They talked and laughed while watching the annual New Year's extravaganza broadcast and eating the dumplings they made together. They ate a steamed fish in a thick garlic sauce and drank sorghum wine to toast the new year. Shao and Zhang had agreed that his parents wouldn't accept their conversion and telling them would only cause them to worry. So, they went through the holiday without revealing their new faith and only offered short silent prayers before they ate. Shao and Zhang spent the night at his parent's apartment and took the train back home the next day.

The sun was bright and the sky was blue on the second day of the Lunar New Year. Shao Huan woke early and read again the story of the spies in Jericho. He imagined the two Israelites in an enemy city, risking their lives and the reward that God gave to his chosen people in the end. Shao Huan prayed for God to speak to him and tell him to stop if it was not God's will to share the information with Jin Xishan.

Shao and Zhang Ying went to the temple fair at Chaoyang Park a little before noon. Shao was nervous and he wanted to be able to leave the fair soon after passing the red envelope to Jin. The park's south gate was decorated beautifully and red arches with wishes for health and prosperity in large gold and yellow letters lined the main path. A mass of people pressed together under the strings of large red lanterns that hung overhead, and more lanterns dangled from the naked tree limbs.

Photographers snapped pictures of the bright red lanterns against the brilliant blue sky, and the people wearing traditional costumes, people dressed as robots and science fiction characters, and small children sitting on their fathers' shoulders. Display boards mounted with elaborate red paper cuttings of the Chinese zodiac lined one of the side paths, and strong black lines of calligraphy on deeply textured paper lined the other side. Vendors cutting stone seals and carving names on grains of rice for children and tourists did a brisk trade and Shao and Zhang could hear the sounds of performances at the stages over the din of the people shouting cheerfully.

Shao Huan and Zhang Ying tried to appear as excited and carefree as the people around them, but the weight of their purpose kept them focused. A dragon dance troupe led by two men with cymbals and a drum made their way down the path. The crowd cheered and cleared a small circle for the dancers. The dancers inside lifted the red and gold dragon overhead and used their bodies to sway and rise with the rhythm of the drum. The crowd laughed and cheered as the lead dancer pressed the dragon's head forward into the crowd and some onlookers put money into the dragon's mouth. The fast beating of the drums matched Shao's racing heart and he pulled Zhang Ying away from the commotion around the dragon dance.

They watched a children's martial arts performance on one of the smaller stages and cheered the loudest for the littlest performer who showed how hard she could punch and kick. They stopped to eat candied haws, five flavored fried bean balls, and warmed their hands on barrel roasted sweet potatoes that melted in their mouths. They always enjoyed the festivities in the park, but Shao kept checking his watch and through all the excitement could only think about passing the red envelope to Jin Xishan.

They reached the bridge just before 2 p.m. and saw the crowd thinned out on the other side of the bridge. Before they reached the bridge, however, Xiaorong ran up and wrapped his arms around Zhang Ying's legs, "Teacher, teacher! Do you also like temple fairs?"

Zhang Ying bent down on one knee and hugged Xiaorong, "Of course! I like the candied strawberries the best. What do you like?"

"I like the drums the most," Xiaorong said and then Bai Yongcheng picked him up and greeted Zhang Ying and Shao Huan.

"Happy new year! It is good to see you. Jin Xishan had a matter to deal with and she can't come, so I brought Xiaorong by myself. Xishan already explained everything to me."

Shao's heart kicked against his chest as he unzipped his coat, reached into his inner pocket and pulled out a red envelope with gold lettering and handed it to Bai, "Happy new year, may all go well with you! This is for Xiaorong, it is very valuable." Shao Huan's hand was steady as he pressed the envelope into Bai's hand.

"Papa, give it to me. I want it," Xiaorong reached for the envelope as Bai tucked it in his pocket.

"I will give it to you later, son. You don't want to lose your money here, right? There are so many people you would never find it again. You can use the money to buy something nice later. Okay?" Bai touched his forehead to Xiaorong's face. He turned back to Shao and Zhang, "Thank you. It is a very nice gift for Xiaorong and for us all. We should go now. See you next time!" Bai turned around with

Xiaorong in his arms and in a moment they had disappeared into the sea of people.

Shao and Zhang stood on the bridge and Shao took a deep breath of the cool afternoon air. Zhang Ying put her arm through Shao's and they looked out over the frozen lake. The ice wasn't thick enough for ice skaters, but it covered the dark water beneath with a sheen of calm stability. Shao turned to Zhang "I did it."

The weight of that simple act lifted from Shao's shoulders. Shao Huan and Zhang walked back along the far side of the lake, where the crowd thinned further. Zhang looked at her husband's angular face and sharp eyes, "Dear, I am proud of you. Whatever happens, I will support you."

"Nothing will happen. We are okay. It is no problem."

Shao and Zhang were both excited by their adventure at the temple fair and exhausted from walking in the cold and the crowds. They both relaxed for the next couple of days, ate left over dumplings and sweet mandarin oranges. Shao read more of the Old Testament and especially liked the book of Daniel.

He kept expecting to receive a call from Liu Wuqing, but was glad the call never came. On his first day back at work he took Liu a bottle of Maotai to thank him for not calling him in over the holiday.

"Hey buddy, happy new year! This is for you," Shao placed the bottle on Liu's desk.

"Aya, you know we aren't supposed to accept gifts like this anymore. You could get me in real trouble," Liu said with a big smile on his face as he took the bottle.

Shao laughed, "Oh that's right, I'll take it back…" he pretended to reach for the alcohol and Liu gently pushed his hand away.

"It's okay. I'll keep it here and we can drink it together to celebrate sometime."

"Like when you get assigned to Hong Kong!" Shao teased.

Liu leaned forward, "Hey talking about celebrating, did you hear about the boss' daughter?" Shao shook his head and Liu continued, "She is engaged. She called to tell him on the Lunar New Year's Eve."

"That's great! We should take the Maotai in and celebrate with Ye Hongqi now!"

"No, no, no. He isn't happy! Not even a little bit happy. She is engaged to the son of the Shandong Province Party Secretary."

Shao Huan was confused, "Isn't that a good thing? Wasn't she dating some foreign guy before? This is better right?"

Liu clicked his tongue ruefully, "No. It's like this. Remember that corruption investigation in Shandong? The boss knows the ultimate target is the Party Secretary there, Wang Zhengong. Ye Hongqi's daughter is tying him to one of the Party Chairman's biggest enemies, right at the moment that the Party Chairman is making a move against him. He doesn't know what to do. I bet he wishes his daughter was marrying anyone else. Even an American!"

"Oh my god, what is he going to do?" Shao Huan knew that Ye Hongqi was clever and capable, but his skill had been in avoiding connections with people who might bring him trouble. He had no way to avoid this connection. "Can he tell his daughter and get her to break off the engagement?"

"No way! If he tells his daughter, she might tell her fiancé, who would tell his father that he is the target. Wang Zhengong might already know that, but having that confirmation would be dangerous, and the Party Chairman would think that the boss deliberately warned Wang Zhengong. For now, I think he has decided to pretend that everything is okay. I am sure he has already told the Party Chairman about the situation. He needs to make sure the Party Chairman knows he is loyal. Loyalty is all the Party Chairman really cares about."

逮捕
Arrest

The guilty knowledge of Shao Huan's transgression against the Party did not weigh as heavily on his soul as he had expected. As each day went by, he felt more confident that the information he shared with Jin and Bai had not been detected, but he still grew anxious about the disruption and arrests that loomed as the Lantern Festival drew closer.

However nervous Shao was, Ye Hongqi was more anxious and frequently lashed out at Liu and occasionally at Shao. Just as Zhang had explained to him before, Shao didn't feel angry at Ye. Instead, he felt sorry for him and prayed for Ye's health and salvation every night. He couldn't imagine how Ye was being torn between his daughter's happiness and Ye's loyalty to the Party. Ye's outbursts, however, were more difficult for Liu to endure. Liu's entire career depended on keeping Ye happy, and there was nothing Liu could do to calm Ye's fears.

The day after the Lantern Festival, the Ministry of Public Security arrested hundreds of religious leaders around China. Just as Liu and Ye had planned, the newspapers and television broadcasts covered the operation extensively, and while the reports announced that thousands of underground leaders of evil cults had been arrested, they only went into detail on ten of the targets. Shao Huan watched the news attentively, but there was no information about the groups that were disrupted or the other religious leaders who had been arrested.

By the end of the day, the Ministry of Public Security had already extracted a confession from one of the leaders of an underground Christian church. They sent the video of the confession to Ye Hongqi through the secure communications network for his approval and dissemination through the propaganda apparatus. Shao received the message just as he was preparing to leave. It was rare for him to receive video messages and he had to download the video to a secure tablet.

He knocked on the door frame of Liu's office, "Hey buddy, seems like the operation is going well. There is a secure video for the boss."

Liu looked tired but satisfied, "Yes, fortunately all seems to be going well. The Party Chairman hasn't called, so that is a good sign. What is the video?"

"I didn't watch the whole video, but it is a confession of the underground Christian leader in Shanghai."

"Great! The boss will be happy to see that. Go ahead and take it in to him," Liu waved Shao toward Ye's door.

Shao Huan knocked lightly on the door and heard Ye summon him, "Come in!"

Ye was watching the wall of television broadcasts when Shao entered, "Boss, I have a secure video for you. It is the confession of one of the targets."

A huge smile came over Ye's normally stoic face, "We already have a confession? That is fantastic. Just wait a minute while I watch it."

Shao watched the screens that nearly filled one wall. The Chinese media was covering the arrests extensively as planned, but it appeared the foreign news stations hadn't even mentioned the operation, just as Ye had hoped.

Ye laughed triumphantly and handed the tablet back to Shao Huan, "I thought he would be the first to confess, but didn't think it would happen so quickly. Go and send this to all of the provincial propaganda heads and tell them to disseminate this to their local media immediately."

Shao nodded and quickly stepped out of the office. He stopped by Liu's desk on his way back to send the message, "You said it, the boss is really happy. He was surprised that this target confessed so quickly, what do you think happened?"

"That bastard has been subverting the state for years. The Ministry of State Security learned that he was in contact with foreign forces to spread his evil teachings among the overseas Chinese communities. His daughter was helping him and when he was arrested, the Police told him that unless he confessed to all of his crimes, his daughter would also be arrested and beaten. I knew he would confess quickly," Liu smiled. "Hey, should we drink that Maotai now? I bet the boss would like that."

Shao tried his best to appear that he shared Liu's satisfaction but couldn't bear the thought of toasting the arrest of so many believers, "That sounds great, but I better send this message for the boss first. You should go ahead and celebrate with him."

"Okay, that is good. That video needs to get out right away. I will go in and toast with the boss," Liu pulled the bottle of Maotai out of his desk and knocked on Ye's door as Shao walked down the hall.

Shao sent the message as instructed and lingered in the office longer than necessary to avoid getting pulled in to drink with Liu and Ye. He heard Liu walking out of Ye's office just as he locked up the communications office and Liu Wuqing spotted him in the hall, "Hey! You should have come to have a drink!"

Shao walked up to Liu, "It took me longer than I expected to send the video message. It is done. Was the boss happy?"

Liu beamed, "He was happier than I have seen him for the last two weeks. Everything went smoothly. I think he will even go home soon, so I will also get to go home."

Shao patted Liu's shoulder to congratulate him and walked away. The lights from the massive bookstore lit the broad sidewalk and Shao looked at the people inside, standing between shelves and tables of books, all carefully curated to support the Party. The after work rush had slowed and the subway car was only half full. Most people on the train looked at their phones and Shao wondered how many of them knew or cared about the barrage of media coverage of the arrests.

By the time Shao got home, the Chinese Central Television news channel was already playing the pastor's confession, and well groomed commentators were lambasting the pastor for not working through the Party sanctioned religious bodies. One slim man with round glasses and short cropped grey hair criticized the pastor for leading so many innocent young people astray and hoped that the

Party would be able to rehabilitate them just as it punished the pastor.

Zhang Ying had prepared dinner, but neither of them could eat. Zhang nodded at Shao and they grabbed their coats and headed back out into the cold night.

Once they got outside Zhang turned to him, "You were right. It is good that we have cancelled church for a while. How terrible, that poor pastor."

Shao grimaced, "Have you heard from Jin Xishan?"

Zhang shook her head, "No. I came home early after school. I didn't see her today. Should I talk to her at school?"

"No. No, you are right. You shouldn't talk to her, but when you see her I am sure you will be able to tell if everything is okay. Just stay a little later at school tomorrow and see how she seems. Okay?"

Zhang Ying agreed, and they returned to the apartment to eat, pray and sleep.

Shao Huan kept a close eye on the news coverage the next day and received several more confessions throughout the day that he delivered to Liu and Ye. Shao was surprised how quickly the people confessed to their crimes, but noted that none of them actually renounced their faith in the videos. They all fit a pattern, the target sat in a sterile room with a neutral background, stated their name and admitted their crimes. Sometimes they appeared to be looking at someone sitting off camera, sometimes they looked directly in to the camera. They all appeared to be tired and broken.

Ye Hongqi kept Shao late at the office sending updated guidance to the local propaganda officials and disseminating the confession videos. Shao tried to hide his eagerness to get home and talk with Zhang Ying, but finally Ye and Liu decided they didn't need to send any more messages and let Shao Huan leave.

As soon as Shao opened the door and saw the look on Zhang's face, he knew something was wrong. He didn't bother to take off his coat, but just set his phone on the table by the entryway and held the door for Zhang as she put on her coat. The night wasn't so cold and Zhang held Shao's hand "Jin Xishan didn't come to the school today. Her mother-in-law came to pick up Xiaorong."

Shao clenched his teeth, "Did she say anything?"

"Not really. I asked how Xiaorong's mother was doing, and she avoided answering. She said it was not convenient for Jin Xishan to come and that she would be helping look after Xiaorong for a while…" Zhang Ying paused, "That is all she said."

Shao Huan's heart sank, "They must have arrested her."

Zhang Ying couldn't believe that, "No. No, there must be something else."

Shao Huan shook his head firmly, "No. There is a problem. She must have been arrested."

"Do you think it was because of the information you gave her?"

"I really don't know. I haven't noticed anything different at work… but they wouldn't tell me if there was. They would put me under close surveillance. I need to be extra careful. I may already be under surveillance. If I am arrested, you don't know anything about what happened? Okay?"

Zhang wrapped her arms around Shao and whispered a prayer, "Heavenly Father, please protect Jin Xishan wherever she is and please look after Xiaorong. He must be so sad and confused about where is mother is. I beg You to also protect Shao Huan. Amen."

"Amen," Shao Huan echoed Zhang. "Okay, all we can do is be very careful. Maybe we should hide the Bibles?"

Zhang Ying hated to be separated from her Bible, but she agreed, "Okay. I will hide them at the school. I know a good place."

The next several days were hard ones for Shao and Zhang. They took comfort in their nightly prayers and their time together, but Shao felt the eye of the Party watching him closely. They didn't get any news about Jin's whereabouts and Zhang avoided talking with Xiaorong's grandmother, even though she desperately wanted to ask about Jin Xishan and Bai Yongcheng. Xiaorong talked about missing his parents but just said they had gone away on a trip.

As the cherry blossoms started to sprout on the trees around Chaoyang Park and all of the trees began to push out young green leaves, Shao and Zhang were anxious to return to church but nervous that they would be seen. They worried that the church was under surveillance, or that they would bring trouble to the church if they were under surveillance.

They walked through the park and talked and prayed about what to do. It had been weeks since Jin Xishan disappeared and no one had asked Shao Huan any questions or treated him with any less confidence and Shao felt more confident that he was not under surveillance. They decided that they would go to Duan Yide's restaurant for a late lunch and see if she could tell them anything and whether the church would still meet the next weekend as planned.

Zhang and Shao arrived at the small restaurant after 2 p.m. as the usual lunch crowd was thinning out. The young waitress, who was also clearly from Sichuan took their orders, but they made eye contact with Duan who was manning the cash register and shouting orders to the kitchen. Shao ordered mapo tofu with rice and Zhang ordered wolf fang potatoes without much spice. They saw Duan watching them carefully as the restaurant continued to empty out. Shao spooned up the tofu and thick red gravy covered in ground Sichuan peppercorn that left his mouth tingling.

Duan made eye contact with Zhang, and then shouted to the kitchen "I'm going out for a smoke!" She pushed open the door and stepped out into the bright spring day. Shao nodded to Zhang to go outside after her and he pushed the rest of her spiced potatoes on to his plate.

"You shouldn't have come," Duan Yide said once Zhang stepped outside.

Zhang stood next to her, "I know it is not convenient for us to be here. We wanted to know if we should come to church next week."

Duan took a long drag on her cigarette and blew the smoke out of the side of her mouth, "No. Of course not. They arrested sister Jin and brother Bai."

Zhang tried not to gasp, she had known that Jin and Bai had probably been arrested, but that confirmation still hit her hard. She worried that Shao was in danger, "Where they arrested because of the church?"

Duan glanced at Zhang and tapped the ash from the end of her cigarette, "No. I don't think so. Jin and Bai were smuggling Bibles in from South Korea. Bai had them published in South Korea and brought them in with the other goods he was importing. Jin distributed them to missionaries and other groups. They were real Bibles, not the state-sanctioned trash. They have a lawyer, and we don't know exactly what is happening, but he has reported that they were charged with subverting the state."

Zhang felt a glimmer of relief to hear that it wasn't immediately obvious they were arrested for Shao's information, "What about Xiaorong? At school he talks about how much he misses his parents and that they went on a long trip to Seoul."

"Those bastards arrested both of the poor kid's parents. Fortunately Bai's mother can help. It is very sad. We won't meet for church again until the first Sunday in June. Come back here then. Okay?" Duan finished her cigarette and went inside.

Zhang stayed outside and thought through everything Duan had said. Shao stepped out a minute later, "Let's go," he said and Zhang Ying followed him away. As they were walking he looked at Zhang, and could see her heart ached.

Zhang Ying whispered, "They were arrested for bringing in Bibles."

天安门
Tiananmen

Shao Huan was relieved that his provision of classified information to Bia and Jin was not the immediate cause of their arrest and hoped that the investigation would be so focused on their Bible smuggling operation that they would not discover the connection between them. He assured himself that he had never called or messaged Jin Xishan and that even Zhang hadn't contacted her through her phone since August.

Shao Huan and Zhang Ying reviewed their explanation for their social acquaintance with Jin all the same and prepared to acknowledge that they had gone out to dinner once, and that Jin had been helpful when Zhang Ying's pregnancy ended in stillbirth, but that they had grown apart from Jin since. Shao Huan redoubled his efforts to present the electronic appearance of a loyal cadre in good standing and Zhang occasionally checked the cabinet where she had hidden their Bibles at the school.

Zhang Ying and Shao Huan were both afraid, but also disgusted with the way the Party had ordered the arrest of both Jin and Bai, leaving Xiaorong without either parent to look after him. Their encounter with the Party's persecution terrified them, but it also strengthened their faith and their resolve. They knew their belief in God shouldn't be a threat to any government and that Jesus had said to "render unto Caesar what is Caesar's," and that other governments all around the world had learned to accept Christians, and that even China had welcomed Christians for centuries.

Shao Huan's conviction that he was now working for God within the Party grew deeper every day that went to work at the Propaganda Department headquarters. He prayed for his colleagues and forgave them for their mistakes, but he saw how the Party shaped and directed everything that they did. Shao Huan realized that Liu Wuqing was right when he said that loyalty was only thing the Party Chairman cared about.

Day by day, Shao saw how the truth was only a tool to measure loyalty, and that the core purpose of thought work was to ensure loyalty to the Party at all costs. He saw that, at its core, thought work was to enable the Party Chairman to point at a deer, call it a horse and have the whole country, even the whole world, agree. He understood why faith was so dangerous to the Party, why anyone who believed in a higher power might stand up and state the obvious, that a horse is a horse and a deer is a deer.

Sima Nan kept messaging Shao Huan and asking to meet for dinner or drinks. Shao didn't want to meet Sima Nan. He feared that he had changed so much that Sima Nan might notice. Shao could hide his thoughts from Liu Wuqing during their brief interactions at the office, and easily kept Ye Hongqi from realizing anything had changed beneath Shao Huan's professional veneer. Sima Nan, however, had known Shao Huan for years. He had known Shao before he became a communications specialist for the Party's General Office, and before he had met Zhang Ying. Shao Huan also worried because he didn't really want to lie to Sima Nan, but knew that he had to.

By mid-April, Shao Huan had run out of excuses and agreed to meet Sima Nan for coffee after work. Sima Nan was standing in front of the book store looking at his phone when Shao Huan left the

Propaganda Department headquarters and stepped into the warm spring evening. Shao Huan walked up to Sima Nan and slapped his shoulder, "Hey brother, have you been waiting long?"

"Good, you finally came. You sure you don't want to grab a beer?"

Shao Huan shook his head, "No, I promised Zhang Ying that I would be home before too late. If we go out for drinks it will end up being late," Shao Huan paused, "But it is too warm for coffee. Let's go to the bubble tea place."

Sima Nan sucked air through his teeth, "That stuff is always too sweet. Let's just get coffee."

Shao Huan shrugged, "Let's go to the Taiwan cafe up the street. You can drink coffee and I will drink bubble tea."

"Fine, it doesn't matter. Let's go. If our social credit score drops for going to a Taiwan cafe, I'll blame you."

"Social credit covers cafes now too?" Shao teased.

"Maybe. Maybe it should. Eating hot pot and drinking beer should increase our social credit. Drinking Taiwan bubble tea should reduce it. Double reduction if you get grass jelly. I can talk to my buddies who are working on social credit and suggest it."

Shao Huan laughed, "Good idea. No grass jelly for me."

Sima Nan and Shao Huan made their way up the crowded sidewalk against the stream of people headed to the subway. The cafe was busy and Shao Huan ordered a milk tea with tapioca pearls and half sugar. Sima Nan ordered straight black coffee and they sat a booth.

Sima Nan looked around, "This place is too… too cute. Japan really poisoned Taiwan with all the cute things. This should be where high school kids come on a date. We should be at a bar."

"Are you a little uncomfortable?" Shao Huan laughed at Sima Nan's expense as he shifted in his seat, "Yeah. A little. Let's get the drinks to go."

Shao Huan asked the server to make the order to go, "Hey, did you bring Hua Chunbao here?"

"No. I wouldn't bring her someplace like this," Sima Nan's face flushed red and lie was transparent. Shao Huan burst out laughing.

"Okay, okay. Forget about it. Let's walk. Where to?" Sima Nan took the insulated paper cup of coffee while Shao Huan punched a wide straw through the thin plastic covering over his bubble tea.

"Let's go east on Changan street," Shao Huan.

They walked back toward Shao Huan's office and Sima Nan asked, "Ever regret going to work there?"

Shao Huan shrugged, "It wasn't really my choice. It was where my boss got assigned. He wanted to keep me. It's fine though. My job is basically the same everywhere I go. Why? Do you regret working for the Internet Information Office?"

Sima Nan smiled at a pretty girl in a long blue dress and sun hat that walked by, and smiled even bigger when she returned his smile, "Ha! I've still got it."

Shao Huan patted his back, "Good. Good, congratulations. I am sure Hua Chunbao will be very proud of you."

Sima took a drink of his coffee, "You are just jealous… I'd don't regret working for the State Internet Information Office, but I am really so tired these days. The technology keeps changing so fast. We have been trying hard to figure out how to stop information spreading on device-to-device networks. It makes my head hurt."

"Can't you just require the companies to disable mesh networks on their devices?" The sun lowering in the west cast their shadows, long and thin, in front of them.

"No. 5G uses so many bands and makes near field communication and device-to-device communication so seamless. It's a basic feature of the 5G ecosystem. The social credit system is good, and focusing on the person rather than the device isn't a bad strategy, but it is our job to be able to stop information spreading and I don't know how we can do it. Foreigners are so worried that we'll use 5G to control them, but we can barely keep up with the technology ourselves."

The golden light of the evening sun sparkled on the glass egg-shaped dome of the National Performing Arts Center to the south, "What would you rather be doing?" Shao Huan asked and sucked the last few black tapioca balls up with a little bit of sweet milky tea.

Sima Nan thought for a moment, "I'd like to take Hua Chunbao to a beach somewhere, maybe stay there for a long time."

"Hey, the boss is going to Indonesia for his daughter's wedding. It seems like it will be at a nice beach."

"Aya, those senior cadre can go overseas but we can't? That's not fair."

"He had to ask the Party Chairman for permission. I don't think he wanted to do that, but he got approval to go for a short time. But hey, don't worry, you can go to Hainan. It's a nice place too."

Sima Nan grunted, "I've never been overseas. I'd like to go someday. Where would you go?"

"Do you mean where would I go if the Party allowed me?"

"No, no, no. I mean, forget about the Party for a minute. Imagine that you can go anywhere in the world. Where would you go."

"Cleveland, Ohio," Shao answered quickly and without thinking.

"Where? What place is that?"

"It's where the Rock and Roll Hall of Fame is. I have always wanted to see it. The Doors, Lou Reed, Cat Stephens. It would be cool, but there is no way I can ever get approved to go to America."

Sima Nan was impressed, "Good idea. I want to go to Iceland."

"Why Iceland?"

"It sounds so cool. Doesn't it? It is so small and so far away. I think I would like to see it," as they arrived at the expansive square swarming with people, "I bet there are more people in this square than in all of Iceland," Sima Nan mused.

The sunlight faded to an orange against the faint clouds above and left a faint blue across the rest of the sky. Sima Nan turned to Shao Huan, "You seem different lately, I don't know what is going on with you, but whatever it is… it seems like a good thing. I was worried about you for a little while."

Shao Huan looked north to the gate to the Forbidden City, where Chairman Mao's portrait hung over the gate flanked by large red flags above it on either side. He felt the history around him, and he wanted to tell Sima Nan that he had become a Christian and found new meaning in life and in learning about God but knew it was dangerous anywhere, and especially in that square covered with cameras and microphones, "I feel better. Zhang Ying and I found strength together. I don't think we could have made it alone."

"You two are good for each other. I hope Hua Chunbao and I can get along so well."

"Hey, are you going to ask her to marry you?"

Sima Nan's bravado fell away for a moment, "I bought a ring for her. I want you to meet her first. Okay?"

"Okay brother. Let us know when. Has she met your parents?" They continued walking east across the square and just as a line of soldiers four across in sharp uniforms marched south through the toward the large flag pole directly in front of the main gate to the Forbidden City. Their boots clicked against the stone square in perfect time and they fell into formation at attention to the flag while it was lowered.

The huge red flag fluttered in as it came smoothly down the flag pole. The honor guard resumed their marching stance with robotic precision, and with the same solemn dignity that they entered the square began their march back north.

Shao Huan and Sima Nan stopped talking to watch the display of control and national pride. As the echo of the soldier's boots marching north faded, Sima Nan turned to Shao, "Yeah. My parents like her. She is the first girl I have dated that my mom liked."

"This is a pretty incredible place isn't it?" Shao marveled.

Sima Nan looked around, Mao's portrait to the north, his mausoleum to the south now lit brightly in the thickening dusk, "Yes. It really is. It's too bad they have all of those camera poles everywhere though."

"I think too many people have done embarrassing things here. This place is too politically sensitive not to be so careful," Shao Huan tried to appear as a loyal cadre.

Sima Nan sighed, "Brother, if someone is able to do something in this square your office and mine, and a few others, have already failed. These cameras aren't the front line of defense, they are the last line."

社会信用体系
Social Credit System

By the end of April, Shao Huan felt confident that whatever led the Party to arrest Jin Xishan and Bai Yongcheng, that investigation had not tied back to him. He continued to be given access to sensitive Party communications, and no one seemed to have any questions about him. Liu Wuqing and Ye Hongqi continued to treat him just as before and Shao decided that he and Zhang could get their Bibles again and return to church.

The night that Zhang Ying brought the two Bibles home from school, they both felt excitement and relief. Shao had not expected to miss the comfort of reading the Bible each day. He opened it and started to read John 4. He whispered to himself, "If you knew the gift of God and who it is that asks you for a drink, you would have asked him and he would have given you living water."

Shao Huan had emerged from a desert. He was sure that it was only God's hand that had kept Jin and Bai from revealing their connection to him, and that had spared Shao from being removed from the Party and arrested. He continued reading the Bible long into the night. He read like a thirsty man who had found a river. Even after Zhang Ying had gone to bed, Shao Huan read.

Though he stayed awake until it was nearly dawn, Shao Huan was not tired in the least the next day at work. Liu Wuqing was making arrangements for Ye Hongqi's trip to Bali when Shao stopped by his desk to deliver the morning reports, "Are you sure you don't want to come to Bali?" Liu asked.

"Sure, I want to go, but the only reason for me to go would be to make sure the boss can communicate with the Center. The General Office won't allow me to take the mobile classified communications package for such a short and personal trip. I am sure it will be a good trip."

"It's a pity. It will be a good chance to get out of the office. I have never been to Indonesia before. It looks nice."

"The Party isn't paying for your trip, right? Do you have to pay?"

Liu smiled, "No, the boss is paying for everything. He said it is his daughter's wedding and he wants me there to help him. There will be a lot of other senior cadre and their wives so it will be a half work trip."

"How will the boss manage Wang Zhengong?"

"Aya. That is still a big problem. He hasn't told me directly, but I guess he is working with the Party Chairman to make Wang Zhengong feel safe while they close in on him. He will hide a knife behind a smile."

Shao Huan didn't understand why the Party Chairman was so concerned about Wang, "Is Wang Zhengong corrupt?"

Liu Wuqing leaned back in his chair, "Probably, but it doesn't really matter. Wang Zhengong is too popular. The Party Chairman sees that Wang could become a rival to him. The most dangerous position in the Party is as a possible successor or rival to the Center. Just look at Liu Shaoqi and Lin Biao. Just look at Bo Xilai, the Party can only have one Center."

"Buddy, you should be very careful in Bali."

Liu agreed, "Yes. I won't talk with anyone, just support the boss. Maybe I can go to the beach. The pictures look so different from the beaches in Guangdong."

Shao Huan wondered what the beaches in Guangdong were like, he had only seen the rough sandy beach at Shanhaiguan where the Great Wall met the Bohai gulf, "Take some pictures to show me when you come back."

"Of course, I'll tell you all about it. There are still a few weeks."

Shao Huan was able to focus enough on work not to make any mistakes or draw any attention, but he was amazed how much his perspective had changed in such a short amount of time and how little he cared about Ye's strategies and plots. He wanted to go home and read more. He wanted to go back to church, to pray together and to hear how the other members of the congregation had fared during the long and lonely spring.

The morning that they returned to church, Shao Huan woke up early. He woke Zhang Ying and they left their phones at home while they slipped out of the apartment much earlier than they needed to before going to church. Shao Huan didn't want to take a taxi, and he wanted to make sure no one was following them. Zhang Ying told him that he was paranoid, and he agreed that she was probably right, but decided that it wouldn't hurt to take a long walk to Duan's restaurant.

After they had walked for some time, Shao Huan felt more comfortable that no one was watching them and grew more excited about going to church. Zhang Ying was also excited. She was confident that they were not in any danger, and longed to return to the fellowship of her first church.

Several of the other church members were already waiting when they arrived at Duan's restaurant. She welcomed them inside, "It is so good to see you both. I was worried when you came here last month, but everything is okay. There is no problem."

"We didn't want to cause you trouble, but we really did want to know what was happening. What about Jin and Bai? How are they?"

Duan put her head down and her brow furrowed with worry as she spoke, "Their lawyer said they were both sentenced to 15 years for the crime of subverting the state. 15 years. It is such a long time."

Zhang Ying thought of Bai Xiaorong and that he would be 20 or 21 years old when his parents were released from prison, "Can his grandmother take care of him that long?"

"Only God knows. She is a strong woman, but she must be 60 years old now. She will be well over 70 when they are released. I don't know if they have other family who can help."

Zhang Ying looked at Shao Huan with deep worry in her eyes, "It is too long. Can we help?"

"We can't worry about what will happen in 15 years. We have to trust in God, and you can talk with Xiaorong's grandmother at school and offer to help. Maybe she will need help, but we must wait for her."

Zhang Ying would offer to help while Xiaorong's parents were away, but knew that it would frustrate her not to be able to tell Xiaorong what had really happened.

The rest of the congregation arrived and Shao and Zhang were relieved to see that, apart from Jin and Bai, everyone else had made it. Duan gathered everyone in a circle. They held hands and bowed their heads. Duan began to pray, "Heavenly Father, we thank You for bringing us together today. We thank You for keeping us safe during this uncertain time. We pray, especially, for our sister Jin Xishan and brother Bai Yongcheng. We do not know where they are or what they have endured, but we know that You have been watching over them. They were only trying to spread Your true word Heavenly Father. We also pray for their son, Bai Xiaorong. He brought so much joy to our church, and we worry for Xiaorong, but we trust in You to take care of him. We pray, Heavenly Father, for Your blessing today and to show us Your way, Your truth, Your light. Amen."

Zhang and Shao listened in rapt attention as their fellow believers testified about their experience during the weeks apart and the Party's crackdown on religious groups. They had all been scared, but put their faith in God and trusted He would see them through. Zhang told how she hid their Bibles, just in case, and how excited they both were to get their Bibles back and study God's word again. One of the congregants asked Shao, "Is it over?"

Shao shifted his weight anxiously, "No. I don't think it is. The Party Chairman is very worried about any groups he thinks aren't loyal to the Party and loyal to him. They will continue to pressure house churches and other religious leaders. We must still be very careful."

"What more can we do?" Another believer asked.

"They don't have enough people to monitor everyone, so the Party is relying on the social credit system to identify people of concern for further investigation. You must pay close attention to your social credit score. You should keep your score above 850. It isn't just about being able to travel, or to book a hotel room. If you are designated untrustworthy the Party will spend more resources to surveil you. Your movements will be more closely tracked and they will look for anomalies. When they do that, they can check the CCTV cameras near your residence and they may see that your phone stays home every Sunday morning but that you go out. When they discover that, they will keep investigating. They will run your face through the CCTV archive and find where you go on Sunday mornings. They will also enter your home, whether or not you are there, and will find material that will show you are a Christian," Shao Huan paused and looked around the room, all eyes were intently focused on him.

"It isn't just about preventing your social credit score from dropping. You must also do things to increase it. Volunteer to help in your neighborhood committees, use the Party ideology app on your phones at least once a day, watch videos online of the Party Chairman's speeches and post comments praising him. All of those things will make the social credit system believe that you are a loyal citizen." Shao thought for a moment, "Don't view speeches by other Party leaders or comment on those. It is impossible to know which senior cadre the Party Chairman supports and which cadre he is targeting for a purge. Go to book stores and buy books by the Party Chairman, but don't pay in cash be sure to buy those with WePay."

Shao looked around the room again, "Does everyone understand?" The group nodded unevenly so Shao clarified, "I am not saying that you should be loyal to the Party. Only that you should do things that trick the social credit algorithms into assessing that you are loyal and don't need any further attention. If you have any financial problems, or your friends have problems, you should be more careful and work extra hard to improve your social credit score. You should also be aware that your social credit score is affected by your family and friends. If they have lower social credit scores, that will also lower your social credit score. You should do what you can to help them increase their scores."

The church said a final prayer and slowly started to leave. Duan pulled Shao aside, "What you said about the social credit system made me worry. The landlord increased the rent on our restaurant at the start of the year and I have had to borrow money to keep up. I am afraid that my finances are no good. What should I do?"

"Can you increase your prices?"

Duan Yide's short tight curls bounced as she shook her head, "No. I tried for a little while but the customers all complained. Most of my customers are migrant workers. They don't make much money. I don't think I can increase my income, but my costs keep going up. I don't want my financial problems to draw attention to our church."

Shao Huan stood silently with Duan. She answered the question that he was preparing to ask, "If I change locations, I will have to move far outside of the city. It would be too far for our church."

"The church will be okay. It will be better for you and for the church if you keep your social credit score high. You can still come to meet with us, and we can meet in other places." Shao saw Duan's normally tough exterior was faltering and tears started to well up in her eyes.

"My business problems shouldn't be problems for the church."

"The social credit system is very strict and we must be prepared to make sacrifices to avoid detection. Maybe it will be a good thing for you to move farther from the city. We will all miss this place, but our church is the people, not any place. You will always be a part of our church, wherever you live."

上善若水
The Supreme Good is Like Water

Zhang Ying kept thinking about Xiaorong. She wished there was something more that she could do for him, but she knew that Shao Huan was right and that it was best he stayed with his grandmother. Zhang had never felt angry at the Party before. She had been annoyed with some of the rules and restrictions, but she had never before felt the Party's cruelty and desperation so sharply.

Shao Huan had seen the Party's duplicity and cruelty, but had never known someone who was arrested. He told himself that Jin Xishan and Bai Yongcheng were aware of the risks, and that they took them anyway to fulfill their calling from God. He wondered if he would have been so brave. He knew that neither Jin or Bai were reckless, but that it would have been nearly impossible to conceal both the importation and distribution of real Bibles. The state security apparatus had too many spies and too many resources to hide that kind of operation for very long.

He was grateful that Jin had given them real Bibles. He had heard Liu Wuqing explain that the Party approved Bibles contained quotations from the Party Chairman's ideology and removed any stories or verses that might be inconsistent with the dictatorship of the proletariat and undermine loyalty to the Party. Shao was ever more detached from the actual substance of his work, and was relieved for some quiet when Liu Wuqing and Ye Hongqi left for Bali.

Shao used the time to organize and review the classified reports. He looked back at some old reports that he had not paid much attention to before his conversion. The orders from the Center to replace pictures of the Virgin Mary with pictures of the Party Chairman in Catholic Churches and the guidance to limit church attendance to only people over 18 years old at churches approved by the Religious Affairs Office, made Shao wonder how any of the State controlled churches could still help people find salvation when their focus was on supporting the Party.

Shao Huan was tempted to take photographs of the classified documents, but the Party had already taken all of those actions, in broad daylight for everyone to see and even though a few people raised an outcry, it hadn't changed anything. He reasoned that providing the internal documents would not change the Party or help the church, so he bided his time.

When Liu and Ye returned, Liu Wuqing was so excited to show Shao Huan his pictures from Bali and from the wedding that he just set the classified folder to the side, "You really should have come! That place is amazing. Here, look at the beach," he held out his phone to show Shao Huan the long white sand beach and clear blue water. Liu thumbed through the photos and held out another, "There was a beach club next to the hotel. It was so cool." Shao looked at the picture of a mix of Asian and Western guests lounging with drinks by a crystal clear swimming pool.

"Why do you need a swimming pool if you are by the beach?"

Liu didn't really hear Shao as he was basking in the fresh memory of his short trip, "Huh? Oh, I think because the ocean is so salty."

"Did you go swimming?"

"Not really swimming, but I went in the water. It was like a bath. So warm. The hotel was amazing too."

Shao Huan did envy Liu for getting to visit such an exotic place, "That's good buddy. Was the boss happy?"

Liu put his phone back on the desk, "I still don't know. He was very busy while we were there. I spoke with him a few times, but he was careful not to say much. He asked me to help look after a few of the other senior cadre who attended."

"Did you meet Wang Zhengong?"

"No, I didn't meet him, but I see why the Party Chairman is nervous about him. He is a very good speaker and people at the wedding all seemed to like him. His son looks like a movie star. With their family background and connections, he must be a very big threat to the Party Chairman. If the Party Chairman had not targeted Wang Zhengong, I am sure Ye Hongqi would be very happy because Wang would no doubt continue to rise."

"What do you think will happen?"

Liu sighed, "I really don't know, but I don't think it will be much longer. The boss told me the Party is collecting evidence against Wang's secretary. Once his secretary is arrested, it won't be long until they arrest Wang Zhengong. If the Party Chairman was going to remove Ye Hongqi, they would first arrest me."

Shao Huan gave Liu a look of sympathy, and Liu shrugged, "There is nothing to be done. That is the way the Party works. We are lucky the boss is so close to the Party Chairman, but not close enough to be a threat. Anyway, you should take your wife to Bali sometime. I have already promised my wife that once I can get approval, we will go to Bali, or somewhere like it anyway."

Liu picked up the folder of classified reports, "It is heavy, we weren't gone so long. What is in it?"

"I don't think anything was too important, just the usual reports from the provincial Party offices and the minutes from the last Politburo Standing Committee meeting. It did not seem too important, but they mention the need for increased thought work overseas to counter negative reporting on China."

Liu nodded gravely, "They still aren't satisfied with our overseas news bureaus. They say they understand that our thought work outside of China is difficult, but they keep demanding more work. We have bought many radio stations and have built influence over newspapers that are struggling financially, we have even pressured Chinese companies not to do business with any media that allow negative reports about China but we can't control the thought environment like we do here. I miss the time of hiding our strength and biding our time. Everything was so much easier then."

Ye Hongqi came out of the elevator and walked down the hall, his face was slightly red but he smiled broadly, "Good morning!"

"Good morning boss, congratulations on your daughter's wedding! Liu Wuqing was showing me pictures. It looks like it was beautiful."

Ye kept smiling, "Yes, it was beautiful. She is married now, and she is happy. That is all a father can hope for. Was there any news from the Center while I was gone?"

"Yes, there was some communication from the Center," Liu Wuqing handed Ye the folder. Shao knew that Liu usually tried to read all of the documents before he gave them to Ye.

"Good, good. I will read them in a little while," Ye took the folder and walked to his office. Liu glanced nervously at Shao Huan, who winked at him and returned to his office to print off copies of the documents from the Party Center, so Liu would be prepared when Ye asked about them. Shao was not supposed to print off extra copies, but he also did not want Liu to get in trouble for being unprepared for Ye Hongqi's questions.

Shao Huan looked forward to meeting Zhang Ying for dinner that evening. She had agreed to meet Sima Nan's girlfriend and Sima Nan had arranged for a table at Din Tai Fung. Zhang Ying was already waiting for Shao outside when he arrived. The golden sunlight lit Zhang's eyes as Shao approached and made them look a light chestnut color and her face smooth and radiant, "You finally made it!" She teased him.

"The boss is back, so it was a little bit busy. Shall we go in?" Shao opened the door for Zhang and they stepped into the busy restaurant. The kitchen had a long glass wall and they watched the cooks pulling noodles and folding dumplings while the hostess found Sima Nan's reservation.

The hostess sat them at a small round table, "He really wants me to like this girl doesn't he?" Zhang Ying joked looking around the elegantly designed and bustling restaurant.

"I don't know why, but I think he is more worried about introducing Hua Chunbao to you than he was about introducing her to his parents. I think he is scared of you," Shao Huan laughed.

"Just right. He should be scared of me! He has put you in too many bad situations."

"He has just taken a little longer to mature. Before I met you, I was a lot more like him than you realize. I think he really is ready to get married now," Shao Huan's phone rang and he nodded to Zhang Ying before answering, "Hey buddy, we are inside. Just come on in." Shao stood up and waved as he saw Sima Nan walking in with a pretty girl.

"Hey!" Sima Nan reached across the table and slapped Shao Huan's hand and bowed slightly to Zhang Ying, "Have you been waiting long?"

"No, no. Not long at all," Zhang Ying smiled at Hua who leaned nervously against Sima Nan.

"Ah, Shao Huan, Zhang Ying this is my girlfriend Hua Chunbao," Sima Nan said with a proud smile. Hua nodded at Shao and Zhang, "I'm really happy to meet you. Sima Nan talks about you both a lot."

Shao Huan tried to set Hua at ease, "He talks a lot of nonsense, but I know he likes you a lot. Please, let's sit."

Sima Nan established from the start that he was treating for dinner and insisted Shao Huan not argue with him. Shao Huan acquiesced and Sima took charge with the waitress. Zhang Ying spoke with Hua Chunbao while Sima Nan ordered. Zhang Ying felt nervous for Hua, she seemed so young but her eyes were bright and Zhang knew she had to be strong to put up with Sima Nan. Hua had grown up in a small town in Hebei Province and finished her undergraduate degree in civil engineering at Shijiazhuang Railway University and moved to Beijing to take a job with the Beijing Municipal Commission of Transportation.

Sima Nan continued to beam with pride as he saw how Hua Chunbao impressed his friends. The waitress brought a plate of steamed mustard greens in garlic sauce and a plate of carefully stacked crisp cucumber drizzled with chili oil and vinegar, and soon after a tower of circular bamboo trays. She took the lid off of the first bamboo tray and set it at the center of the table. Sima Nan insisted that Zhang Ying be the first to lift one of the perfectly wrapped dumplings filled with hot soup and tender pork and crab meat.

Zhang Ying blew on the xiaolongbao on her spoon while the others all took dumplings as well. Sima Nan was not as patient as Zhang and Hua, and bit through the soft doughy skin to let the soup spill out onto his spoon, "This place is so good," he said and slurped the soup out of his spoon before pushing the remaining dumpling skin and meat in his mouth.

Hua Chunbao carefully poured a small amount of black vinegar into the dish next to her plate and waited for the dumpling to cool before she ate it. She was a little shorter than Zhang Ying and had a round, strong face with thin lips and fast, dark eyes. Shao Huan noticed that under her long white sleeve she wore a bracelet of dark wooden beads with the character "Dao" etched in them. Shao smiled at Sima Nan. He was marrying a Daoist. Shao Huan couldn't restrain himself and complimented Hua on her bracelet.

"Oh, thank you…" Hua started to blush

"It's okay. I like Laozi quite a lot. I used to think of myself as Daoist in college, I especially like the beginning of the Dao De Jing, 'The way that can be walked is not the constant way, the name that can be named is not the constant name,'" Shao Huan offered.

Sima Nan laughed and slapped the table, "That's right! I forgot, you used to talk about getting a tattoo of the eight trigrams!"

Shao Huan blushed, "Yes, good thing you talked me out of it. But I still like the idea."

"My favorite part of the Dao De Jing is the eighth chapter, 'The supreme good is like water, which nourishes all things without trying, it goes to the low places people despise, and so it is like the Dao.' I try to remember that when I am unhappy. I should be like water."

Hua's voice was soft and vulnerable and Zhang Ying placed a shrimp and pork shao mai dumpling on her plate, "It is good you are like water. I think Sima Nan is too much like fire. You are good to balance him."

The two couples feasted on dumplings, friend rice and finished the meal with small bowls of noodles in spicy peanut sauce. Hua Chunbao completely won over Zhang Ying and as they left the restaurant, Zhang told Sima Nan "She is too good for you. But if she will marry you, you should hang on to her tightly."

Sima Nan laughed and pulled Hua Chunbao close, "Okay! I will." He said and opened the door to the taxi for her.

Zhang Ying laughed as they drove away, "She really is too good for him, but maybe you are right that he is ready to grow up."

"I told you. They will be a good couple," Shao Huan laughed, "Hey, maybe they can get married in Hainan so we can go to a beach wedding."

Zhang clicked her tongue, "No matter where they get married, we will go."

That night before bed, Shao Huan remembered his college dalliance with Daoism and contemplated Hua Chunbao's quotation from the Dao De Jing. He turned again to John 4 and read, "Everyone who drinks this water will be thirsty again, but whoever drinks the water I give them will never thirst. Indeed, the water I give them will become in them a spring of water welling up to eternal life."

思想工作
Thought Work

Shortly after the dinner with Sima Nana and Hua Chunbao, Sima called Shao and told him that Hua had agreed to marry him and they were organizing the celebration for just after the mid-Autumn Festival. Sima Nan sounded happier than Shao Huan could ever remember, and he was glad that his friend had finally found a good partner.

Shao and Zhang continued to study and pray. They prayed for Duan Yide, for Jin Xishan and Bai Yongcheng and all of their fellow believers. They prayed especially for God to take care of Bai Xiaorong. Duan had closed her restaurant a few weeks after Shao spoke with her and relocated to a quiet street just outside of the satellite city of Tongzhou. They didn't hear any more news about Jin and Bai, however, and Zhang Ying's heart ached for Xiaorong.

In mid-June, Ye Hongqi received news that Wang Zhengong's secretary had been detained, and Liu Wuqing confided in Shao Huan that they were caught in a dangerous game. Wang was more popular and better connected than Ye Hongqi had realized, and perhaps that even the Party Chairman had underestimated Wang's supporters.

Shao Huan received a notification that the Center wanted to hold a secure conference call with Ye Hongqi, the head of the Internet Information Office, the Minister of State Security and the Minister of Public Security. Shao assumed that it was related to the Party Chairman's maneuvers against Wang Zhengong and promptly informed Liu Wuqing, who shared Shao's assessment. Ye Hongqi dropped all of his other activities and prepared for the call.

Shao connected the phone and then stepped out of Ye's office to wait with Liu next door. They listened for Ye's voice through the door, but he only spoke a few times and neither of them could discern what the phone call was about. When Ye hung up the phone he immediately summoned them both to his office.

Ye looked worried and rested his hands on his desk, "There has been a serious compromise of State secrets. The Ministry of State Security has detected the compromise, and have no way to control the information. They expect that it will reach the foreign media very soon. We must be prepared to counter the foreign propaganda."

Liu Wuqing nodded, "Okay. We can issue instructions to remind all Chinese media not to report on any foreign media stories that spread rumors or gossip about China. Should we also instruct the Chinese journalists overseas to counter the false reports?"

Ye agreed, "Yes. That will be the first step. We must try to prevent the news from reaching the people inside China and portray the foreign journalists reporting the story as gossip mongers and running dogs for anti-China forces. Fortunately, the story is so outlandish that we can describe it as a complete fabrication designed to undermine the Party."

Liu looked at Shao and then turned back to Ye, "What exactly is the information that has been compromised?"

Ye sighed and shook his head, "I will tell you both because I need you to help me manage the situation. The compromised information is related to sensitive research into extending human longevity. I do not know exactly how much of the research data has been compromised, and the Ministry of State Security is just beginning to investigate how the information was compromised. Right now, we need to send the instructions to all Party propaganda offices reminding them not to allow any reporting on negative rumors about China or the Party. We will also send instructions to all Embassies overseas to instruct the Chinese journalists to aggressively counter the news stories as fabrications and slander," Ye thought for a moment and continued, "Liu Wuqing, also schedule an emergency instruction session with the editors-in-chief."

Ye dismissed Liu and Shao. They returned to Liu's office worried and confused. "That was really weird, the boss seems nervous," Shao said.

"There must be more that he is not telling us. Right now, we should do what he asked. I will organize the emergency instruction meeting. Can you draft the message to the propaganda offices and the Chinese Embassies overseas? You should be able to copy the guidance we issued after the protest in Malaysia. Just make it more general for now."

Shao returned to his office, prayed quietly for the wisdom to navigate whatever storm was building, and prepared the instructions for the domestic and overseas journalists. Shao printed them for Liu's edits and approval before he sent them out. Liu was on the phone when Shao reached his office, "I know it is inconvenient, but it is required by the Center. The meeting is at 6 p.m. today. Goodbye."

Liu shook his head in disgust, "Sometimes I think these editors forget who they work for," he reached for the two short documents that Shao Huan had drafted. Liu quickly read them and made a few small edits. As he handed them back to Shao he stated, "You better let your wife know you won't be home for dinner tonight. I think we will have a few busy days."

"It seems that way. I will transmit these messages. I can go out and get dinner for us later," Shao offered.

Shao wondered what Ye Hongqi had withheld from them. It did not seem that research into extending human life spans could be so damaging to the Party. Shao was sure that many research institutions around the world also studied that same topic. The level of concern from the Party Chairman, however, indicated that there was something more.

Shao received a few more reports for Ye over the course of the afternoon, but none of them seemed important compared to Ye's immediate focus and Shao set them aside. The editors-in-chief arrived a little before 6 p.m. and Liu had arranged everything for them. Once they were safely secured behind Ye's office door, Liu breathed a sigh of relieve, "Finally, they are all here."

Shao stood near Liu's desk, "They must realize that there is a big problem to attend an emergency instruction session."

"Yes, of course. The smart ones will not try to ask any more questions, but I am sure at least one of them will try to find out more about exactly what rumors and slander they should not report."

"If it really was rumors and slander, there wouldn't be an emergency instruction session," Shao observed.

"Of course, that is obvious. They know the Party well enough. They know that whatever may be reported in foreign media is likely true."

"Hey, what do you want for dinner?" Shao asked.

"It should be something fast. How about McDonalds? I would really like a bacon cheeseburger."

Shao tilted his head and agreed, "That does sound good. Okay, no problem. I'll be back soon. Do you want fries?"

"Yes, fries and a large coke," Liu handed Shao a few red bills, "My treat this time."

Shao didn't protest and grabbed his phone on his way out. He had a half dozen messages from Sima Nan and the last one asked him to call. As Shao walked north from Xidan Station he called Sima Nan.

"Hey! You finally answered!" Sima Nan exclaimed, "What is going on? I got some strange instructions from the boss that we need to be extra vigilant. I have put extra Internet monitors on duty, but don't know what we should be looking for. Can you tell me anything?"

"Not really, and definitely not on the phone. Can you meet at McDonalds at Xidan? I am going there now."

"Dammit. I… Okay, okay. Just wait there. I will be there as soon as I can," Sima Nan hung up.

Shao Huan used the automated touch screens to order and pay for three bacon cheeseburger meals with large cokes. He loved Chinese food, but ever since he had his first hamburger in high school, he had loved the soft bread and warm meat of McDonalds burgers. Shao also liked the friendly efficiency of every McDonalds that he had ever visited. Shao stood in front of the fast food restaurant sipping his coke in the warm summer evening.

A taxi pulled up and Sima Nan jumped out, "Hey! What's up? What is going on? I have to get back soon."

Shao Huan handed him a bag with a warm burger and fries and a cold coke with water beading on the waxed paper cup, "Me too. At least you can go back with dinner."

"Hey! Great! I didn't eat lunch, I am so hungry. Okay, what is going on? I haven't seen my boss so worried before, but his guidance was so vague."

"Me neither. I don't know exactly what is happening, but some sensitive information was compromised. The information was from a research institute that studied extending human longevity. I am sure there is more that the Head of the Propaganda Department isn't telling us, but right now that is all that I know. You can't tell anyone that I told you this."

Sima Nan took a long drink from his large coke, "Okay. That is useful. We have already blocked access to the major foreign news outlets, but I can start to direct the algorithms to flag any news reports about longevity. If we can automate that search, it will be much easier and we can stop the stories before they get started." Sima Nan reached into the brown paper bag and took out a handful of warm salty fries. "There must be something more to the story. Why would they be so worried about such common research? Why are they withholding information? We can't be effective if they don't tell us."

"I don't know, but I think we will find out soon enough," Shao Huan stated with his usual calm.

"Dammit. Why aren't you worried about what is going on?" Sima Nan took another handful of fries.

Shao Huan wanted to tell Sima Nan that he wasn't worried because he trusted that whatever happened was part of God's plan, but simply explained, "Worrying isn't very useful. It is better to keep our minds clear and not worry."

"Brother, you are too cool for your own good. If your boss is worried, at least try to look a little bit worried."

"That is well said. You are right, I will try to look worried. Hey, when this is all over we still need to go out and celebrate your engagement," Shao Huan patted Sima Nan's shoulder.

"Good. Hopefully this will just be a few days and we can go out after that. I better go. Let me know if you learn anything more. I'll do the same," Sima Nan wiped his greasy fingers on his blue jeans and hailed a cab.

Ye's office door was still closed when Shao returned to Liu's office. Liu greedily bit into the thick, juicy burger. "They are still going?" Shao Huan asked rhetorically.

"Yes, it is going longer than I expected. We may have a long night."

Shao sat with Liu and they ate their sandwiches in silence listening to the muffled sounds of an argument and waiting for the door to open. Finally the door swung open and the editors-in-chief filed out. Liu wiped his mouth and after the last of the editors had left the floor he knocked softly on the door frame and Ye summoned him in. Shao listened through the open door as Ye unleashed his fury, "Damn that guy! He thinks because he is editor of the People's Daily that he knows how to do propaganda better than I do! He wants to publish stories about this great research and work by the Party before it appears in the foreign media and say that it was not yet ready for release to the public when it was stolen. He thinks that we can get in front of this story. He doesn't know what information the enemy actually has. Keep a close eye on the People's Daily and let's begin planning to replace him. There are hundreds of editors who would be better than him."

Ye paused and then yelled again, "I'm not going to do something different than what the Party Chairman instructed because some damn editor thinks he has a better idea. Send another message to all the Party propaganda offices emphasizing that any violation of the Center's directive to avoid publishing stories about foreign slander will be met with severe punishment!"

Liu Wuqing didn't say anything as he backed carefully out of Ye's office nodding his understanding, he turned to Shao Huan and pointed down the hall toward Shao's office. They hurried down the hall and Liu carefully dictated the instructions. They both realized that the second set of instructions and the threat of severe punishment only served to highlight the matter and indicate that the alleged foreign slander was probably based on truth.

Liu and Shao waited for a couple more hours before Liu told Shao that he could go home. Shao reflected on the strange day as he rode the subway home. He had never seen Ye so angry or Liu so worried. Whatever was actually happening must be a much bigger problem than he realized. He was glad for Sima Nan's recommendation to at least try to appear worried, and had done his best to reflect Liu's concern.

Zhang Ying was getting ready for bed when Shao returned home. "My dear! What a long day, you must be very tired," She greeted him with a hug.

"It was a long day. It was a very strange day. Something big is happening, or is about to happen. I don't know what. I may be working late for a few days. I need to relax a bit before bed. I will come to bed soon," he kissed Zhang on the cheek and sat on the sofa. Every time he sat there he still remembered the terrible morning when the old sofa was covered in blood and their daughter was stillborn. He put a dramatization of the War Against Japanese Aggression on his phone and picked up his Bible.

Shao Huan opened his Bible to 1 John 2 and read, "Do not love the world, or anything in the world…." He read on, "The world and its desires pass away, but whoever does the will of God lives forever." Shao re-read the passage several times and realized how much Ye and Liu were bound by the pride of life that came from the world, and that whatever was happening, or about to happen, would be very hard for them both. Shao prayed for strength and wisdom and for God to show Ye and Liu God's way and to free them from the pride of life.

Shao's heart was calm when he went to work the next morning. Liu was already in the office and appeared haggard, "Hey buddy, did you sleep last night?" Shao asked.

"A few hours, but the foreign media has already started reporting on the compromised information. It is quite bad. They have tens of thousands of documents from more than fifty years of research. They are just starting to go through the documents, and the main things they are focusing on are that the Party was keeping secret sophisticated stem cell treatments that could keep people alive much longer than normal. I don't know how much the boss knew about all of this. It seems like he knew a little bit, but not everything. He is already in his office watching the Taiwan news."

"So maybe the People's Daily editor was right that we should have been the first to announce the discovery?" Shao Huan asked in a whisper.

"Be careful! Don't say that. The boss would be furious, and it isn't true. The reports in the Taiwan media show documents from the late 1990s that the Party allowed the researchers to use fetal tissue for their research, and there is even one document signed by the Party Chairman at the time ordering the continuation of the one child policy even after the demographers recommended relaxing the policy to avoid abrupt population decline. They didn't keep the one child policy to prevent a population explosion, they continued the one child policy to to ensure that the researchers could have access to unlimited fetal tissue."

"What? No way!" Shao Huan realized he had raised his voice and whispered again, "That isn't possible. That just isn't possible."

Liu Wuqing shook his head, "It looks like it might be possible. The documents all look authentic. The reports say that the life extending treatment is available for senior cadre at the Vice Minister level and above…" Liu lowered his voice again and continued, "I know that the boss get's visits from doctors about once a month, but I don't know what they do. I never ask. I guess he has been getting the treatment as well."

"So they are using the tissue from babies to keep the Party leadership alive longer?" Shao asked.

"I… I don't know exactly. But that sounds like the basic point of the reports in the Taiwan media."

"Are we going to change our strategy?"

"No, I don't think so. Not yet. So far it seems like the news has not been reported in China, and that even the People's Daily editor understood the meaning of the second message we sent yesterday. The State Internet Information Office has blocked all access to overseas media. Let me know if there are any secure communications about the issue. The boss has been summoned to a meeting at the leadership compound at 11 a.m. this morning to discuss the matter. I will go with him."

Shao Huan checked the incoming messages and found only a handful of reports from Chinese Embassies overseas that documented the beginning of new slanderous rumors against the Party. He updated Liu while he busily prepared for the short drive to Zhongnanhai. Liu was summoned to Ye's office and Shao listened again as Ye yelled at Liu, "These foreign bastards are spreading such slander against China! Why aren't our journalists overseas responding? Send them guidance immediately! They are to call all of these stories ridiculous lies by foreign powers who are racist and do not want to see a strong Asian country. That these stories offend 1.4 billion Chinese people and are completely baseless. That the so called documents are obvious fabrications and that they are reporting science fiction and not reality! Go!"

Liu again backed out of Ye's office and followed Shao Huan down the hall, "Well, at least this time the guidance can be more specific," Shao offered.

Liu grimaced, "Yes. I am sure that the Embassies and journalists who received the instructions yesterday are waiting for more detailed instructions before they make any public statements. They know that if their public statement is counter to what the Center wants them to say, that they will be punished severely. They are smart to wait for clear guidance rather than to take the risk to say something the Party will have to correct later. They must be especially careful now, because I am sure most of them realize the rumors they are supposed to denounce are probably true."

Shao sat with Liu and prepared the detailed instructions for overseas journalists and officials to respond to the media inquiries about the alleged Party documents. They sent the classified message just before Liu had to drive with Ye Hongqi to the high red walls and imposing gates of the Zhongnanhai leadership compound.

After they left, Shao stepped outside and got his phone. He went to the street outside and tried to call Sima Nan, but there was no answer. Shao was sure that Sima Nan was busy as well. Shao wasn't hungry but decided to get some Shanxi sliced noodles while Liu and Ye were out of the office. His phone buzzed in his pocket a few minutes later as he walked along the street and he saw that it was Sima Nan calling.

"Hey brother. Are you okay? It is a crazy day."

Sima Nan's voice on the other end of the line sounded tired, "Crazy day. My boss just went to Zhongnanhai. Yours too?"

"Yeah. It can't be a good sign."

"No, definitely not. We were able to block the foreign news, but it is so hard to block on WeChat. We are blocking accounts and news feeds as fast as possible, but the bastards are starting to use the character '子 zi' for child to criticize the Party. Some people are just sending messages that say that character once, sometimes they say it a dozen times. Those ones are easy to filter, but other people are more sophisticated. When we had to filter for Malaysia or Winnie the Pooh, it wasn't so hard but this is crazy! How can we filter out one of the most common characters in the Chinese language?"

"Do you think it is true? I mean, what they are reporting?" Shao asked.

Sima Nan hesitated, "It doesn't matter what I think. We have to do our jobs, this is going to be a big problem. People online are really angry. We have filtered and blocked millions of posts and messages just this morning. The system is slowing down and we are struggling to keep up. Someone actually suggested completely shutting down the Internet until we have this under control. I don't think it will come to that, but that is still possible. We should talk more about it next time we see each other. I have to get back to work."

Shao Huan quickly ate a bowl of hand sliced noodles with pickled mustard greens and ground pork and reflected on Sima Nan's comments. If there were millions of people commenting on the foreign press reports, Ye Hongqi's strategy to prevent the news from reaching inside China had already failed. The pork fat glistened on Shao's lips as he slurped up the hearty noodles. The reports were so outrageous that if he hadn't seen how Ye Hongqi was reacting, he wouldn't have believed the reports were true. He was disgusted to think that the senior cadre had been using the tissue from aborted babies to extend their own lives.

Shao thought of how God had created each of those little lives and that it was the ultimate perversion of God's creation to kill those babies to extend the lives and power of men who worked so hard to stop the spread of the gospel, and of every other belief that didn't lift the Party up in the place of God. Shao prayed for God's guidance and waited for a sign, some voice, telling him what he should do as the Party scrambled to hide and divert attention from such a damning revelation of the callous indifference for life and imperious effort to subjugate even the laws of nature to the Party's service.

Shao Huan's disgust with the Party only grew as he returned to the office. It wasn't long until Liu Wuqing and Ye Hongqi also returned. Ye went straight to his office and closed the door. Liu came to Shao's office and sat down in the extra chair where he usually sat when dictating messages, "In my whole life, I have never been in a meeting like that. The Party Chairman was furious. He yelled at everyone. He blamed the Minister of State Security for failing to prevent the compromise of such sensitive information. He blamed us for failing to conduct sufficient thought work outside of China, he blamed the United Front Work Department for lacking the influential contacts in foreign governments to prevent the spread of the news.

He blamed the State Internet Information Office for not being able to stop the slanderous rumors from entering China. It was very bad," Liu put his head in his hands.

"Did the Party Chairman just yell at everyone or did he provide instructions?"

"He gave instructions. I don't know how we will implement the instructions he gave us. He directed the Propaganda Department to redouble our thought work. We must not cover the story being reported in the international media, but we will publicize efforts by the black hand of foreign forces to embarrass the Party and undermine China's unity. We will publish some embarrassing news about a few foreign journalists here in China and expel all of the foreign media."

"Will that work?"

"Who knows…Whether it works or not, it is the Party Chairman's guidance. We cannot refuse. At least we are not the Ministry of State Security. They say they have identified the source of the information compromise, but the Party Chairman did not accept that as success. He threatened in front of everyone to have the Minister of State Security removed from his position for such a grave failure. The Party Chairman didn't yell at the People's Liberation Army, but he did notify them to be on a war footing. It is really quite serious."

"A war footing? Are the Americans preparing to attack?" Shao Huan had not imagined the situation was so extreme.

"No. He isn't worried about the Americans. He is worried about the people. If this news reaches the people, they may become angry. I think he just wants the army to be prepared to defend the Party."

"So should we send a message to the provincial propaganda offices?" Shao Huan suggested.

Liu Wuqing sighed, "Yes. We should. Let's begin… The black hand of foreign powers will not rest and continues to threaten China. Take every step to educate the people that China's enemies will not stop and they have no limit to the baseless claims they will make against China. It is the duty of all Chinese people to defend our country from lies and rumors from outside of China. They hate China and their only purpose is to weaken and divide China. They cannot accept a strong China. We must rally together to support China. Every classroom must hold a mandatory education session on the efforts of foreign powers to undermine China beginning with the Opium War and through to the American slander against China during the novel coronavirus pandemic. Every newspaper and magazine will provide top coverage to efforts by the Party Chairman to protect China." Liu continued to dictate a strong message of resolve and patriotism against foreign threats and after Shao finished typing and preparing the message Liu took it to Ye for his approval.

Liu returned to Shao's office, "The boss approved. Send the message. Our thought work is more important now than ever before."

黑手
The Black Hand

Zhang Ying was already asleep when Shao Huan returned home that night and he fell asleep on the sofa while reading the Bible. He forgot to turn his phone off before he fell asleep and it was completely drained of battery when he woke up the next morning. Zhang Ying was getting ready for work and turned on the television when she saw that Shao Huan was awake, "My dear, something strange is going on. The news on my phone was all about the danger of foreign forces, and even the television news is talking about the danger from foreign powers that want to divide China. What is happening?"

Shao watched as the morning news broadcaster spoke about the State discovering a plot by foreign powers to undermine and divide China while the screen showed images of the U.S. Embassy in Beijing, the Japanese Embassy and the British Embassy. Shao Huan turned to Zhang Ying, "They are trying to distract the people and prepare them for bad news."

Zhang sat down next to her husband, "Is it true?"

"No. There is no foreign plot. The problem is inside the Party, but they can't admit that. They must find a foreign threat to distract people, I need to go I will tell you more tonight," Shao Huan plugged his phone in while he prepared for the day and got enough of a charge to get him to the office.

The electronic billboards and television screens on Shao's commute to work all showed images of foreign embassies and military vessels and aircraft. He had not seen the Propaganda Department's efforts translated in to action so clearly and quickly. As far as he could tell, however, there was no real information about the nature of the foreign threat, only that the Party authorities had discovered a great danger to the people of China and were preparing all available measures.

In the subway car, however, Shao saw a small character written in black marker. He hadn't seen graffiti in the subway in years and took a closer look and saw that it was the character "zi" for child. As overwhelming as the Propaganda Department's dominance of the media was, it was not complete and Shao took comfort in the knowledge that some brave soul had made a small act of defiance and scrawled one simple character that undermined the thick and relentless lies around them.

Shao was sure that Liu Wuqing would be exhausted from another long night and picked up two lattes with double shots of espresso before he went to the office. Shao greeted the guards at the front entrance as warmly as ever and they opened the door for him. Shao gave one cup of coffee to the guard at the front desk, "How's it going buddy?"

"It is strange. We are on high alert. All of the security elements around the country have been placed on high alert. I am not sure, however, what we are supposed to be watching for."

"It seems like there is a big threat, so I thought you might need an extra coffee," Shao left the coffee on the counter as the guard started to receive a call over his radio.

Just as Shao had expected, Liu was in his office and appeared to be in desperate need of a coffee. "The thought work has certainly been redoubled. All the media outlets are talking about the foreign threat and the Party Chairman's work to keep the Chinese people safe."

"Yes, that seems to be working. Thanks for the coffee. The boss is not here yet, but I took a look in his office at the foreign media, they are all covering the information compromise. The Taiwan news seems to be the most accurate, they have experts from their intelligence services who have verified the documents are internal Party documents. We will be able to accuse the Taiwan separatists of collaborating with the foreign powers to draft fake Party documents."

"What else did they say? Is the treatment real?" Shao asked.

"There was an interview with a Japanese professor from Kyoto University, he said the research is persuasive and the treatment should be viable. He said the technique is sophisticated and far beyond what he was working on. He actually called it a great leap forward in stem cell therapy."

"Well, maybe that is a good thing? The research could help people. I will go check the messages and bring them before the boss arrives." Shao Huan found many more classified messages than usual, but took notice of one from the State Internet Information Office. They did not normally receive any communication from the State Internet Information Office and he immediately remembered Sima Nan's concerns that they could not continue to filter such a common character.

The report described the tens of millions of messages and web searches about the compromised information. The report concluded that the general public was already aware of the Party documents that had been published overseas, that the search terms were too common to be easily blocked and the proliferation of news articles made it impossible to control. The only effective way to stop the transmission of the information was to completely shut down the Internet, but that would also have grave consequences for commerce as most business transactions were conducted electronically. They could try to segment and preserve WePay but that would leave open channels for transmission of information over WeChat which meant that they could not guarantee complete control.

Shao printed that report first and delivered it directly to Liu Wuqing, "It appears that our thought work may not be as effective as we believed."

Liu glanced at the report and commented while he read, "We will need to adjust methods. I will let the boss know, but I am sure that we will now focus on the threat of these false reports from overseas. This is moving more quickly than we expected. We will have to expel the foreign journalists immediately."

"Okay. I will bring the rest of the reports soon. They are mostly from Embassies overseas and a few from provincial propaganda offices. It looks like they are all listing their accomplishments and their response to the Center's guidance. It didn't seem like anything too important, but I will let you know."

Shao printed off the reports and noticed that one report from the Guangxi Party Office in Nanning was not a simple report on their successful thought work. He put it at the top of the folder and delivered the documents to Liu, "Most of these are probably not so important, but the report from Nanning may be interesting. There was a big protest in Chongzuo not far from the border with Vietnam. The protesters carried banners with the character 'zi' and shouted anti-Party slogans. They overwhelmed the local police and the Party had to activate the nearest garrison to disperse the protesters."

Liu read the report quickly, "We will have to adjust our methods immediately. This probably will not be the last protest. Thought work has always been hardest along the borders. But it will spread from there. Please let me know immediately if we receive any more reports like this."

A steady stream of reports of sporadic protests around the country came in through the rest of the day and Shao Huan delivered them to Liu one-by-one. Ye Hongqi's door stayed closed through most of the day and Shao only saw him once as he escorted the head of the United Front Work Department to the elevator. When Shao delivered a report about another protest in Zhejiang, Liu sucked air through his teeth sharply and clicked his tongue, "The Party Chairman will call a special meeting today or tomorrow morning at the latest. This is very bad. I will talk with the boss."

Shao Huan returned to his office and waited. A short while later Liu arrived at his door, "We will hold another emergency instruction session this evening. After that instruction session, we will send new guidance to actively counter the slanderous allegations."

"Okay. No problem. I will be ready," Shao Huan paused before commenting, "But the news is true. Can we really counter the truth for very long?"

Liu smirked, "The truth is whatever the Party says it is. The Party says these documents are part of a foreign plot to weaken China. We will make sure that the public understands the truth as the Party Chairman wants."

Shao Huan was amazed that the Party would be so brazen to fight the objective reality of their own mistakes and embarrassment, but he realized that the Party must have done this many times before. Whether they were reshaping reality to suit the Party's objectives or completely reversing the facts, the Party's control over history, over the media, over all elements of education and even over the religious groups that were allowed to operate in the open gave the Party's thought work every advantage over the real facts on any matter. Shao remembered how they portrayed the novel coronavirus as an American biological weapon, when they knew full well that the new disease had come from within China and that they had spent months trying to cover it up. In a moment of quiet panic, Shao wondered if some day the Party would have so completely eliminated the original version of the Bible, that Christians would only know the version of the Bible that supported the Party and quoted the Party Chairman.

Shao prayed for God to show him what to do. He prayed for God to stop the Party from rewriting history and the present reality. He looked through the reports that he received and the guidance that he had sent, and nothing in the guidance acknowledged the foreign media reports were true. People within the Party would understand clearly, but anyone outside would just read guidance from the Center to protect China against foreign threats.

That evening Shao went out to pick up dinner again. Sima Nan had tried to call several times so Shao returned the call. Sima Nan answered his voice sounded panicked, "I think they are really going to turn off the Internet. It is going to be a big problem."

"No way, they can't do that. The economy in the cities would stop, and people would know there is a real problem. They can't turn off the Internet."

Sima Nan was not convinced, "They are having a leading group meeting tomorrow morning. I am sure your boss will be there too. My boss will propose turning off the Internet to regain social control."

"Okay. We should meet tomorrow evening."

"Good idea. Let's meet at the bookstore tomorrow. Confirm the time tomorrow, okay?"

Shao agreed and returned to the office with two plastic bags weighed down with fried dumplings. Liu wasn't at his desk so Shao left a bag for Liu and returned to his office. Shao was nearly done with his warm, oily dumplings when Liu came in to the office, "That instruction session was very difficult. The People's Daily editor didn't argue, but they all wanted to know more about the situation. The boss did a good job telling them to focus on their new task. Do you mind if I eat while we draft the guidance message?"

"No problem, you must be hungry. Please eat. I will type."

Liu sat down, "The black hand of foreign forces has infiltrated China and disseminated ridiculous and obviously false information slandering the people of China. All propaganda offices and all media outlets are to begin a total assault on these treacherous lies. Use all platforms and all resources available to refute allegations that the Party has a secret research institute working on the problem of longevity as complete fiction. Use any expert resources available on the subject of stem cell therapy to portray the alleged therapy as pure science fiction. Refute all allegations of misuse of fetal tissue and embryonic stem cells as abhorrent and highlight the Party's commitment to improving the quality of life for all people and the success of the one child policy as a difficult but wise decision by our leaders that averted an economic disaster. Portray anyone organizing or leading protests as agents of a fifth column organized by foreign powers, especially the United States and Japan, who have been waiting for this moment to destroy China from within."

Shao Huan typed diligently as Liu dictated the message between bites of the heavy pork dumplings, "That is really not bad at all. Is there anything else?" Shao tried to appear supportive but his heart burned with anger that the Party was about to portray any protestors as agents of foreign powers, when the Party knew they were just normal citizens who were outraged at the Party's abuse of power.

Liu finished his dumplings and set the styrofoam container back in the plastic bag, "No. I think that is all for now. There is a leading group meeting tomorrow morning. We will get more guidance from the Party Chairman then. I expect that the Party Chairman will give us a few days to see if our new thought work campaign is successful. If not, he may take more drastic measures to close down the country and protect the Party."

Shao nodded, "Okay. I will be ready tomorrow. Do you need me to stay longer?"

"No, you should go home. Let's hope that everything goes smoothly tomorrow."

On his way home, Shao saw that the news feeds still focused on an ambiguous foreign threat, and he wondered what the coverage would look like the next morning. He was tired, but he noticed a few more "zi" characters scrawled on the corners of buildings, one was large and drawn in red paint and maintenance workers were already trying to remove it. Those displays of anger were growing bolder, and harder to miss.

Shao Huan got home before Zhang Ying was asleep and nearly collapsed in her arms, "I don't know what to do. They are lying to everyone. The Party really did all of those things."

Zhang held Shao and sat down on the sofa, "Keep strong in your faith, my dear. God will show you what he wants you to do. When the moment comes, you will know. What exactly have they done?"

"Aya, that's right. You don't know. The Party had a secret research institute that was working to extend the lives of Party leaders. They used fetal tissue and embryonic stem cells. They destroyed lives so the Party leaders could extend their own," Shao looked down, "I keep thinking about our baby, and wonder if the Party took her body for their research. It makes me so angry. It is making a lot of people angry. The Party is scared, they are having more meetings about this than they did about the novel coronavirus."

"Is that the foreign threat they are talking about?"

"There is no foreign threat. Just like when they talk about the black hand of foreign powers in Hong Kong, they know it is the common people. Now they are using the same method inside China. Tomorrow they will blame any protest leaders as foreign agents, a fifth column working against the Party. If the protests don't stop, I am afraid a lot of innocent people will die.

招供
Confession

Shao Huan couldn't fall asleep. His heart was heavy with the sins of the Party and his mind kept turning over his own complicity in covering up those sins, in shaping reality to permit and even praise the Party's deception. He got up and read the Bible. He started reading Matthew 6 and recited the Lord's Prayer, but it was the words after that he felt God speaking through, " For if you forgive other people when they sin against you, your heavenly Father will also forgive you. But if you do not forgive others their sins, your Father will not forgive your sins."

Shao realized that as angry as he was at Ye and Liu and the entire Chinese Communist Party, he had to forgive them. Their sins were terrible, but they were not beyond redemption. Shao prayed, "Heavenly Father, I know I must forgive the Party cadre for the terrible things they have done. I am angry at them and don't want to forgive them, Heavenly Father, please help me to accept them as Your children who also deserve forgiveness and salvation."

Shao Huan lay down on the sofa and woke with the first light of day. He checked the news on his phone. All of the top stories were about foreign powers using these false documents to undermine China. There was an interview with a stem cell researcher from Tsinghua University who lambasted the alleged research as a laughable fiction that was dreamed up by a madman. There was an investigation of a factory worker in Guangdong Province who had led a protest and carried a large banner with the character "zi" on it. The investigation alleged that he had been recruited by foreign forces and showed that his bank account received a large payment days before the protest.

Shao Huan put his phone down in disgust. He reminded himself that he needed to let go of his anger and listen for God's voice and to find the right moment to act. Shao left early for work, and in the morning light saw more maintenance workers covering advertisements that had been defaced with the character "zi." He saw at least a dozen characters of protest etched, drawn, painted on any surface out of the view of the almost ubiquitous cameras that kept a watchful eye over the city.

The cafe near the Propaganda Department headquarters just opened as Shao arrived. Shao was the first to order, but while he waited for his drinks he overheard other guests talking about the news. One man in a sharp business suit said, "They are obviously lying. There are no foreign forces. Besides, if there were so many foreign agents inside China, the Party has failed already."

A slightly older man who was with him answered, "The foreign powers still want to split China apart. Why would the Party lie about something like this? It is nonsense that they could have found a way to extend life."

"They landed a robot on the far side of the moon. Not even the Americans have done that. Why couldn't they extend the human lifespan?"

Shao Huan wanted to stay and listen but his coffees were ready and he couldn't linger. He was amazed to hear people speaking so openly about the Party's thought work. He delivered a coffee to the guard, "Is everything okay?" Shao asked.

"Everything is calm. There has been some vandalism around Fengtai District, Haidian and Chaoyang but so far no disturbances in Xicheng or Dongcheng."

"Hopefully it stays quiet!" Shao Huan tried to sound encouraging for the guard.

Liu Wuqing was in his office as usual, but appeared more anxious and was busy preparing for the leading group meeting to manage the crisis response. "The new approach is already taking effect. I will check the reports, but it appears things are working," Shao said.

Liu nodded and straightened his red tie, "Yes, this all out assault on the false stories from overseas is more effective. If the Party Chairman gives us a few more days, I am sure that we will be successful."

There were many more reports than normal and Shao Huan found that more than half of the reports were about protests around the country. The Party cadre who submitted the reports tried to identify leaders for the protests, but it appeared that most of the protests were spontaneous and they could not identify a single leader or group that organized the protests. The most surprising report was from Ningbo where the police who had been dispatched to disperse the protest not only failed to make any arrests, but several of the police officers joined the protest.

Shao Huan printed off the reports and delivered them to Liu, "There are many more protests, and in at least one of the protests, the police not only failed to stop the protest, what is more they joined the protest."

"Those bastards. If the police, the military or other Party cadre join the protests or argue against the government, we will have a much bigger problem. Our thought work can only be effective if we all work together. I will report this to the boss immediately. We have to leave for Zhongnanhai soon. Please let me know if there is anything else important that comes in before we go."

Shao Huan didn't see Ye Hongqi before they left for Zhongnanhai, but Ye left the door to his office open and Shao slipped in to see what the foreign media was reporting. Shao was amazed to see that it was still the top story on the foreign television stations. One of the Taiwan stations even had video footage of the protest in Ningbo and the images of police who joined the protests. The American and European news switched between images of the documents, footage from some protests and distinguished looking people talking. The Taiwan news commentators assessed that the unrest in China was the greatest threat to the Chinese Communist Party since the student protests in 1989.

Contrary to the dismissive attack against the quality of the research that Shao had read that morning, a senior professor from the Taipei Medical University praised the breakthroughs in stem cell treatment as some of the most creative and meticulously researched methods that he had ever seen. He assessed the treatments could at the very least cure many degenerative disorders and could possibly extend human life spans by decades.

Shao Huan didn't dare stay in Ye's office for more than a few minutes, but the Chinese domestic coverage of the protests was so different, and focused more on protests in front of the fortresslike U.S. and Japanese embassies in the Liangmaqiao neighborhood. Those protests appeared obviously staged, with uniform banners and organized chants, completely unlike the foreign coverage of the spontaneous, sprawling and poorly organized protests across China.

Liu came by Shao's office in the early afternoon, "It was a long meeting, but in the end, the Party Chairman agreed to give our thought work more time and not to cut off the Internet yet. The boss even persuaded the Party Chairman to make a statement himself against the foreign interference in China's domestic politics. Of course, that will be the top news tonight and all day tomorrow."

"Okay, I will be ready whenever the boss wants to send the instructions out. There have been a few more reports that came in, but no big changes. Was there anything else interesting from the meeting?"

"Ah, yes. The Minister of State Security confirmed that they had identified the source of the information compromise and had obtained a confession. The head of the State Internet Information Office also explained their assessment of completely turning off the Internet. It is possible but would be very costly. That is still possible, but it seems unlikely unless things go very badly."

Shao Huan remembered that he had to forgive Liu and the other cadre and slowly let go of the anger that started to burn in his bones, "Let's hope that everything stays peaceful."

Liu provided the guidance from Ye to maintain the total assault on the false stories from foreign powers and attack any people who appeared to support or organize the protests, but also to ensure the Party Chairman's speech was broadcast on every media platform. The national broadcast was scheduled for 9 p.m. Liu decided he was too busy to eat as he ran back and forth between Ye's office and his own. Shao left the office to make a quick call to Sima Nan.

"Hey buddy! This is crazy. I can't believe they aren't shutting off the Internet. We can't keep up with the messages. They are adapting so quickly and using other homonyms now too. I don't think the Party Chairman really understood how bad things are online. The only way to stop this from spreading is to turn off the Internet," Sima Nan sounded anxious but glad to vent his frustrations to Shao Huan.

"The Party Chairman is making a big speech tonight at 9 p.m. so I can't meet tonight. But I don't think it will be effective. The reports of protests all over the country are growing. I even saw some 'zi' characters painted around Beijing. The common people are very angry."

"Brother, you really have no idea. The people are furious. They always hated the one child policy, but now the rumor that the Party kept that policy longer than they needed to, just to help their own chances of living longer has really angered everyone. We saw some recordings being shared on WeChat of police joining a protest. It is really bad. Maybe we can catch up tomorrow? I have to go."

"I also should go. Let's talk again tomorrow," Shao Huan hung up and returned to his comfortably cool office. He checked for messages again and there was a video message from the Ministry of State Security.

Shao Huan opened the video of a thin woman with big glasses and small eyes. She looked tired and broken. She also looked vaguely familiar, but Shao Huan was sure he had never met her before. He started to play the video. The setting looked all too familiar as well,

Shao Huan had seen so many confession videos from the neutral setting of a Party detention room.

The woman's voice was heavy as she said "My name is Doctor Chen Yunbo, and this is my confession. I was a researcher at the 484 Research Institute developing advanced stem cell therapies. I stole secret data from the institute and sent it overseas to a foreign researcher who is an enemy of the Chinese Communist Party. I put my own interests above the good of the Party and believed that I knew what was best. I acted on my own and I will accept the consequences of my actions."

Shao Huan's jaw dropped and he watched the video again. This woman looked so small and meek. He couldn't imagine that she was the mastermind who had compromised such sensitive information. Almost as a reflex, he downloaded the video to the secure tablet, but the power of this confession from someone who looked so honest and so defeated, struck him. He felt the fine hairs on the back of his neck stand up and he knew he needed to copy her confession. He casually stepped out of his office and picked up his phone. He quickly deactivated the data connections and slipped it in his pocket. In Shao's office he placed the secure tablet against a blank wall and used his phone to record the short video. Shao saved the video to his micro SD card and put the micro SD card in his shirt pocket.

Shao quietly returned his phone to the cabinet outside of his office before he delivered the video to Liu. Liu noted it was almost time for the Party Chairman's speech and invited Shao to sit in Ye's office and watch the speech together. Liu knocked on Ye's door and then delivered the secure tablet to Ye Hongqi.

Ye watched the video twice and his face shifted from shock to a look of fear like Shao and Liu had never seen from him before, "This is terrible!" Ye shouted, "This is absolutely terrible! Destroy this at once!"

Shao and Liu looked at each other and Ye saw their confused glances, "That woman is my daughter's best friend! I sat next to her at my daughter's wedding! I must tell the Party Chairman as soon as possible. I had no idea it was her. I didn't even know where she worked. She was always so quiet. Dammit!" Shao quickly took the tablet away from Ye and returned to his office to clear the tablet, but he couldn't delete the message and knew that regardless of what he did, the Ministry of State Security had that recording and could use it against Ye Hongqi.

Shao returned to Ye's office where Liu was seated watching the television screens and Ye paced anxiously up and down the long office, his hands folded behind his back. At exactly 9 p.m. all of the domestic television channels played the national anthem and showed the same images of Tiananmen and Chinese flags flapping boldly against a bright blue sky.

The Party Chairman sat behind a large dark wooden desk, with a Chinese flag at his side and a painting of the Great Wall behind him. He began to speak, "My comrades, friends, ladies and gentlemen, our country is facing a great danger from foreign powers who want to destroy our great nation. They fear our growing economic power, they fear our military will soon become the strongest in the world, and they fear that the ideology of decadent so called democracies cannot compete with our Chinese dream. They cannot defeat us in the market or on the battle field, so they turn to lies and slander.

Many of you may have heard reports about a secret research institute working on extending human life."

The Party Chairman's voice was sincere and his face calm and warm, he spoke with the authority of his office and like a stern but concerned father, "These reports are completely false. There are many talented researchers and scientists who have made great achievements for China, but we have not hidden those efforts. If we had discovered treatments to help heal diseases, we would share those treatments with the people of China and the world. The foreign lies are baseless and ridiculous. Their only goal is to weaken and divide us. We must all stay together as one people, as one nation, strong and defiant against the foreign forces that have tried to destroy the Chinese people since before the Opium War. They will not stop, and we must not relax our efforts. Tonight I tell you, the Party has protected the people of China for more than 70 years and we will continue to protect the people of China for hundreds of years to come. Protect China, resist the foreigners. Trust the Party, oppose our enemies. Good night."

Ye hadn't stopped pacing throughout the speech and Liu's face was pale and his eyes tired. Shao looked at the scene of anxiety and in that moment forgave both of them for their sins against the people of China and against God. He put his hand to his chest and took comfort in the tiny square of silicone tucked safely in the corner of his shirt pocket.

温柔的人有福了
Blessed are the Meek

Zhang Ying was sound asleep when Shao Huan returned home. He sat quietly on the sofa and took the micro SD card out of his pocket. He felt the weight of it, lighter than a feather and smaller than his finger nail, but knew it held a truth that could shake the Party and push the country to revolution. Shao thought of someplace safe to keep it until he decided what to do with the video. He looked around the apartment. He looked in the kitchen but in the end decided to tape it inside his Bible. He would trust in God to keep it safe there.

Shao opened his Bible and turned to Matthew 5:5 He taped the micro SD card over the verse "Blessed are the meek, for they shall inherit the earth."

He prayed for guidance, strength, wisdom and for God to bless the people of China. Shao did not want foreign powers to undermine China, but he also knew that China had been a great power before the Chinese Communist Party and with God's blessing it would be an even greater power after the Party.

Zhang Ying's cool hand on Shao's warm cheek woke him the next morning and he smiled at her, "I know what God wants me to do. He showed me last night. I will need the church's help."

Zhang Ying beamed at him, "I knew God would use you. I watched the Party Chairman's speech last night, and knowing what you told me… I can't believe he would tell such a clear lie to all of China."

"It is only clear to you because you know the truth. We will help everyone else know the truth too. I should get to the office. If anything happens to me, remember to read Matthew 5:5."

Zhang Ying smiled, "Nothing will happen to you. I will see you tonight. I hope you won't be so late."

Shao Huan was not surprised to see that all of the news stories were about the Party Chairman's speech and he had to scroll far down his news feed before he reached stories about the arrest of foreign agitators and agents working in a fifth column against China. Even though the maintenance workers had cleaned up some of the 'zi' characters that had been marked in quiet corners across the city, Shao noticed that still more continued to appear. It seemed that for every character that they cleaned, another ten appeared.

Shao delivered the morning coffees as usual and checked the classified reports. There were dozens of more reports about protests around the country, but it did not seem that there were as many as the day before. Shao printed the reports and delivered them to Liu. Liu's face still looked pale and weak, Shao tried to give him some good news, "It seems there are not so many protests."

"The protests are not such a big problem for us now. The boss is much more worried about that confession. He learned that his daughter asked his brother at the Ministry of State Security to allow the traitor to travel overseas to the wedding. She worked in a sensitive facility and should never have been allowed to travel overseas. The boss and his brother are both very worried that they will lose their jobs," Liu set the folder down without opening it, "And the Party Chairman was happy with how his speech was broadcast throughout China, but the foreign media portrayed his speech as a desperate attempt to restore political stability. He is angry about that. I don't think we can do anything about it, but the boss seems to be in a very vulnerable position right now."

"Maybe he will be okay if the all out attack on the foreign news is successful? How do you think?" Shao asked.

"The best scenario is that he might not be forced to retire or to resign from the Party, but even if this campaign against the foreign lies is very successful, now there is no chance that he will reach the Politburo Standing Committee. His career will be finished whenever he leaves this job."

"What does that mean for you?"

"I need to find a new patron. I cannot go any further with Ye Hongqi, and he probably won't be able to get me that assignment in Hong Kong," Liu couldn't hide his disappointment and exhaustion.

Shao Huan was relieved that the rest of the day passed in relative quiet. The flurry of reports and guidance from the last few days slowed and while there were still problems around the country, the guidance was clear and appeared to be working. Ye Hongqi and Liu were more focused on making every effort to appease the Party Chairman and to distance Ye from the treachery of his daughter's friend, but Shao was fortunately removed from that seemingly impossible task. Shao stepped out of the office at lunch to call Sima Nan and confirmed they could meet for a quick meal after work.

He met Sima Nan in front of the bookstore. Sima Nan appeared more relaxed as they walked together, but he confided that he was not yet completely at ease, "The immediate crisis as passed, but people are still searching for information about the compromised information. It seems that the Party Chairman's speech slowed the protests, and that people are more scared of being seen as supporting foreign powers against China, but this will be a problem for decades. The foreign news organizations are still analyzing the documents and finding more information. Some journalists in Taiwan are even starting to identify the patients who received the treatment. The documents used patient numbers, but some of the patients are so well known that their ages and diseases can be identified. They have even found the Party Chairman's patient history. He is so angry about that!"

"I didn't know that. I am sure he would be very upset. I'm not so hungry, let's just get some kabobs. Okay?"

Sima Nan agreed, "As long as we get beer, I will be very satisfied."

"My boss is pretty distracted. He knows the person who sent the information overseas. It is his daughter's best friend."

Sima Nan stopped walking, "No way! That's horrible!" He shouted and then quickened his pace to catch up to Shao Huan, "He is done for. There is no way the Party Chairman will forgive that."

"Liu Wuqing also said the same thing. Maybe the General Office will assign me to another senior cadre, or maybe they will just ask me to return to the main office to work there."

"Just be very careful. At least you have good technical skills. Even if the Party won't give you another job, because you are too close to Ye, I am sure you can still get a job for one of the Internet companies. You will make a lot more money. Then you can take me out for better meals than kabobs and beer."

"Hey, I thought you said you'd be very satisfied as long as there is beer," Shao Huan laughed as they reached the small kabob stand and ordered six kabobs each and two cold beers.

Sima Nan asked, "So, imagine that the treatment really works and that the Party leaders kept it for themselves. What would the world be like if they could live for hundreds of years and stay in power forever while the rest of us lived and died like humans always have?"

Shao clinked the neck of his beer bottle against Sima Nan's, "That would be completely unfair."

"Of course, of course. It would be completely unfair, but just imagine. It would be like there were actually two different species of humans. One that could live for hundreds of years and one that only lived for 70 or 80 years. They really would look at the common people as even less valuable than they do now."

The cynicism in Sima Nan's comment surprised Shao. Sima Nan was always so critical of foreign governments and supported the Party, it was strange to hear him criticize the Party. Shao felt comfortable letting his own disillusionment show a little, "It would be a little different than now, but would it really be a huge change? For Ye Hongqi, whatever happens to the common person is not so important. All he cares about is reaching the next level of power."

"He must be so upset. His thought work saved the Party from the Ministry of State Security's failure and he won't get to benefit at all."

The service person called out their number and Shao Huan picked up the twelve long skewers of seasoned meat. Sima Nan and Shao Huan both quickly ate the first kabob and then Shao asked, "What was the hardest information to control during this crisis?"

Sima Nan answered without hesitation, "It was the volume. There was just so much. The other thing that made it really hard was how common the terms were. At one point we blocked any message or website with the character 'zi' in it, and later we blocked any message with any homonym for 'zi' it was hundreds of millions of messages and websites that were blocked, most of them weren't even related to the protests at all. Many companies complained that their businesses couldn't operate. There is a dumpling restaurant owner who happens to be married to the sister of one of the senior leaders in the Internet Information office, and he said he couldn't do business if everyone who searched for 'dumpling' was blocked because the word contains the character 'zi'… and he has a point. It was just about impossible."

"What would have happened if you had shut down the Internet completely?" Shao asked after finishing another skewer.

"Everything would have stopped. Almost all businesses in the cities now depend on the Internet, and they would have lost a lot of money. It would have been a big problem. It is still possible that we would shut off the Internet, but it seems like we don't have to worry so much about that for now."

Shao Huan and Sima Nan toasted to the apparent ebbing of the immediate crisis, but Shao Huan still wondered what would happen when people saw Doctor Chen Yunbo's confession. They finished the spicy roast mutton and said farewell. Shao had noticed several 'zi' characters along the walk with Sima Nan but neither of them said anything about the characters.

Zhang Ying was awake and reading her Bible when Shao Huan returned home, "You are home so early! Was everything okay at work?"

Shao Huan hugged his beautiful wife, "It was okay for me, but the boss is in trouble. I don't know how much longer he will be able to stay in his position. But, I want to show you something." Shao opened his Bible and took the micro SD card out. He rummaged through his drawer in the bedroom and returned with an old phone. Shao disabled the network connections and put the micro SD card into the phone.

Zhang Ying's mouth opened wide as she watched the video, "It is moving isn't it? She is clearly telling the truth."

Zhang Ying agreed, "It is incredible. She looks so small and so sad."

Shao Huan took Zhang's hand, "I need you to buy a new 5G phone. I will use that to send this video. Can you go to a phone store after work? Don't get an expensive one, just a normal 5G phone. Okay?"

Zhang smiled, "Of course. I will do that tomorrow."

The reports the next day continued to show a decline in protests, and Shao Huan felt the tide turning back in the Party's favor. Their lie was working. Liu Wuqing and Ye Hongqi, however, did not enjoy their success. Ye had appealed to the Party Chairman, and was allowed to keep his position but it was clear that his career was over. Ye seemed disinterested in all of the reports, and he even allowed Liu to run the meetings that day. A few weeks earlier, Liu would have taken great pride in running the daily meetings, but under the circumstances he only led them because he had not decided on his next move.

Zhang Ying was waiting for Shao at home with a broad smile and a new phone. Shao carefully set the phone up. He disabled all of the network features except for device to device communication and then loaded the micro SD card. Shao opened the video and saved it to the new phone. He made sure to strip the metadata from the video and saved it again under the name M55, with the faith that the meek would inherit the earth, as Jesus had promised.

Shao Huan and Zhang Ying prayed, studied and waited for their church to gather. They returned to the mechanics garage in Wangjing on Sunday morning. Shao and Zhang arrived early and prepared. The church members looked to Shao to lead the service. Shao Huan had never led one of the worship services, but he felt at peace as he invited everyone to hold hands and bow their heads in prayer.

Shao started to speak but felt the voice in his throat was not his own, "Heavenly Father, give us the strength and wisdom to bring glory to You. These are dangerous times for Your children in our beloved China. We pray, Heavenly Father, for Your will to be done, for Your truth to spread, for all of our brothers and sisters in this country to have the chance to find true salvation in You. The Party leaders wanted to chase eternal life in this world," Shao Huan's voice built in a crescendo, "Heavenly Father, we know that eternal life is only possible through You. We trust in You with all our hearts. Lead us through the valley of death, let us fear no evil, for Thine is the glory and the kingdom forever," Shao Huan almost shouted, "Amen!" And the rest of the church joined him.

They all knew that something terrible had happened, and guessed that the Party was lying about the documents that had been published overseas, but their rage at the Party boiled over as Shao Huan explained everything for them. Shao Huan urged them not to rush out into the street, "The Party has done such thorough thought work for decades. They are in trouble now, but if we are not careful, they will just make us look like foreign agents. We must do this very carefully."

Duan Yide narrowed her eyes and asked with her fiery intensity, "What is your plan?"

"I am going to show you a video now. Then I will show you how to set your phone for device to device transmission. Later today I will sit on a bench in Chaoyang Park reading a book. You will all walk by over the afternoon and I will send the video to your phones. After that, you will teach all of your friends and family how to do this and you will send the video to them. Every person who receives the video must share it with everyone they can. If we only send the video from device to device, and never over the data network the Internet Information Office won't be able to detect it. At least, they won't be able to detect it until it has spread too far to control. Also, you must turn off all of your automated data back ups so the video stays only on your phone and doesn't go on to any network. Does everyone understand?"

The fellow believers all nodded and expressed their resolve. Shao then placed the new phone on a work bench so everyone could see it. The smell of grease and metal dust filled their noses as they pressed together to watch a meek woman deliver the damning truth of the Party's perfidy.

救救孩子
Save the Children…

That afternoon, Shao Huan and Zhang Ying sat on a bench near the bridge in Chaoyang Park where they had last seen Bai Yongcheng. The summer sun was strong and the air humid and hazy. Shao Huan held up a copy of Lu Xun's 'Call to Arms' and read the short story 'A Madman's Diary,' while watching for the other church members to pass by.

As instructed, they disconnected their phones from the network and only enabled device to device transmission. One by one, they waked past and Shao Huan sent them the file. Shao Huan had calculated that if each of the more than 20 church members could share the video with an average of 10 people, and that continued for seven iterations, the video could reach 200 million people. Duan Yide had assured Shao that she alone would share it with at least one hundred of the migrant workers who came to her new restaurant. She said they were furious about the reports but were scared the government would send them back to their villages if they joined any protests.

Shao read Lu Xun's story about a madman who began to see the characters "eat people" in traditional texts and to see the vicious cruelty of the traditional Chinese culture that Lu Xun and his contemporary revolutionaries had rebelled against. He read to Zhang Ying 'It has only just dawned on me that all these years I have been living in a place where for four thousand years human flesh has been eaten…" Shao shook his head at the irony, "I wonder what the first generation revolutionaries would say if they saw China now?" Shao read a little more silently and then read to Zhang Ying again, "perhaps there are still children who haven't eaten men? Save the children…"

Zhang put her hand on Shao's leg to let him know another church member was passing by. He quickly connected to their phone and transmitted the file. She looked at him, "I am so proud of you."

Shao laughed, "Why is that?"

"Do you remember how nervous you were passing one scrap of paper to Bai Yongcheng just a few months ago? And now, you are sending this video to more than 20 people. God really is using you my dear."

"I really feel like it is the right thing to do. It may hurt the Party, but it will help China. This time I don't want the information to stay secret, I want it to become so wide spread that the Party doesn't know where it came from."

Shao Huan and Zhang Ying waited more than thirty minutes after the last church member passed before they returned home. Shao Huan's heart raced more walking away from the park than when he had sent the video to the church members as they walked by. He knew that his plan was in motion now, and that just as when he passed the paper to Bai Yongcheng, whatever happened with the video was now beyond his control.

The next day when Shao returned to work he was glad to see a few 'zi' characters still appearing along his commute. Even though the Party seemed to be winning, the fire had not been extinguished. When he arrived at the office, Ye and Liu were even less interested in their apparent success than they had been on Friday. Liu Wuqing confided to Shao Huan that Ye Hongqi had already written his letter of resignation and was just waiting for the crisis to fully pass before he informed the Party Chairman, and that was likely what the Party Chairman expected from Ye.

The international news still had some coverage of the longevity incident as the Taiwan press had called it, but it now appeared to be just one story among many. Ye had not allowed foreign journalists to return to China, and the State Internet Information Office continued to block access to all foreign media, but it seemed the crisis was waning and the domestic thought work continued to investigate and humiliate any of the people who had been identified as leaders in the protests.

The police officers in Ningbo who joined the protests were all fired, arrested and publicly humiliated as foreign agents. The television and radio stations continued to broadcast the Party Chairman's speech and at Ye's direction his speech remained at the top of every news web site and news broadcast across the country.

As the week went by, things gradually returned to normal at the office. Shao Huan delivered the daily reports and sent out Ye's guidance. The only thing that seemed slightly different to Shao was that even though the state media continued to attack the foreign agents hiding among the good people of China, he saw more and more displays of protest. Some of them were brazen like a red 'zi' character spray painted on a bus stop. Some were more subtle like the character 'zi' being circled in advertisements in the subway stations.

Sima Nan called Shao Huan on his way home from work on Thursday, "Brother, is everything okay at your office?"

"It is still a little strange. Before this situation, my boss was still ambitious. But now it is like he has given up. Why? How are things at your office?"

"Really strange. We are still on high alert and blocking millions of messages a day, but something weird is happening. We see people talking about a video, but haven't seen the video anywhere yet. At least, I don't think we have. I don't know what is going on. I just wanted to check if you have heard anything about this video. We are starting to filter for the term video, but it is such a common term."

Shao Huan was glad that Sima Nan couldn't see the smile on his face, "No, I'm not sure what video that is. Maybe the Ministry of State Security will know something more about it?"

"Aya, of course they would but I can't call those bastards. They never tell us anything. Just let me know if you hear anything, okay?"

"Okay. I will tell you if I hear anything more about a video."

Shao Huan was excited to return home to Zhang Ying and when she hugged him, he quietly whispered in her ear, "It's working." Zhang Ying pulled back and gave Shao Huan a huge smile and a kiss. Shao Huan's phone rang and he answered the call from Liu Wuqing, "Hey, is there an issue?"

"We need you back right away. I will explain everything when you get here."

"No problem. I will be right back," Shao Huan hung up. Zhang looked disappointed but Shao kissed her again, "Don't worry. I think this will be a good thing. Don't wait up for me."

Liu Wuqing was not at his desk when Shao Huan returned to the office. He heard Ye Hongqi shouting behind his closed door. Shao waited in Liu's office for a few minutes. He couldn't make out what Ye was yelling about, but was sure that he was yelling at Liu. Ye's office door opened and Liu carefully, submissively, backed out and turned towards Shao, "Good, you are here. We have a big problem. Somehow a foreign journalist got the video confession of the traitor who compromised the sensitive information. It is already all over the news in Taiwan and other foreign media are starting to pick it up. The Party Chairman already knows. We have to send instructions immediately to attack the video as a fabrication. We aren't going to wait this time and try to stop it. The Party Chairman risked his own credibility when he delivered that speech and this video is a direct attack on him."

"Okay. I will get everything ready. Sounds like the boss is very angry."

"I have never seen him so angry. The Ministry of State Security is beginning an investigation, and we will all be questioned. Anyone who had access to the video will be questioned."

Liu and Shao sent a message to all of the Party offices to immediately call in the head of propaganda to receive the message and for them to use every element of the propaganda apparatus to attack the video as a fabrication but forbidding them from showing the video or repeating any information contained in the short video.

Shao sent the message and waited for another hour before he stopped by Liu's office, "It seems like there is no more work to do tonight. I can still come back if you need me later."

Liu looked up from his computer, "Oh, okay. You should go home. I should have let you go earlier. Come early tomorrow. It will be a bad day. There will be a meeting at Zhongnanhai early tomorrow."

Shao Huan called Sima Nan as soon as he walked out of the Propaganda Department headquarters, "I found out about that video."

"A little bit late brother, it is all over WeChat now. We are blocking it as fast as we can but it keeps popping up. It is somehow getting around the network. We are going to disable the ability to share or send videos. This is really bad. Have you seen the video?"

"No," Shao Huan lied.

"I saw it. It is bad. It shows that everything the Party Chairman said in that speech was a complete lie. I've got to go."

Shao Huan noticed a group of people in the distance, moving quickly toward him. Shao Huan dashed up the stairs to the bookstore to get out of their way and watched as they ran by. All of them wore face coverings. Some carried spray paint, some carried broom sticks. As they raced by one of the men ran up to the bookstore and spray painted 'zi' in huge black strokes on the glass window. A handful of police chased after them, but they were outnumbered. Their radios sparked with static and voices calling in other disturbances.

Shao Huan tried to enter the subway but a transportation worker informed him that all public transportation had been shut down suddenly. Shao tried to get a taxi but they wouldn't stop. He finally gave up and got an orange share bike. As he rode home, he saw more people scurrying through the dark, some chased by police, others making their marks of protest unmolested by the police who were clearly overwhelmed.

Shao was relieved when he reached home and he tucked the bike in a quiet corner, sure that he would need it to get to work the next day. Shao called Liu "Hey buddy, I just got home. I had to ride a bike. There are protests all over the city. Be careful."

Shao felt the capital was on the brink of something historic. He knew that the video he had disseminated was the catalyst, and he prayed for the police not to shoot anyone, and for the protestors not to attack or hurt the police. Shao had a few hours of uneasy sleep and woke at dawn.

Fortunately the bike that he had used the night before was still there and he rode the bike back to Xidan. The roads were eerily quiet. There were no buses or cars and no people walking to the subway. Shao saw "zi" written in large characters on the road, sidewalk, doors, and cars. It seemed that any surface had become a target for the character of protest.

As Shao Huan approached the second ring road he saw that a few officers from Central Guard Regiment had established a checkpoint on Inner Jianguomen Street, just west of the Second Ring Road. Shao was surprised to see the Central Guard Regiment there and not normal police officers. One of the officers held up his hand for Shao Huan to stop and two others readied their long guns. Shao stopped and held up his hands, "I'm a communications officer with the General Office assigned to the Propaganda Department headquarters. I have to go to work."

The officer who appeared to be in charge motioned for Shao to approach. Shao dismounted from the bike, offered a silent prayer and walked calmly to the soldiers. Shao felt their anxiety and tried to set them at ease, "It has been crazy. It's okay. I can give you my ID card."

"Okay, move slowly and hand it to me," the lead guard stated. He looked like he was in his early twenties and his eyes were tired. Shao handed him his ID card and the soldier stepped away and used his radio to call in Shao's name and ask for guidance. Shao waited for several minutes and looked at the Second Ring Road, which always had at least some traffic even at 2 or 3 a.m. and was amazed to see it completely empty. The city was beautiful in the morning light and the absence of the normal bustle gave a peaceful veneer over the most tense morning that Shao Huan had ever experienced.

The officer approached and returned Shao's ID card. You can proceed, but no one is allowed near Tiananmen or Zhongnanhai. You will have to go to the south and then go north to Xidan."

Shao accepted his ID, "Thank you. Stay safe today." He rode off and turned south as directed. The city seemed empty and when Shao finally reached the Propaganda Department headquarters, the sun was bright and its strong light was nearly blinding as he walked the rest of the way to his office. The guards had erected barricades along the sidewalk and were armed with their long guns. Shao could only see their silhouettes against the rising sun but heard a familiar voice, "It's Shao Huan! Let him through!"

Shao Huan crossed the barricade and greeted the guard, "What happened?"

"There were protests most of the night, we have deployed our first line here to defend the headquarters. Our second line will be at the building if we have to fall back."

"Are Liu Wuqing and Ye Hongqi already here?"

"They didn't leave all night," the guard grimaced. After you left the situation became too unstable for anyone to leave."

Liu Wuqing was dozing in his chair when Shao entered, "Good morning. Are you okay?"

Liu woke with a start, "Good! You made it. I shouldn't have let you leave last night. I didn't know about the protests until you called. I really shouldn't have let you leave. The situation was so unstable. What is it like outside?"

"It is very quiet. All of the roads are closed and the public transportation has stopped. No one is out on the streets. The Central Guard Regiment is deployed around the Second Ring Road. It feels like it will be a very bad day."

Liu nodded, "Yes. The Party Chairman accepted the Minister of Public Security's recommendation to shut down the city. The State Internet Information Office also shut down the Internet. There is a meeting at Zhongnanhai at 8 a.m. Can you check the reports to see if there is anything the boss should know before the meeting?"

There were hundreds of messages from all over China. Most of the reports described protests that emerged from no where, overwhelmed the police and disappeared again as well as reports of police and military officers who joined the protests. Based on the reports, police had shot several hundred people across the country. Shao knew he had not fired those bullets or built the tinder box that was now catching fire, but he felt that he had put that final match to the kindling and that those lives would not have been lost if he hadn't stolen and disseminated the video. Shao prayed again for strength as another day of fire and fury lay ahead.

中国梦
Chinese Dream

Shao Huan waited anxiously for Liu and Ye Hongqi to return from Zhongnanhai. He slipped in to Ye's office and watched the foreign news play the confession video over and over again. They reported that China had completely cut off the Internet and that Beijing appeared to be under lock down, but they couldn't confirm anything. The Chinese media, however, followed their instructions and attacked the alleged video as a total fabrication. The Party had not yet realized how many people had actually seen the video, and Shao Huan wondered how many people still accepted the Party's thought work.

It was nearly noon when Liu and Ye returned. Liu asked Shao to follow him to Ye's office. Ye's face was long and tired, "The Ministry of State Security has determined the video has been spreading around the country for a week or more, and that it had been sent with device to device transmission which the State Internet Information Office was unable to detect until it was too late. They estimate that several hundred million people have already seen the video. Even though the telecommunications system and Internet have both been turned off, people are still sending the video to each other. The Party Chairman has instructed us to have all media stations send one last message that the country is under attack by a fifth column and the military will use every measure necessary to protect the Party and save China from our foreign enemies. After that, they will only broadcast the emergency message instructing everyone to leave their televisions and radios on and remain inside until the situation is stable."

Shao Huan sent the message as instructed and by 2 p.m. all of the television and radio channels had announced the country was under attack by a fifth column and then switched over to the emergency broadcast message. Shao continued to check secure communications system for updates. The Party offices around the country continued to send in reports about protests breaking out all over China including some more reports of police units and even People's Liberation Army units that either refused to break up the protests and in some cases joined the protestors.

Shao delivered the reports to Liu, "It seems like what is happening in Beijing is happening everywhere. I think the only communications system that is working in the country now is our secure network, but even with the other communications shut off people are still protesting against the Party everywhere. What happens now?"

Liu Wuqing shook his head, "I really don't know."

They heard Ye Hongqi shout in his office and Liu carefully approached the door, and motioned for Shao to follow him, "What is the matter?" Liu followed Ye's eyes to the wall of television monitors and noticed that the Shandong Television broadcast had switched off of the emergency broadcast and a slender man with a distinguished face and dark hair began to speak.

"I am Wang Zhengong, Party Secretary of Shandong Province. Our great country is on the brink of a terrible tragedy. My countrymen, you have no doubt seen the Party Chairman's speech denouncing foreign lies and interference, and many of you have already seen the video confession of Dr. Chen Yunbo from the 484 Research Institute. I am speaking to you today to verify Dr. Chen Yunbo's confession is true. The Party has developed these advanced stem cell therapies. I know because I have received this treatment."

Ye Hongqi shouted at the screen, "No! No!" He turned to Liu Wuqing, "Make him stop. He must be stopped!"

Liu Wuqing didn't know what to do and they continued watching as Wang Zhengong continued, "The Party Chairman has put his pride ahead of the good of the country. I call on the Party Chairman to step down immediately and spare this country more trouble. He has lost the mandate of heaven and the only way forward for our country is under new leadership. The People's Liberation Army Northern Command and the Eastern Command have agreed the best way to fulfill their duty to the country and to the Party is to call on the Party Chairman to resign. The moment has come for change in our great country. As leaders we owe our people a safe, stable and prosperous country, but we also owe them leaders who put the country ahead of their own ambition, and freedom to choose their own futures, to travel freely, to trade freely and to make this country even greater. I call on all of the people of China, all of our patriots, to stand with me in demanding a peaceful transition of power. I urge the patriots in our police, security services and in the People's Liberation Army do not fire your weapons on your fellow patriots. We will, together, make China even greater. Thank you everyone."

As they watched the Shandong broadcast end and switch to images of Chinese flags flapping against a blue sky, the Hebei Television broadcast switched over and began to retransmit Wang's speech. Dragon TV in Shanghai and Shenzhen TV followed close behind. Ye put his head in his hands, "Damn him!"

Shao and Liu looked at each other helplessly. "Damn him! That bastard knew they were coming for him! He knew he was done for and now he is launching a coup!" Ye Hongqi shouted again and stood up. He walked to his desk and started to put papers into his briefcase. Liu cautiously asked, "Boss, what should we do?"

Ye didn't bother to look up, "I don't know what you should do. I am leaving. That bastard has just ended me."

Shao was curious that in all of the turmoil, Ye's focus was still on his own career. Ye continued bitterly, "The traitor is my daughter's best friend. I was the one who encouraged the Party Chairman to stake his own credibility to crush the reports about the longevity research. And now... now the father of my son-in-law has just launched a coup and called on the Party Chairman to step down. If the Party Chairman wins, he will see me as one of the key conspirators against him and will execute me. If Wang Zhengong wins, he knows that I was working against him and may have me executed as well. I will get my wife and we will take the next flight out of Beijing."

Liu looked at Shao, the worry and anxiety clear in his dark eyes, "Boss, it can't be that bad."

Ye slammed down his briefcase on the desk, "Damn it! It is exactly that bad. There is no way to win. Of Sun Zi's 36 stratagems, fleeing is best," Ye picked up his briefcase and pushed past Liu and Shao toward the elevator. Liu and Shao shadowed him down the hall, and just as he pressed the button to summon the elevator, the power in the building stopped. "Damn it!" Ye shouted again. He turned around to Liu and Shao, "Where are the stairs?"

Shao Huan led Ye Hongqi to the stairwell at the end of the hallway. All of the gravitas and dignity that Shao Huan had come to expect from Ye evaporated and he saw the desperation and fear in Ye's eyes in the dim light before Ye disappeared down the dark stairwell.

Shao and Liu stood in the hallway. The normal electrical whir had ceased and the building had fallen almost completely silent. Liu walked back to Ye's office and sat down in Ye Hongqi's chair behind the big desk. He looked at the wall of black screens, "I don't know what to do," he admitted in a voice just above a whisper. "I guess they turned off the power to stop people from seeing Wang's speech."

"I think we should go home. There is nothing that we can do here. We might not be able to get a plane to take us away from here like the boss, but we shouldn't stay here. I am going to go lock up the office and try to go home. Who knows if we can even get home. It was hard enough getting to the office today. It must be more difficult now."

Shao Huan used the light on his phone in the dark communications office, he found a large flashlight in the desk and used that to disconnect the servers and locked the key equipment in a safe. Shao set the electronic alarm which still had battery power to last for several days. He bolted the door and wondered if he would ever return to that office.

Liu Wuqing was still sitting in the large and gloomy office as Shao prepared to leave. Light streamed through the blinds on the far side of the office that were open just a crack. Shao took a peak out of the window and saw hundreds of people gathering in the street below. They had managed to get through the Central Guard Regiment's

275

checkpoints around the Second Ring Road and seemed to be coming from all directions. "We need to get out of here now buddy," Shao said and tried to lift Liu from the chair.

"You go ahead, I will stay here a little longer," Liu seemed completely defeated and unwilling to move, but Shao argued with him. "No, really you have to leave now. There are so many people outside. We need to go. Take off that tie and leave your jacket. You don't want to look like a cadre outside."

Liu reluctantly stood and removed his jacket but carefully took the Chinese Communist Party lapel pin that he wore every day and put it in his pocket. He carefully folded his jacket and tie and left them on the desk in his office.

The light outside was blinding and Shao Huan lifted his hand to shade his face. They saw that there were hundreds of people walking east toward Tiananmen Square. Shao wanted to follow them, but knew that he needed to get home to Zhang Ying. Shao tried to pull Liu Wuqing with him across the crowd and to the south side of the street but Liu stood frozen as students, workers, parents and grandparents kept moving eastward around him.

The crowd wasn't violent, but they were resolved. Years of corruption, control and abuse that had hurt all of them welled up in that moment and drove them to the center of control that had governed every element of their lives. Shao pulled on Liu again, "I'm going home!" He shouted at Liu, but decided that no one would hurt Liu and left him standing dazed in the middle of the street.

Shao heard the sound of gunfire in the distance. It sounded like a hand gun firing somewhere ahead. The crowd didn't stop, however, and Shao started sprinting south. He retraced the same route he took to work, and his lungs burned as he weaved his way between thousands of people who all seemed to be instinctively converging at the physical center of Chinese political history. Shao wanted to join them, but he wanted to see Zhang Ying more.

He prayed as he ran that God would keep the people safe and that whatever came next for China would make it stronger and safer for all of God's children. The checkpoint that Shao had passed that morning at the East Second Ring Road was abandoned and people walked down the street. Shao kept thinking about how Ye Hongqi had simply abandoned his position and wondered what the other senior cadre would do.

Shao Huan's legs ached and he was drenched with sweat when he reached their apartment building. He noticed some familiar faces standing around outside and nodded to the neighbors that he recognized. He hunched over and put his palms on his thighs to rest and catch his breath. He noticed the door for the convenience store across the street was open. He was so thirsty. The shop keeper was standing just outside in the warm evening air.

"Where did you run from? What's happening?" The middle aged man asked Shao.

"I came from Xidan. So many people are going to Tiananmen. I heard a few gunshots, but just one time. I don't know what else is happening."

The shop keeper went inside and got a liter of water for Shao Huan, "I know what is happening," he said as he opened the bottle and handed it to Shao, "It's over."

The cold water running down his dry throat felt like a timely rain on a parched land. The shop keeper continued in his thick Beijing accent while Shao drank, "They are done for. Those bastards thought they could get away with anything. Now they will eat their own fruit."

Shao offered to pay for the water but the shop keeper declined, "Just come back and buy some things after this is all over."

Shao saw Zhang Ying walking out through the apartment building doors and raced back across the street to her, he threw his arms around her, "It is really happening!"

Zhang held him tightly, "You are so sweaty! Did you run all the way here?"

"Yes, there was no other way to get back. There were so many people going to Tiananmen."

Zhang Ying's voice filled with worry "Will the army shoot them?"

Shao Huan shook his head and smiled, "No. I don't think they will. I heard a few gunshots earlier, but that was it. Even if they did decide to shoot, there are so many people, the Party would never recover. No thought work could hide that. It all happened so fast, they weren't ready for it."

A soft evening breeze swept down the street and blew gently against Zhang Ying's black hair and kissed Shao Huan's sweat streaked face. "We should pray," Zhang Ying whispered.

"Here? Now?" Shao Huan was surprised. They had hidden their faith from the beginning, it felt strange to pray openly with hundreds of people around them. Zhang Ying smiled and bowed her head.

Shao Huan pressed his forehead against hers as she began to pray, "Heavenly Father, You saved us from our sins. You led us to this moment. Please protect the protestors and the soldiers. Please forgive the Party cadre for their sins. We trust in You, Heavenly Father to fulfill the dream of a China where Your children can sing Your praise openly, where reading Your word is not a crime. We pray for a China that is stronger than ever, and for a China that accepts all Your children and their dreams. Amen."

Dedication

For the faithful who know their God is bigger than the CCP.

For the believers who know scripture is the word of God, not the CCP.

For the truth tellers who will call a deer a deer.

For the persecuted who endure and will overcome.

Made in the USA
Middletown, DE
24 June 2020